For Ganga & Grace

Printed in the United States of America
First Edition

The Secret of Enduring Love may be purchased online at amazon.com, barnesandnoble.com and at your local bookstores.

ISBN: 978-0989649605

HotCore Yoga Press

October 19, 2013
Boston, MA

The Secret of Enduring Love

by Peter Sklivas

Or for as long as this universe existed. Which is a pretty long time. The sacrifice of Shakti had happened so long ago no one could remember what the goddess looked like. No one except, of course, for her beloved Shiva.

The original yogi agreed to take on his first disciple. Shiva told the creator of the universe to sit in silence. Along with other instructions Lord Shiva whispered the mantra into Brahma's ear. The guru was guiding the creator of the universe to open seven inner gateways and discover the secret of enduring love.

01 Rousing Shakti – Root Gateway

Where resides elixir of love
Shimmering temple inside seven gateways
Too long have you sought to conquer
my heart and soul
Be like Shiva who yields all to me
Counsels Shakti ... if & only if
The root burns to peel back
The veils of your million-question mind

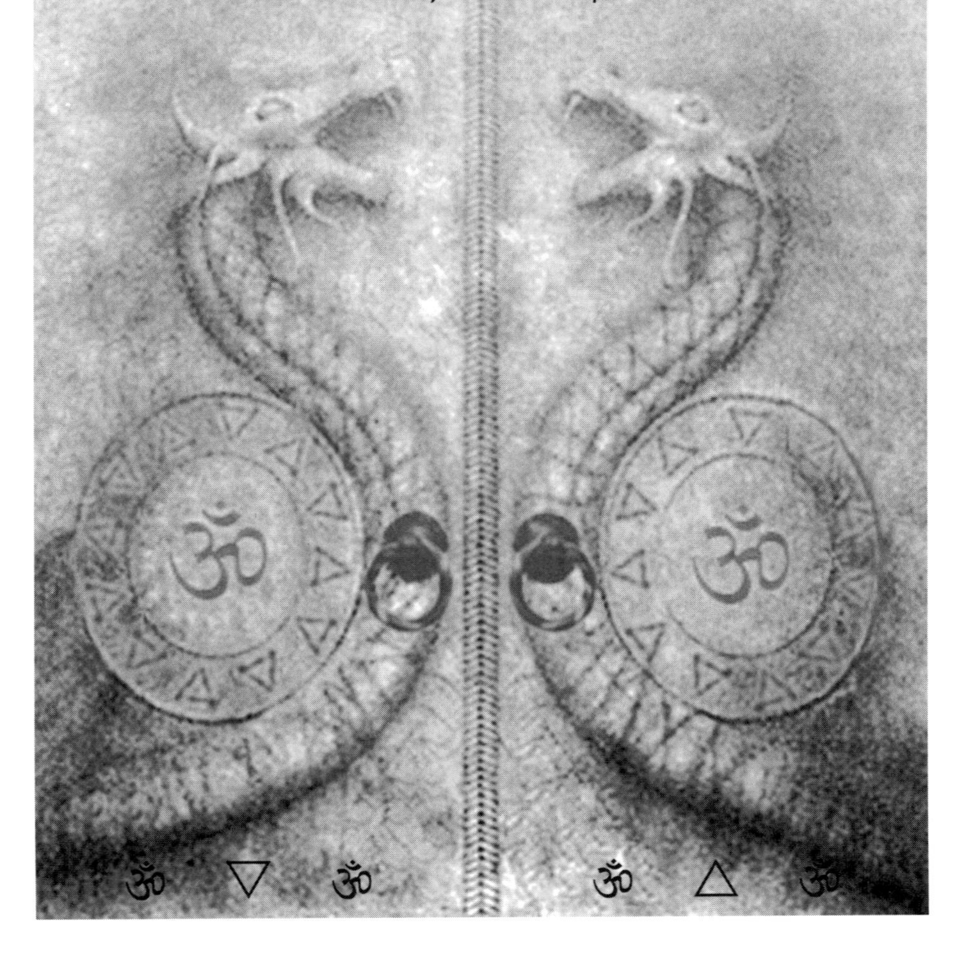

"How beautiful you are," the girl exclaimed. Although not used to being given orders, Damayanti did as she was told. Bowing down to one knee she stroked Great Swan's white feathers. "You must be the most beautiful swan in the world."

"Princess, the Wheel of Dharma turns to attract like forces. So beauty is drawn to beauty. Hansaram and I have been in every land, and we have never seen a girl as beautiful as yourself. It is for this reason we swim in your lake."

"You say these words just to be polite."

"Do you not realize, Damayanti? It is no kindness to be made so beautiful. Wherever my mate and I land, people try to catch us and keep us as pets. Just as you did now. But who is worthy of me except my mate?"

The princess realized she was standing at one of those life-altering moments known as a crossroad. Something had driven her down to accost Great Swan. But what was it?

"He is as handsome and graceful as I am. And I believe Hansaram was created just for me. And I for him. Do we not glisten more brightly beside one another than now when you see us apart?"

Truly Great Swan's white feathers reflected the light in muter hues than normal. Admirers claimed when swans mated, shafts of rainbow light radiated from their bodies broadcasting their secret of enduring love for all beloveds across the universe. It must certainly be wishful folklore. But who could really say for certain? I mean, unless you had been there.

"For as long as I remember, I have been watching both of you." With each word the princess was stalling. She thought that if she could just have a little more time beside the swan, life would start happening. Just a little more time. And suddenly everything would make sense. The girl was playing a hunch. "Today something flashed inside me when the two of you swam apart. A spasm of fear, perhaps."

"Or was it something else, child?"

"I just knew I had to swoop you up and hold you in my arms. Tell me about your mate."

"Long ago Goddess Saraswati brought our hearts together. We are perfect beloveds destined for each other. I could never find another like Hansaram anywhere. Or he another like me."

"Ah! Great Swan, I am so perplexed."

Great Swan slowly waddled back to the water's edge. Damayanti matched her deliberate pace.

"Princess, what is it you want?"

Her first impulse was to gallop into the palace and leap into her mother's arms. For no one ever posed such a question to Damayanti about such an important matter. In fact, while she was unacquainted with exercising her mind this way, the princess kept hearing the swan's words ring like a haunting conundrum in her ears. *'We are perfect beloveds destined for each other.'*

Even before she was old enough to understand the spoken word, Damayanti had heard Queen Bhavani recount how she selected Bhima to become her husband. Bhavani had been playing rivals against each other: Prince Bhima of Vidabhar and King Salya of Madra. Tradition called upon a princess to select her husband from a line of noblemen in a ritual known as a swayamvara. Throughout the appointed day, ancient prayers were recited by Brahman priests while purified butter was spooned over sacred fires. Tournaments were enacted for the noblemen to prove their worth. All the events were a preparation for the dramatic moment when the princess walked the line of suitors and hoisted her lotus garland. The swayamvara represented the highlight in the life of a princess.

From a tender age something in these stories always seemed missing for Damayanti. During her swayamvara Bhavani calculated what had weighed heaviest in her decision. Which combatant swung the mace with cruelest abandon? From her new husband's palace, would she be able to swim in the milky ocean where once upon a time gods and demons churned out the nectar of immortality? Or, would she stroke the locks of Shiva's matted hair streaming down from the Himalayas into the holy Ganga river? On her swayamvara day Bhavani had just turned twelve. So she viewed the world with both whimsical innocence and the pressing weight of family expectations.

The fortunes of these powerful men were assessed to fine minutiae. Bhavani's mother had whispered counsel toward Salya for his famed army of elephant riding warriors. Calculating planetary positions along columns of numbers gleamed from stacks of old parchment, the court astrologer presaged a great destiny with Bhima.

In the quintessential decision of her life Bhavani draped the lotus garland around the neck of young Prince Bhima. And why had she stopped in front of the Vidabhar lord? On an otherwise drab day, it was in this moment the god of the sun Surya burned through thick grey clouds. As the golden rays fell upon young Bhima, the princess fancied the glittering emerald jewel mounted on the hilt of his sword.

In all the times listening to her mother's recount of the Who's Who of royal suitors standing on the line, the gold thread sari and glittering jewels Bhavani wore that day, what stood out for Damayanti was the absence of love. If draping the lotus garland around a man's neck was the most important decision in the life of a princess ... and Damayanti had this mantra drilled into her head a million times ... then how was Bhavani swayed by the glint of a stone? It made no sense to the princess who was now two years older than her mother had been on the fateful day.

"Above the esteemed noblemen and sages traveling through Vidabhar," said Damayanti, "it is you whom I admire most. Great Swan, teach me the secret of enduring love. For it seems to be elusive among humans."

Here the bird stopped before reaching the water's edge. In a single graceful swivel of her long regal neck Great Swan dipped her beak to one side. The bird was taking note of this teen on the cusp of self-inquiry. "You show wisdom beyond your years."

"Why do you say that?" asked Damayanti.

"You could have asked me to find your perfect beloved. Instead you ask to learn the secret of enduring love."

Great Swan looked for signs of artifice. In rarified court social circles a princess gained power by learning to twist the world to her furtive whims. But there appeared to be none. Brushing fingertips to push the long loose strands of hair away from her flawless face, Damayanti asked, "Isn't love what all girls and boys yearn to understand?"

"Alas, no, sweet princess. Most humans only think of conquering love. Not to be conquered by love."

From the day he first wielded the Vidabhar scepter Damayanti's father Bhima had earned universal admiration as a fierce warrior on the battlefield and a king of virtue in his court. However the same could not be said for the queen. Aside from a slim waist and seductive neck, it appeared Bhavani had ceased striving for nobility. Most of the hours in the days of her life were spent scheming to retain the power she had won on the day of her swayamvara. At all costs Damayanti yearned for something more out of her life. Something worthy of a princess. Something to make a girl's heart flutter not just on the day of her swayamvara.

"When I saw you alone, Great Swan, I knew this was my chance. Will you guide me?"

"Daughter of King Bhima, you are so young." The swan stood up and turned to the center of the lake to face Hansaram. Without emitting a sound he stared back intently across the water. Then both looked skyward. As though conferring with someone hidden above the clouds, Great Swan muttered, "The girl has no idea what she is asking for."

Waiting motionless by the lake Damayanti swallowed her pride. Of course she knew what she was asking for. After all she was not just a princess in name. For years Damayanti had sat beside her father and listened to the petitions of subjects from every sphere of society. So she had gleaned the ways of coaxing the truth out from under the questioning nature of the mind. Sometimes though it was prudent to keep silent.

"Damayanti, are you prepared to give up everything?"

"What do you mean?" asked the princess.

In the last year speculation had grown across the continent around whom Damayanti would choose as her husband. Great Swan relayed gossip heard from passing birds. Kings of considerably greater wealth than Bhima would be vying to be the one chosen in the swayamvara. Adding fuel to the gossip mill were rumors gods were arguing among themselves as to which of them would wear Damayanti's lotus garland.

"Do you see how simply my mate and I live?" asked Great Swan. "Enduring love takes away everything that gets in the way. So think twice before you take me as your guru."

Great Swan recounted an ancient aphorism. For a pauper to renounce wealth is like a eunuch renouncing sex. One must possess something in abundance before it has any real meaning to give it up. The swan asked Damayanti if she was prepared to give up her inheritance of wealth, power and stature. Among various probable outcomes Great Swan raised the possibility that Damayanti's actions would earn her mother's scorn and break her father's heart.

Damayanti distilled all the court intrigue and complexity down to the heart of the matter. "All I want is to be the perfect mate alongside my perfect beloved. I see no reason to turn away just because others might want something else for me."

"So you think you are ready to learn the secret of enduring love?"

"With all my heart and soul."

"As a precursor, you must pass through seven inner gateways. Just now you snuck a peek through the first one."

"How can you be certain?"

"When you observed Hansaram and me moving away from each other, you said you felt a burning light but you didn't say where."

The princess blushed and turned to look at the lake.

"Was it at the seat of your spine?"

Damayanti nodded without taking her eyes off the water. Great Swan instructed the princess never again to feel embarrassed about the awakening of her body. The first place enduring love stirs is not in the heart. It is at the seat of the spine where the body's three primary energy channels start. The central one is a long hollow tube called Sishumina. A two-headed serpent named Kundalini crisscrosses through Sishumina seven times. At each crossing lies a gateway.

"Would it be accurate to describe the light as luminous heat rising from a burning ember?"

Again the princess nodded. Great Swan explained how the secret of enduring love fit in with the seven gateways. Back when the gods and goddesses were divvying up the tasks necessary to birth the universe, Brahma got the job of creating it. Vishnu is the one who sustains it. And Shiva transforms or destroys it. Ever notice how these gods are all male? So what were the goddesses up to? Well, while the big-shot gods were working on the outside structure of creation, the goddesses were designing the inner structure which is where the really important work was happening. Out of the chaotic void Saraswati plucked the strings of a musical instrument which inspired her beloved Brahma to stop his endless meditations and start creating the universe. One by one the soundwaves struck open the seven gateways inside Brahma. Stunned by the flurry of emotions awakened inside himself Brahma lumped the mishmash of feelings into one emotion: love. It was Saraswati's love which inspired Brahma to create galaxies, stars, planets, oceans, lands, animals, plants and the other sentient beings necessary to populate the universe.

Picture Lakshmi as the universal interior decorator arranging form and matter from the newborn creation. It was Lakshmi who gave the world the feminine touch of luxurious charm and beauty. Shakti brought the fervent yearning to merge with God which she called devotion. Both Shakti and Shiva expressed their devotion to God through their love for each other. In her infinite wisdom Shakti noticed how men of all races and castes were feverishly plotting to conquer the most loving, beautiful and devotional women.

Even the gods occasionally lost themselves in the quest to conquer love. So Saraswati, Lakshmi and Shakti distilled the purest essence of love, beauty and devotion into a single elixir. Shakti devised a plan to hide the elixir in a location so secret that no conqueror could ever find it. Saraswati hugged and kissed her sister Shakti. And Lakshmi did the same. Next the goddess performed one final act. Shakti's gift to creation was that she dissolved herself into the elixir so that she could put a drop inside each of the seven gateways locked inside every sentient being. In so doing Shakti scattered herself across all creation, concealing with her, the secret of enduring love.

When the first gateway opens, you are changed. Nothing is ever quite the same again. Your capacity to receive and transmit the love energy is upgraded. Starting at the seat of the spine and progressing upward through seven gateways exposes the veils of illusion created by the mind. Opening a gateway carries a responsibility. Like pilgrims lost in the wilderness at night, people will look to you as a wayshower. How you conduct yourself will determine how far you travel on Shakti's journey to enduring love.

"But where do I fit into this story?" asked Damayanti.

"You have roused Shakti from her slumber. The mistake everyone makes is to shun her because of where she sleeps. Curry favor with the goddess. Feed her with your breath. Let her energies rise inside you. I will teach you yoga. When you are ready, Shakti will usher you through the first gateway. Then we will see how far you get. Young princess, this journey is not what you think it is."

To be clear, the princess had no memory of asking this spark of light to awaken at the seat of her spine. The wheels of dharma were turning. Damayanti had her role to play in this drama of gods and humans. What set her apart from other girls and boys was her refusal to stifle a deep yearning inside. Even if it meant exposing herself to great risk.

"Enduring love," shouted Damayanti loud enough to be heard by Hansaram and whoever was cloaked above the clouds, "is the fuel kindling the flame of my soul. I will not stop until I find the way to its source."

Great Swan waded into the lake. Without looking back, she paddled her webbed feet. Gliding elegantly along the water toward her mate, the swan pronounced in a barely audible voice, "Then let it begin."

2. Mantra

Four years passed with King Bhima and Queen Bhavani feeling the pressure build day after day. In other realms princes and queens of powerful kings were breathing down the necks of soothsayers and pundits to determine whether to wait for the beautiful princess or move on. From faraway northern isles to the west and east edges of human civilization, captains of commerce were eager to pluck this exquisite lotus blossom as a trophy to showcase. And so it was for Damayanti reputed to be the most beautiful of all women. Entering her nineteenth year, her every action and delay of action influenced millions of human beings, most of whom she would never meet.

Seated with legs crossed on a bench Damayanti opened her eyes and stretched her arms. After a time she turned to her guru and shyly asked, "Am I ready yet?"

Earlier that morning over a breakfast of papaya, curds and almonds, Bhavani had lobbied hard to announce a date. Why belabor the inevitable? Just pick a day! Like other mornings the princess forestalled with the excuse of needing to better understand herself to make a wise selection. The queen responded by quoting numbers: ten, thirteen, nine, twelve, twelve, eight, thirteen, seventeen and twelve as to the ages when her great grandmothers, grandmothers, mother and herself had walked the swayamvara line. Then came the names of princesses in neighboring lands and their ages when they married. During a pause in the verbal joust Damayanti rose and touched her mother's feet.

Just as quickly she darted outside to check on the irrigation channels distributing water to the fruit and nut trees and plants in the extensive palace gardens, fields and groves. After that she paid her respects to the plant devas who were the spirit beings assigned within the plant realm to protect each of the species of the fruit and nut trees, vegetables and flowers. Kneeling down she dug her hands into the earth. Here she talked to the devas as though they were her dearest aunties and uncles. This morning it was the tulsi, mint and thyme devas on whom the princess showered her love.

The devas responded by dancing with delight around the princess. Among themselves these beings conferred and negotiated before telling Damayanti the best places to plant new seeds or saplings. Year after year the Vidabhar gardens were producing such harvests that the subjects of the land had not known a famine since before Damayanti's birth. Far and wide this fortune was acknowledged as part of the beauty the gods had bestowed on Damayanti. And the princess was not so naïve as to be unaware of the power she wielded in dealing with her mother. Normally Bhavani left her entirely to her own devices in the groves and gardens. Just as she kept out of Damayanti's dealings with Great Swan. But not on this day.

Trailing after her daughter Bhavani demanded to know if getting a man's education had rendered Damayanti into a dimwitted girl. Why couldn't she perform a daughter's most basic duty? Rather than halting Damayanti's progress Bhavani went through the vegetable garden insisting that the great reputation of the Vidabhar princess would be irreparably tarnished if she failed to: one, marry into a noble family, two, produce healthy progeny, and three, please her husband's mother and father. A woman's time to act decisively was in her early years when her lifeforce was strongest.

Damayanti smiled as she examined the moisture content of a banana leaf. She whispered to the banana tree that the lessons of Great Swan were working. A few months earlier she would have quarreled about the queen's pitiable state of knowledge as to how her own kingdom operated. Now she no longer felt the need to defend her journey by disparaging her mother. The banana tree whispered back that he hoped the princess would ever remain faithful to the earth and the sentient beings whose voices went largely unheard by humans.

Beneath the canopy of the mango grove Bhavani continued expounding on the source of a woman's power. Damayanti could quote what was coming next. No princess would ever be more powerful than the moment she hoisted the white petal garland. Even the power of a queen or a mother paled in comparison to holding the undivided attention of the most accomplished men in the land. Though fleeting this moment represented an eternity in the life of a woman. To see the look on those men's faces like an army of little boys pleading helplessly for a mother's love. What good was Damayanti's famed beauty if she didn't spend it at her prime?

Bhavani failed to see how the consequence of a princess holding her greatest power during this singular event only supported Damayanti's decision to postpone it. From one plant to the next the mother followed the daughter. The arguments shifted to the inherent merits of motherhood and then to the secret pleasures of being alone with a man.

When Damayanti refused to feign interest in what Bhavani considered the sanctity of mother-daughter intimacy, the queen launched into a bitter harangue against Bhima for always pampering Damayanti. As their firstborn child Damayanti was encouraged from a young age to sit beside her father and listen to the happenings in the court. When the first of her two younger brothers was old enough to learn his ABC's, Bhima made sure his clever daughter studied right alongside her brother under the pretext of acting as an additional tutor. Now Bhavani chastised her husband for failing to honor the differences between boys and girls. Damayanti had become overly free-thinking to the point of forgetting her place within the kingdom. The clock of nuptial obligation was ticking so loudly that everyone else in the universe but Damayanti felt the sense of impending urgency.

Back in Vedic times it was not unusual for humans to study the wisdom of monkeys, snakes, elephants, swans, eagles and other animals esteemed for their knowledge. In fact from the outset of his daughter's yoga training Bhima was keen to observe her progress and sought permission to be initiated by the wise swan. As the queen followed the princess around the garden trying to bully her into naming a date, Damayanti's mind traced back to when she and her father received mantra initiation. Dressed in white robes the king and the princess walked down from the palace at sunrise single-file through the colorful flower gardens with lilies in one hand and a coconut in the other. By the lake Bhima dropped to his knees and placed his forehead on the webbed feet of his new guru. Great Swan took his offerings and set them on the altar facing the sun. Damayanti knelt down in pranam as her father had done. Only she maintained contact longer. A warm tingling flooded through her forehead.

The princess rose to sit on her heels and watch Great Swan whisper words to King Bhima that she could not hear. Then the swan instructed him to close his eyes and take in long slow breaths. When he achieved a state of mental stillness, Great Swan crept close and whispered briefly. Afterward the swan listened while Bhima whispered back to confirm he had accurately received the mantra. Then they sat in silence as the rays of the sun revealed the subtleties of aging gathered on her father's face and shoulders. It meant so much to the princess that her father not only approved but was participating in the path right alongside her. Damayanti's heart heaved with so much emotion that a cry escaped from her lips when Great Swan pecked her slender beak once on his forehead. When Bhima opened his eyes, Great Swan nodded her approval. Without glancing at Damayanti, the guru and disciple rose and walked out of sight into the garden. Here Great Swan selected a site for him to meditate on the new mantra.

Upon returning the swan sat down on the soft grass. In a solemn voice she explained how the mantra was like a raft on the stormy ocean of human suffering. Before life challenges arise, recite the mantra to start and end each day so you are prepared. In the midst of life challenges, recite the mantra constantly as though it charges the air you breathe with lifeforce. In the midst of life celebrations, recite the mantra to prevent indulging in acts that deplete your soul. The mantra quiets the mind and liberates the soul. It is the password to open gateways. Before you eat, sprinkle your food with mantra. When you bathe, wash every body part with mantra. When you sleep, dream mantra. When you perform your life's work, work mantra. When you make love, love mantra. When you give birth to life, envelope your child in mantra. When you die and lose all your possessions and loved ones, recite the mantra even as Yama lord of death ties his noose around your wrist and leads you to The Footsteps of God. It is your first and last friend. It connects the disciple to the guru. And it connects the beloveds Shakti and Shiva. In their embrace lies the secret of enduring love.

Damayanti closed her eyes and took in a long slow breath. Great Swan whispered the most important sounds the princess would hear in her lifetime.

Om Shakti Om ... Om Shiva Om

Damayanti whispered the mantra back.

Om Shakti Om ... Om Shiva Om

Great Swan led Damayanti to a spot all by herself in the garden. The princess closed her eyes and took in a long slow breath. And she silently recited the mantra.

Om Shakti Om ... Om Shiva Om

The princess wondered how long Great Swan would leave them meditating. All day? Who was holding the royal umbrella to shade her father's head? Why was Shakti first? And Shiva second? It wasn't long before her stomach started growling. Was a special meal being prepared to celebrate? Who was preparing it? Damayanti's mind drifted to an enchanted grove where teams of white-haired monkeys were climbing along high tree limbs in search of the sweetest fruits to celebrate Damayanti's boon of receiving the mantra and taking Great Swan as her guru. She imagined Hanuman, the most beloved of monkeys, feeding wildly sweet dripping slices of mango into her mouth while she thought she was meditating in peaceful bliss.

When thoughts seduce the mind away from the mantra, Great Swan had instructed the princess to return to the silent repetition. Her guru told her to refrain from getting lost in judgments about wandering. Just return to the mantra. If judgment arose, fine. Notice them and return to the mantra. Great Swan explained that the ordinary mind was lazy and subject to endless loops of the same fluctuating queries of thoughts that she dubbed *the million-question mind.* Mantra repetition was designed to train the mind to dissolve this loop of illusion in order to merge with Shakti. Great Swan declared that nothing less than extraordinary discipline would suffice. Bhima and Damayanti pledged to meditate on the mantra every morning and night. Damayanti would meditate with Great Swan here by the lake while Bhima would practice in places suited to his duties as lord of the land.

Damayanti was surprised how easily the mantra worked. It was as though she had already heard herself repeating it a million times before. Her mind became completely still. She heard her guru state that when we die, the only possession we take with us are the steps we take on our spiritual path. Not fame, money, children or even the beloved. But the merit of our practice goes with us into the great mystery. So each mantra repeated with love is like a gold coin dropped into our own goddess vault. Over time the yogi earns a great fortune that no one can take away. Not even Yama the lord of death.

After repeating the mantra enough times that the princess lost count, she felt something hard nudge her forehead just above her eyebrows. Was it Hanuman tempting her with an invitation to swing from the limbs of the fruit orchards with the other monkeys? After careful consideration Damayanti decided to decline Hanuman's attempt to break her concentration. Or could it be someone else? Perhaps an interloper sent by the gods? The princess traced the identity of this mischievous tapping to a handsome gandharva *celestial warrior* drumming the love beat of her heart. If she could just remember to stick with the mantra, Damayanti convinced herself this celestial warrior would carry her in his blazing arms all the way to the gates of Indra's heavenly palace where they would be welcomed and, along with so many others, together they would drink Indra's immortal nectar and sing and dance in celebration of God's love.

This was the way the princess meditated the first day with her guru's mantra. At least part of the time she lost herself in vivid girlish fantasies. Eventually she realized who was doing the tapping. And it wasn't a monkey god. Nor a celestial lover. Just then the princess remembered she was still in the middle of her mantra initiation.

Throughout the thread of wandering thought Great Swan had been pecking the same spot above the brow of her forehead. Without warning during one of these strikes Damayanti felt her guru's beak penetrate her skull. Oddly the princess felt no pain. Instead what she experienced was a yummy warm expansion as though her skull was being filled with wonderful nectar. The dimensions of her cranial cavity were being pushed out to hold more of the liquid. Damayanti dared not open her eyes for fear of halting whatever was happening. Calling upon the months of accrued faith in her teacher, she recited the mantra with extra fervor. The next thing the princess felt was a narrow tool reaching into the opening in her forehead to scoop out a tunnel. Then she felt her guru's long slender tongue slipping through a gateway. There Great Swan buried a seed deep in the center of her brain. This seed emitted the vibration of the mantra.

Om Shakti Om ... Om Shiva Om

In any ordinary state of mind the princess would have screamed for her life. *Great Swan, what are doing to me? Get that seed out of my brain!* Instead she followed the instructions to notice the fluctuations of the mind and return to the mantra.

Om Shakti Om ... Om Shiva Om

Damayanti felt the warm nectar washing the glands in her brain. Eventually the liquid overflowed so much that it dripped down from the roof of her mouth onto her tongue. The princess marveled at its taste and the coincidence of her earlier fantasies of Hanuman feeding her succulent mangos in the enchanted grove of fruit trees and her gandharva lover taking her into heaven and feeding her Indra's immortal nectar. Her secret wish was being fulfilled. To keep this nectar ever flowing she silently promised Great Swan to never miss a day or night of meditation. Then she ushered her mind back to the practice while the nectar slid down the back of her tongue and dripped into her spine. The mantra was filling her from the inside out.

Om Shakti Om ... Om Shiva Om

Great Swan's voice spoke over the mantra uttering words that streamed tears down the cheeks of the princess. Even as she heard the words the princess kept repeating the mantra and feeling the nectar fill her. From this day forward Damayanti understood there was no turning back. Implanted in the seed along with the mantra were her guru's words.

The victory you are seeking is the one
Where no one has to lose
In order for you to win
Feed this seed with mantra
And your victory will feed countless hungry souls
Enduring love is right here
Locked inside seven gateways

From the seat of Damayanti's spine to her crown, the seven gateways suddenly swung open. For an instant the princess experienced the surging power of Shakti pulse through every cell in her body. Was this what it felt like to merge with the Great Elusive Goddess? The unseen cosmic target of Lord Shiva's eternal embrace? She looked inside herself for a face to go with the energy. Then the meditation was over. The gateways closed as suddenly as they opened. Damayanti was instructed to open her eyes. Great Swan gave her a plump ripe guava. As she savored the fruit Damayanti was convinced she had completed the work ... Shakti had bestowed the blessing upon her ... Great Swan had exaggerated the difficulty of this inner journey ... and she would meet her perfect beloved the next day.

Since that morning nearly four years ago the princess had been meditating twice a day. But she had not so much as cracked a glimmer of light inside the first gateway. Receiving his own private guidance, King Bhima had stopped attending his daughter's lessons. Becoming a yogi, it turned out was not all sweetness and bliss. Sometimes she chaffed at the effort required to satisfy her guru. In moments of loneliness the princess would think back to the memory of her mantra initiation.

After saying goodbye to the plant devas and promising her mother to consider setting a date, the princess walked out to the palace lake where she had been sitting in meditation. Even though Great Swan had sounded Om to announce the completion of the meditation, she was taking longer than normal to open her eyes. So this morning was one of those times when the princess observed her mind drifting back to her brief but exalted glimpse of merging with Shakti.

"Yes," replied the sage swan. "You are ready."

Instantly Damayanti wanted to exclaim in jubilation. Mother, I am finally ready for the next stage! Instead she closed her eyes and resumed her meditation. But her mind was busy retracing each footstep after the mantra initiation. This period of study had been the richest time of her life. Was she really ready, she wondered. Would this moment signal the high-water mark of her spiritual journey? Or would her husband turn out to have a guru like Great Swan? Would Great Swan take flight to her new home so the princess could continue her practice? Perhaps her husband would study with Great Swan as Bhima had done. Might other women join her in creating a new lineage of passing along feminine wisdom?

All her life was a preparation to hear this word of affirmation. Damayanti tried her best to shield herself from jealousies and expectations. While the gossip went unspoken in her presence, women and men and girls and boys held Damayanti up as the ultimate fantasy goddess born into human form. *If only they could live in her body for a day? A week? A year? Especially when Damayanti draped the lotus garland around her future husband's neck.* The scene was being enacted between girls and boys in village fields everywhere throughout the subcontinent. The notion of a woman selecting her husband was indeed a rare occurrence. The days and nights of the honeymoon were beyond conjuring.

What if this young princess got up from the wrong side of the bed on the morning of the swayamvara? What if she chose poorly? Or the gods refused to bless the union? Now that the long anticipated approval had come, Damayanti could not fathom how she could be ready when the path ahead looked so steep.

Over the last year she had come to recognize Great Swan's admonition about the burden of beauty. Once her father made the announcement, a million covetous eyes would set upon her. The roads to Vidabhar would be flooded with traffic. In spite of her refusal to acknowledge the world of betrothal, Damayanti received a procession of gifts including parcels of land and palaces constructed along sacred rivers, Nubian servants of great strength and beauty, armies of seasoned soldiers and armaments to defend Vidabhar from any foe, garments of more hues than the human eye could discern, every accessory a woman could dream of, scented oils and perfumes distilled from the most precious flowers, masterfully crafted statues dedicated to every god and goddess. Without exception Great Swan instructed her disciple to return each item.

Enduring love cannot be conveyed in objects. No matter how lavish or romantic. Love starts with a pure frequency rising from the seat of the spine. Great Swan taught the princess how to peel away the trappings of love to discover what about it was enduring. The princess had taken to wearing a simple terracotta robe with crystals hidden inside to correspond to each gateway along her body. Practices of yoga and healing arts dominated Damayanti's waking hours. Such was the influence of Great Swan that every day was dedicated to Damayanti awakening an authentic connection between her own body and the universal body of Shakti.

The natural order stated that it was the feminine destiny to guide the masculine along the pathway of love. The teaching required many months of practice for Damayanti to even begin ushering its secrets into her own body. Despite the preferential treatment she had received in her education, Damayanti's childhood training told her that women were born to yield to the wisdom of fathers, husbands, lords and priests. After all so few women received any formal education. Great Swan explained males were born with an innate proclivity to analyze, conquer and create inanimate things. The corresponding gifts of the feminine were to intuit, nurture and create life. Love dwelt within the province of the female.

Great Swan predicted in the future women would stand as equals with men in the centers of education. For now, though, this imbalance could be turned to a woman's advantage. By forgoing worship at the altar of the mind, Damayanti could focus on her own body as the creator of life where the feminine is naturally dominant. The journey required an initiation that Damayanti sensed was waiting just over the horizon.

"So," Damayanti coughed. She cleared her throat and continued, "What exactly am I ready for?"

"To study men," said Great Swan.

"To study men?" Damayanti echoed her guru's words in the first volley into an emerging full-blown hissy fit. The princess jumped away from Great Swan as though she was leaping off a hot frying pan. "Me? How? Where? Ahmmmmmmm?" The princess stomped her feet down the path toward the palace. Then she turned around and stomped back. "Do you really think my father and mother will let me walk outside the palace gate to study men?" Each time she uttered the word *men*, Damayanti increased the volume of her voice. "Great Swan, are you crazy? Men? And me?" The princess clenched her fists and started hitting herself while she paced. "Men? You above everyone should know the sort of attention that hovers around me."

"Silence!" honked Great Swan. "Stop pacing now! Where has your center gone? Have you retained any of the yoga I taught you?"

Damayanti retreated to her seated position on the grass. Sinking her head into her hands, she muttered, "I can't do this, Great Swan. Don't you get it? It's not my place. Even if I am a beautiful princess, I'm just a girl."

"Listen! It is not enough to still your body. Stop the pacing of your mind. Now!"

The princess folded her legs into lotus petals. She closed her eyes and took in a long slow breath. She recited the mantra.

Om Shakti Om ... Om Shiva Om

By the third repetition she felt the connection between her body and the universal body of Shakti. Using techniques gleened from Great Swan, the princess controlled her breath and her million-question mind slowed to a halt. Hot tears flowed and her body demeanor softened. Before long she was resting her head at her teacher's feet.

Great Swan reiterated that the next stage of training for the princess required peering into the souls of men. It is impossible to select a perfect mate without understanding the opposite gender.

instead of pining for a handsome prince to lift you in his arms, all you had to do was take Shakti's hand to fly out of the chasm. Last night we carried you out because you did not know how to do it yourself. Sweet child, fly now with us. Practice lifting the rainbow shaft. The Goddess within you lies behind seven gateways. Do not beat yourself up with small thoughts. In the beginning, it is this way for all of us.

5. Flock of Sisters

For weeks the flock flew from one capital to the next in kingdoms throughout the greater Asian subcontinent. Then weeks turned into months as the winged sisterhood journeyed across vast mountain ranges and oceans to foreign palaces of untold wealth and power. Damayanti studied men of different cultures and bloodlines. From her cloaked bird's eye perch she observed the phases of development necessary for men to become sage kings and maharajas, respected ministers of commerce and diplomats, luminous yogis and healers, skilled farmers and masons, trusted fishmongers and carpet merchants, wise philosophers and scholars, feared assassins and warlords, great athletes and orators, hunters and foot soldiers, holy rishis and saints. From boyhood to adolescence to young adulthood to full maturity to declining faculties and finally death. The princess paid extra attention to the cause and effect of why some men soared in their arenas of achievement while others degenerated into compulsive gamblers and charlatans, drunkards and thieves.

Great Swan taught her to peer into the souls of men and examine their deepest yearnings. What fascinated Damayanti was the frequency to which success hinged on one or two insignificant events later affecting other decisions which stitched together the fabric of a man's life. For the holy rishi presently acting as the trusted guide to kings and beggars, it was observing the illness and death of his elder brother in adolescence which solidified his resolve to leave his home and journey alongside a wandering sadhu. In the life of the feared assassin, it was observing his own frozen face of betrayal as a small boy being ganged up on by other boys. After days without a single catch the trusted fishmonger learned the value of an honest day's labor when in his father's fishing net they reeled in a gold jewel bracelet that his father later entrusted to a local Brahman. She wondered what future event would be decisive in the life of her husband. Perhaps among the many lives she was observing the key event was happening right now in front of her eyes.

On many occasions the princess was moved to tears by acts of kindness or cruelty. Where she had expected to encounter so much certainty and strength, the princess discovered that inside the hearts of these men of great accomplishments, they were every bit as afraid of life as she was. Perhaps more so.

Damayanti asked her guru many questions. Where do men find the confidence to act boldly in life? Why do men hold more power in this world than women? How does a man know when he has found his perfect mate? What is a man's greatest fear? Is his success in life defined by his capacity to dissolve this greatest fear? Or does he simply push forward in spite of it? Great Swan replied with silence. So the princess took her questions inward. In her moments after meditating she asked Shakti. Then she listened. In this way Damayanti learned many secrets about the ways of men.

Night after night though there remained a single question which plagued her dreams. What if I fail to recognize my perfect beloved on the day he crosses my path? What then?

When she posed this question to Shakti, all the princess heard was agonizing silence. In her heart she was becoming acquainted with her own greatest fear.

At each stop the sister swans seated themselves in concentric circles around Damayanti. Together they meditated. The princess of enduring love was learning to trust the rainbow light igniting at the seat of her spine. The voice of many-as-one now comforted her. Surrounded by so many sisters who were becoming as dear to her as her father, mother and brothers, Damayanti felt a level of nurturance which words could not capture. She was learning to trust the radiant light of Shakti ... that she was ... that they were ... that is, intrinsically, the feminine mystique ... embracing her inner language of expression among her sisters. It was at this time she began to hear her own voice among the chorus of many-as-one, which came as a surprise, because there was no conscious effort on her part. Everything simply flowed in these moments of effervescent interconnectedness.

Om Shakti Om ... Om Shiva Om

After observing so many men unbeknownst to her presence, Damayanti began contemplating a new direction of inquiry. Who am I seeking in my perfect beloved? What qualities are important to me? Over time the princess had shifted priorities. The accumulation of material wealth which so many prized in their beloveds lost luster in Damayanti's eyes. At the same time she was a princess accustomed to fine things, not just for herself, but for the subjects depending on the leadership of their king. The notions of what comprised a noble man had actually become more nebulous than ever. The use of power by influential men to acquire more of it made her soul cringe. From her new perspective she wondered how she would view her own father when she returned home. If he were her age, would she fall in love with a younger version of Bhima? Despite the teachings and meditations dedicated to embracing the goddess hidden inside Damayanti's seven gateways, the princess was embarrassed to admit her mind kept gravitating toward discovering the identity of her perfect beloved.

One chilly morning three years after leaving Vidabhar the flock of white swans set down on the wide calm waters of the holy river Kshipra running alongside Avanti the capital of Ujjain. Downstream they spied a crowded east-facing ghat where a city of men were performing daily ablutions. Each of them recited a prayer of salutation to Surya the sun god and Kshipra the river goddess. Then they immersed their bodies completely in the water. Without haste they washed their bodies and minds yielding impurities to Kshipra. Then they got out and seated themselves on recently vacated sections of long tiered rows of stone ledge. Here thousands of men let the rising sun dry their goose pimpled skin in preparation for the day of labor. This procession of purification had been reenacted in the river every morning for as long as men had inhabited this fertile valley.

Among them was a charismatic handsome man who in no way attempted to set himself apart. Great Swan identified him as Mohanna the king's chief minister and broker of a series of longstanding peace agreements between neighboring kingdoms. His gift of political negotiation had gained him fame in faraway courts. Yet he bathed among men from humble origins. Instead of pitting one party against another to curry favor, Mohanna possessed the rare capacity to listen for the purpose of shared mutual benefit. Though kings and queens had offered their daughters as a way of elevating his status to nobility, out of principle, he had steadfastly refused. For Mohanna knew that if he married into a single kingdom, the alliance whose number had grown to seven would inevitably unravel. All his life he placed the greater good for the many above personal gain for himself.

Damayanti could see how her father would be well pleased to embrace Mohanna as a third son. The prosperity of Vidabhar would surely grow with Mohanna assuming the role of lead counsel to Bhima and eventually to her eldest brother when he assumed the throne. What's more Damayanti would not have to abandon her studies with Great Swan to assume a new life in Ujjain. Her mind was adding up one reason after another to welcome courtship with Mohanna. She pictured birthing four beautiful children adored by this man. It was a picturesque life any woman would envy.

"What do you observe in this man's soul?" asked Great Swan breaking the reverie.

"So much love. Not for one person. But for everyone. Mohanna is the most pure man we have met."

"And what do you feel for him?"

"Awe," said the princess pausing to get a better view of his physique. "And respect."

Great Swan asked if Damayanti could envision making a happy life with Mohanna. The princess wondered if her teacher had been reading her mind. She smiled and nodded her head. Then Great Swan asked, "Would the light of your soul grow stronger in the arms of this man? Or weaker?"

"I don't know."

Great Swan changed the subject by asking the princess to identify why she thought so many men were attracted to her.

Damayanti feigned modesty at her elevated stature in the eyes of men. With her beak she pecked at pebbles along the dry bank of the riverbed. In retort Great Swan listed the gifts kings and gods had showered upon her any one of which would have removed poverty from an entire city. Still Damayanti pleaded ignorance.

"Think fast, princess, or the fears haunting your dreams will come true. As soon as this conversation is complete, the flock is flying back to Vidabhar."

"Men see me as beautiful," admitted Damayanti.

"And what is beauty?"

"A pleasing shape of my hips, mouth, face, hair, thighs. A quality in my voice. The way I walk. A mysterious scent no man can quite name but keeps him awake at night."

"Now we are getting somewhere. What is this scent?"

Damayanti's mind went blank. Although it was universally agreed she possessed beauty in greater abundance than any other woman, the princess had never given it much thought. She considered the subject a slippery slope of feminine vanity. The last thing the princess wanted to grow up to become was the sort of woman who plied guileless tricks and powders to cling to beauty.

"Whenever you look at men," continued Great Swan, "it is vital to remember you are the beacon of their deepest yearning. You send out a brilliant light that allows men to find their way. Most women fritter away their essence searching within the male polarity for the beacon they will follow. When in truth a woman's power lies within. If you walk freely among these men right now, every single one of them will try to steal your light."

"Even Mohanna?" asked the princess. Her voice sounded crushed as Great Swan's words landed like a physical blow.

"Yes, even him."

In a second Damayanti's fantasy of their conjugal life vanished. All hope of enduring love seemed like a girl's dream. Did not Great Swan tell Damayanti that dreams were a bottomless chasm? The princess felt more confused than ever. Adding to her distress was Great Swan's intimation that the flock of white swans were homeward bound. In her mind it seemed the subject of enduring love was impossibly vast and arcane. There was so much to learn and so little time. How would she ever gain the slightest glimmer of mastery?

"Not because he is evil. But because, in your presence, Mohanna would see a magnificent light of unsurpassed beauty. And he would become so infatuated as to forget that he possessed it himself. In a moment he would cherish you above all sentient beings only to resent you later as the cause of his own forgetfulness. Do you recall what I said on the day you snatched me into your arms? 'The perfect mate is the one who was created just for me. And me for him.' Do you understand? You must shine among all men without taking advantage of their weakness or allowing any violation of your luminous mantle."

"But how?"

"All these months you have been doing it. Only these men have not been able to see you. Soon this will change."

"And I will no longer be enveloped in a flock of sister swans."

"Take back those words! Damayanti, listen to me. For the rest of your life you will *always* be surrounded by us. This is what it means to be initiated into our sisterhood of Goddess Shakti. You are one of us. And we are one of you."

Why had the rainbow shaft traveled outside the sisterhood to a specific target? How was it that the light became suddenly visible to these men when no such problem had occurred before? Was the swan clan spell dissolving? The princess anxiously swiveled her head left and right. In the midst of arcing light with its threat of attack and all the shouting, the sister flock of so many feathers remained unruffled. This calmness was in stark contrast to her own. In different places she stabbed her beak into her own plumage and spat out feathers. Damayanti was frantically checking to determine what was happening. She looked down at her webbed feet. Sure enough, she was still a bird.

"What does it mean?" pleaded the princess.

Great Swan interrupted a most exquisite avian cackle long enough to whisper, "Mission accomplished, girl. Ready to go home?"

02 Swayamvara – Sex Gateway

Salutations ... Gods & Goddesses, Saints & Sadhus
Lords of Light, Men & Beasts
Earth Elementals & Spirits of the Sky
On the vernal equinox
In the bountiful land of Vidabhar
King Bhima & Queen Bhavani request
Your darshan (blessing & presence) for the ancient swayamvara
Where our daughter Princess Damayanti
Will walk the lines of noble suitors
& hoist high her white lotus scented garland
Might you be the One
To win the trophy of her enduring love?

"Excuse me," interrupted Indra. "What's going on here?" Gandharvas ... that is, celestial warriors in service of defending all known realms of existence from demons ... unable to resist the sweet heavenly sounds of the apsaras were also roused to lend their booming voices and chiseled bodies to the song and dance. "Why is everyone so happy?" demanded the lord of heaven. "And can someone explain why no human warriors have been joining our rank?"

"Have you not heard, Lord Indra?" replied Narada over the festive din. "No one on earth is quarrelling. "

"No wars? No fits of pugilism? How can this be?" demanded the commander responsible for upholding light against the forces of darkness. Into his celestial army Indra accepted fallen human warriors among his mighty gandharvas until such time as they choose to return to earth. Such was the vertical cycle of life and death. Like the falling of rain that flows into rivers and oceans only to one day expire back into the sky as vapor in clouds. Indra could not recall a time when the flow of warriors into his army had been interrupted for so long. Of course, as a celestial being possessed with divine insight, Indra knew exactly what was transpiring on earth and in his celestial realm. But he had a role to play in this cosmic drama. And naturally he played it to the hilt.

"What spell of blissful coexistence has intoxicated the human spirit?"

"Her name is Damayanti, Lord Indra," said Parvata. "For a fortnight all humanity has ceased aggression in the common cause of rejoicing her much anticipated swayamvara."

As Narada described the grand array of suitors and retinues as well as auspicious omens for the event, the rank of luminous immortals swelled in the main chamber. Parvata focused his ascetic mind to project multiple streaming images onto the crystal wall for the preparations happening below on earth. The twain saints captivated everyone amid the aura of love inspired by a beautiful princess and her declaration to take a mate.

"Why am I always the last one to hear about the really juicy human gossip?" snapped Indra. Typically his involvement with humans was devoted to slaying demons and providing otherwise much needed providence at the darkest hours of humanity's troubles.

"Why ask why?" teased a winking Chandri goddess of the moon.

"Let's party on earth!" chimed Agni god of fire.

All the gods and celestial beings shouted a unanimous second. The god of oceans and rivers Varuna enlisted one of the gandharvas to hang up a sign on heaven's gate:

Gods on Vacation

Come back later

Weeks ago Varuna had squared away a deal with mermaids and dolphins to cover for him. Agni left apprentices in charge of making sure sacred fires stayed lit everywhere. And the lord of death Yama declared an amnesty that underscored in everyone's mind that these big fellows meant business. "Nobody is going to die for the next 24 hours."

"You rascals were holding out on me," boomed Indra. "Hoping to scoot down and win the lotus garland without your thunder daddy. Well, I always knew there was a reason to be nice to saints." As he was speaking Indra touched two fingers to his forehead. Bowing his head the lord of heaven shot two beams of light into the feet of Parvata and Narada. "Today I finally discovered what it is," he shouted. "Let's go!"

"Don't flatter yourself, Mr. Thunderbolt," countered Agni. Waves of heat shimmered from the god of fire's body. "The princess will never get cold in my bed. On winter nights that goes a long way with beautiful princesses."

"Hey, Agni! Can you bodysurf with Damayanti on tidal waves of oceanic nectar?" So saying Varuna tumbled through the air flailing his four arms wildly in all directions. The contagion set in motion by Damayanti's acceding to the spring swayamvara had indeed leaked into the heavens.

"Fellows, chill out," Yama hollered. "None of you stand a chance. I can give Damayanti immortality with my touch. Besides I'm the stud-liest looker in this god group." Normally the most taciturn member of divine ensemble Yama swung his infamous noose, used to usher spirits out of their empty husks of departing physicality, into the air like a bronco-bucking cowboy poised to lasso the beautiful princess of Vidabhar. "So who wants to be my best man?"

The goddess of creation, wisdom and arts Saraswati caused everyone in the crystal palace to stop what they were doing and reflect. "My sources on earth assure me," she announced with a voice of serene authority, "the princess plans to cross up all you chest-thumping fools." From every direction the celestial ones turned to her. Finally the singing and dancing stopped. Saraswati continued, "Didn't you know?" Saraswati paused long enough to insure she had everyone's undivided attention. "She's been training to take the orange robe of a sannyasin renunciate and put the lotus garland around her own neck?"

"Is that really Damayanti's destiny?" asked Indra mischievously. "Or yours, sweetest Saraswati?" All beamed with blissful mirth including the goddess herself. For Saraswati, as the feminine counterpart of Lord Brahma the Creator of the Universe, dwelled in regions of truth that left the other gods guessing. It was all part of the *lila* ... that is, the divine universal play ... for each being, including these illustrious deities, to perform his or her role in this great drama of unfolding consciousness ... without taking any of it too seriously.

"Leave it to the most beautiful woman ever to grace the earth to leave us all in the lurch," cracked Agni.

"Hey, guys!" sang Chandri. " Every night for years I've been spying for you. So don't screw it up!"

In this manner the gods and goddesses hopped aboard Indra's majestic golden chariot Puskpaka and descended toward earth. Members of the celestial entourage danced to an irresistible pumping beat. Of course having a good time was nothing new to the gods. But today felt especially choice. Among these ancient lords and ladies of light there was a consensus that things might actually get and stay better for those poor suffering sods down on earth.

A stunning apsara named Urvasi grabbed the steering wheel of Indra's famed chariot which would be more accurately described as a convertible spaceship the size of a mid-sized city. Pushpaka contained flowering gardens with soaring trees, magical nectar-filled rivers with water fountains and flying fish. Anyway, the apsara could not resist driving this bad-ass golden hovercraft in loop-tee-loops through the clouds. When she got to unfettered blue sky over the capital of Vidabhar, Urvasi whispered seductively into Varuna's ear. It didn't take much coaxing for the sexy nymph to get Varuna to show off his aquatic powers. Working together they spelled out in big neon pink letters.

We Love U, D!

Pick a god hunk for your Sweetie!

These divine antics went on for considerably longer than it took to reach terra firma. Only after Indra decided to assert some cosmic authority did things simmer down. "Let's get it together," commanded Indra. "Come on, now. Gods and goddesses, are you with me?" Indra chanted. "'One love.' I can't hear you!" The band of gandharvas and apsaras amped the music to a thunderous volume. "'One heart.' Okay? Everybody, are you singing with me? 'Let's get together and feel all right.' This is the last song. So get it out of your systems. We can't let the humans see us horsing around like a bunch of monkeys."

8. Indra's Favor

Drawn by pairs of well-trained steeds down on earth, Virasen and Nala traveled astride lightweight chariots over seldom used cow paths without attendants or ministers. Carrying little more than bedrolls, change of formal clothes, skins holding oils of sandalwood from the sacred royal grove as their nuptial gift, the king and prince sped over the earth with feigned masculine fury. Tomorrow when the sun blazed across the western sky men and gods would battle for the attention of the celebrated princess who would select her mate in front of all the world. But this morning's journey was a series of jousts strictly between a father and his son.

In a booming voice Virasen shouted to the sky a wager to wrestle the god of time. If the king were to defeat time, he would keep the lad forever by his side. Just the way they were today. But not even kings possessed such power. No, he thought, *time* reigned supreme over kingdoms. Not men. And love reigned over time. But, feeling his own mortality, Virasen marveled at the strength and gait bursting out of this young man and he pondered what his son would accomplish in the years ahead that the king had left untouched. Already Nala had gained acclaim for his mastery with horses and throwing dice. In his short life he had never lost an equine race or a game with the six-sided stones.

Since the incident by the pond Nala seemed possessed by a passion for life. Together they cavorted like boys making up wagering games out of nothing. Who would spot the first rhododendron blooming along the brook? Or predict which direction a pair of falcons soaring high above a grove of tall neem trees would turn? Whose team of horses crested the hill fastest? From the first time Nala ambled into the palace stable as little more than a toddler he had possessed a rare gift with horses. They adored him. As a child he was found sleeping in the stable more nights than in his own room. Nala's winning streak remained unbroken today. For three days it had been this way since setting out from the capital Hastinapura. Neither of them wanted it to end. They shared in the pleasures of men that were rarely so simple.

Spiraling down from the clouds, Indra called out, "Salutations and honor, Virasen venerated king of Nishada." Indra's charioteer Matali conveyed Indra, Agni, Varuna and Yama on a separate smaller emerald-studded chariot off the massive main vessel. Without emitting the slightest mechanical sound the chariot nimbly hovered forward until it settled inches from the earth.

"Salutations and honor to you, great Indra, lord of heaven," replied Virasen. "What an extraordinary blessing to receive the darshan of so many gods. May I present my son, Nala?"

In the last demon war Virasen had made his bones as the bravest warrior among human kings fighting on the front line alongside the Celestial Legion. While he was acquainted with the others, Virasen had never been so close that he could reach out and touch them. To receive the darshan of four gods simultaneously portended great happenings. Virasen was certain this meeting was connected with the mysterious light arcing into his son back at the hunter's pond. Whenever there were gods present, there had to be a goddess nearby operating the levers of cause and effect. At least this was Virasen's theory. And in his heart the center of devotion was always Goddess Shakti.

The king and prince placed their palms in prayer together over their hearts. They closed their eyes and bowed their heads. And the gods did the same. It was a poignant moment of yielding together to the Great Mystery.

"First, tell me, Virasen," boomed Indra shattering the silence. "Are the humans in your realm happy these days?"

"Not so much as the gods."

"Don't be so sure, Virasen. No matter whom Damayanti chooses, before tomorrow's sunset, all but one will languish in misery. My friends and I have made a pact that it will not be all four of us. What a splendid looking son. What did you say his name is?"

Nala stepped forward to speak for himself in greeting the immortals. First was Lord Yama distinguished by the long jet black mane running down his shoulders, the glittering rings of gold dangling from his ears and his shimmering black-as-midnight obsidian skin. At his belt the lord of death tapped the knotted noose with his fingertips. "Young Prince, the next time you gaze into these eyes," said Yama pointing to his own face, "the circumstances will be far different."

"Yama, why are you always scaring everybody? Kid, don't listen to him. I'm Agni and he's Yama the lord of Death." To lighten the mood Agni

9. Little Things

As noblemen, neither the father nor son's head were easily turned by displays of power or wealth. But to be greeted by four gods and asked a favor by Lord Indra, Virasen and Nala felt as though they had just ridden through heaven's gate. Now everywhere they observed blessings from the gods. The closer they got to Vidabhar the more they marveled at the multitude of terraced rice paddies engineered with such clever irrigation channels along the steep rolling hills. Dominating the valleys were manicured groves of bananas, dates, almonds, pomegranates and mangos. Bhima and his citizens had cultivated the fertile land to muster levels of abundance in excess of any kingdom through which they had passed. On the faces of common people Virasen observed a contentment which only comes from a genuine sense of belonging to a shared destiny. While industrious in their labors, none showed signs of being worn down by their efforts.

With the forward cantering strides of his pair of horses Nala felt energized by the newness of the moment. Wending their way down alongside a river, the father and son recognized it was time to put aside their prankish ways. Amidst a grove of almond saplings Nala alighted his chariot and loosened the leather bridles. He picked out thistles and brushed road dust from the thick coats of the horses while the sinewy beasts slaked their thirst from a stone trough.

Not far away a foreman directed a team of young men to widen the irrigation trenches between rows of the skinny trees extending further than the eye could see. Pointing his tawny weathered hands to the places where excess water was puddling, the bushy browed Vidabhar commanded attention like a captain directing his infantry. There was no doubt in the mind of the prince that this grove was going to grow delicious almonds.

When he eventually noticed Virasen and Nala, the foreman smiled broadly and waved to them in greeting. Then he set the men to work and walked briskly to introduce himself. Within minutes the prince was peppering the savvy farmer with questions. How many seasons did he expect to wait for the first harvest? Why had he chosen this location? From where were they getting their water? How did the foreman calculate the number of trees this water source would feed? Who designed this almond grove? What could he tell them about his famed young princess? Could he describe her beauty?

All Nala's thoughts streamlined into questions about Damayanti. Exactly what did the most beautiful woman on the planet look like? Why all this fuss about a girl? Could she really be so special? Wasn't she just another spoiled pretty princess fortunate enough to select her groom?

Against the formidable famed nobles traveling from faraway kingdoms laden with the wealth of seaports, gold mines, spices and the silk trade, the smart money would have put the Nishada prince's chances of winning the heart of the princess at less than a million to one. Born under the constellation of the gambler both father and son shared a destiny of feeling most ease when the odds were stacked against them. It was this full-tilt fearless attitude which made the Nishada noblemen a force on the battlefield and attracted the eyes of women. Unlike so many others Nala had not come merely for the bragging rights of being able to claim to his children and grandchildren that he had competed at this once-in-a-lifetime spectacle. From his father's first mention of the swayamvara they had been planning his assault to win the white lotus garland.

"When you meet her," said the humble Vidabhar foreman, "You will see for yourself. Our princess cares about the little things."

In an earthenware vessel Nala collected cool spring water. The prince turned back to the foreman and asked, "Little things?" Kneeling on the earth Nala removed one of the king's sandals and washed the dust off his father's foot in the water.

"Where others waste their fortunes trying to cheat life with shortcuts, Princess Damayanti is always examining the little things right in front of her. And that's where life is lived. In the little things. In Vidabhar we are twice-blessed to be ruled by a king who teaches us such lessons."

"With the second blessing being," said Nala then pausing to lean his head to one side to dry his father's foot using his long black hair. The prince slipped his father's foot back into the sandal and refilled the vessel with fresh water. Wringing the day's tensions from his father's other foot, he turned toward the foreman's to finish his sentence, "that his daughter is his best pupil."

One child was taller than the next in a line of three village sisters walking single-file in the direction of the men. On their heads the girls carried impossibly large baskets of almonds, mangos and pears. Under one of the shadier trees they lowered their loads to the earth and huddled close to one another. Whispering secrets to each other, the pony-tailed girls studied every nuance and gesture of the young prince. When the foreman beckoned them, the girls rushed forward to present the Nishada men and horses with much-needed sustenance.

"May your land be twice-blessed as well," said the foreman. "By the way it was Princess Damayanti who laid out this almond grove. The plant devas who reside on the land of Vidabhar adore her. It is they who tell her where and how many trees to plant. And she listens to them. And we listen to her."

Before moving on with his day's tasks, this man of the earth smiled and looked softly into Nala's eyes. "Tell me your name so I can introduce my daughters to the prince who will win our lady's heart."

10. Evening Heat

At sunset the riders passed through a series of gates into the city. Upon entering the court of the palace Virasen stifled embarrassment at being praised as a paragon of kings by Bhima. The Nishada nobleman relayed to his host that he had been living too long off his reputation. Journeying through Vidabhar had opened his mind. Here ruled a leader from whom all leaders could take inspiration. Virasen looked to introduce his son but discovered he was nowhere to be found.

It took Nala several encounters walking back and forth in front of the palace guard to realize Indra's dust had rendered him invisible. He could walk with impunity wherever he wished. As one acquainted with palaces, Nala quickly discovered the way to the women's quarters.

Once in her bedchamber Nala sat against an open window ledge and quietly watched. Clothed in a simple terracotta robe the princess was being attended by three handmaids. With musical precision the youngest girl brushed Damayanti's long wavy black hair over and over into her hand. The others rubbed a mixture of turmeric, sacred ash, frankincense and sesame oil into Damayanti's hands and feet. The trio softly chanted the hundred and eight names of Goddess Shakti. The task of preparing their princess for sleep on the most important night in her life was one they too had long awaited. Nala wondered how he would ever move his tongue to speak Indra's words. In his heart Nala felt an itching burn like a fire eager to leap across a river for dry wood.

Armies of men would sacrifice themselves to gain even a single one of the three hundred noblemen encamped in Vidabhar this same access. From her chair the princess turned to face her altar. It was a simple slate of marble with a burning candle in front of two gold swans entwined in love's embrace.

Nala had promised a favor, not just to any god, but Lord Indra, Agni, Varuna and Yama. Now the burning pain spread across his chest. Nothing mattered. Only the need to speak of love to a woman whom he had never met. Was there not a higher calling than favors to gods? He wondered. As high within the celestial realm as Indra reigned, it was known there dwelled higher more elusive gods. Perhaps Indra had been sent to bring Nala and Damayanti together. These were the Nishada prince's hopes as he sat mesmerized across the room from the famed Vidabhar princess. Perhaps it was their destiny to live together and build a life of enduring love. If this wish residing in his heart were true, might not the universe conspire to make it so?

Out of respect for this beautiful woman Nala kept his eyes closed. He wanted to have permission before joining Damayanti in this sanctuary of her altar. In so doing he was astonished by two things. First, he could see the fire leaping out of his chest. And, second, he watched the flames engulf the princess. Indra's dust had gifted the prince an inner vision. Even when he turned away, he saw only the princess and this fire threatening to scorch her.

Nala expected Damayanti to scream for palace guards to douse the flames. But nothing of the sort happened. Instead the princess smiled as though basking in the glory of the morning sun. Nala had never encountered anyone like her. What if the Vidabhar foreman has been right and Damayanti embodied that rare breed of human who understood the value of little things? How could he miss this opportunity to win her heart? How could he risk losing her to the gods?

Nala debated whether to open his eyes or turn away. The decision was moot for his entire body became paralyzed. Only the fire moved. From his being into hers. It was a mystery how it did not disturb her. The flame did not burn her. Even with his eyes closed Nala could see that no woman's beauty could ever surpass the princess. Except Damayanti herself if tomorrow she placed the garland around his neck. Then he would rub sacred oils into her hands and feet for as many decades as the gods granted them life. In his mind Nala saw the two of them together.

When the handmaids completed their tasks, Damayanti sent them away without moving from her seated posture. Several minutes passed. And then she spoke. "Are you the god of love come to bless my selection tomorrow?" Not even slightly did she turn in Nala's direction or open her eyes.

"Tell me." In reply to her question, Nala finally found the freedom to loosen his tongue. "How would you know if I were the god of love?"

"Well, anyone would know you must be a god. Who else could get past my father's guards?"

"Actually I'm just Indra's messenger."

"*Just* a messenger?" smirked the princess. Without bothering to cover her body she shook her head. "I think not. Only the god of love could replicate the energies flooding through my body." Placing her hand over her heart, Damayanti sighed. Then her manner softened as though poised to melt into the sofa. "But I'll play along with your game. Speak Indra's message."

When Nala had finished, Damayanti grew visibly annoyed. "Have you no more to say, messenger?"

"Much."

"Then open your mouth and speak! My body is aflame to hear why you came to my bedchamber after sunset on this swayamvara eve."

"I am not the god of love. I am a prince from a land not nearly so prosperous as your own. My name is Nala born of Virasen and Uttani of Nishada."

"What else?"

"Like everyone else I had heard of your great virtues so I came to witness the spectacle. Never did I imagine such beauty could be real. All day my father and I reveled in journeying through your kingdom. Meeting your subjects and seeing the opalescence of the land, our respect for Bhima and his daughter grows with each step we take in Vidabhar."

"What else?"

"From the clouds the gods hailed us as we trod on a seldom traveled cow path. Yama warned me of a future encounter. Agni made light of it. Varuna cast a mist upon me and forecast a long virtuous life. And Indra begged a favor which I just now fulfilled."

"What else?"

"My heart aches to hold you and no one else for all eternity."

"What else?"

"Tell me your lotus garland will be mine. Or I will kill myself this night. I cannot bear to watch you bestow it upon another. Tell me it will be my unimagined fortune to embrace you as my beloved."

"What else?"

"I pledge enduring love to you. Through this life and beyond. As Goddess Shakti is my witness, will you be my enduring beloved and wife?"

Drawing her knees into her chest, Damayanti cooed like a morning dove calling ecstatically to her mate in a cool summer breeze. Then she straightened her heels to stretch her legs. Quick as thought, the princess bolted upright seating herself with lotus feet facing in Nala's direction. The room was silent as the princess examined her intruder from head to toe. Nala was pleased that while he was invisible to everyone else, Damayanti could see him.

"Now, Damayanti, do not torment me with silence. Is it not your heart's turn to speak?"

"My father and the many armies of men outside will kill you if they discover you here."

"What else?"

"They will kill me if they find out I am speaking to you on my swayamvara eve."

"What else?"

"This is not the first time you and I have met. Not long ago your father, brother and you were hunting near an isolated pond. I was traveling with an enchanted flock of sister swans. We had stopped for a moment to rest and graze."

"What else?"

"Light burst out of me across the pond and landed in your chest. At the time I had no clue what was happening. I only knew I had left my kingdom in search of my perfect beloved. After three years of wandering I thought I had failed. Even on that day I did not understand."

"What else?"

"Tonight my prayers are answered. You have come to me. You opened your heart and filled me with your light."

"What else?"

"Now I understand what my guru Great Swan meant when she said beauty is drawn to beauty. For you are the most handsome man I have laid eyes on."

"What else?"

"Now I understand what she meant in saying her beloved was created just for her. As I gaze upon your face, I feel the same way about you. I feel you were created just for me. And me for you. A match of perfect beloveds."

"What else?"

"She said it is in the nature of most men to steal beauty from the women they love. But when perfect beloveds embrace it is not necessary because both hold a similar radiance. I cannot bear to sleep this night without your arms wrapped around my body."

"What else?"

"Rest assured, Nishada prince, my lotus garland will be draped around no one else's neck. All my dreams are fulfilled here and now."

"What else?"

"My lifelong quest for the perfect beloved is fulfilled here with you. As Goddess Shakti is my witness, I pledge enduring love to you. Through this life and beyond."

For so long as either of them drew breath, Nala and Damayanti never tired of recounting this night to their children. Nor the children recounting it to their children, grandchildren and great grandchildren. Such was the power of love that it fueled them and their heirs to face the great day and days ahead.

Tomorrow the princess and prince would pretend none of this had happened. Astonishment would buzz through the amphitheater when Damayanti passed over the impressive line of kings and gods to choose a little known prince.

Right now the young lovers gazed at each other with a depth of intensity that caused the clock of time itself to stop. And with it the stars, planets and even the wind in the sky. Rivers, oceans and rainfall ceased motion. All plants, insects and animals, including humans were frozen in suspended animation. Even the gods found themselves stunned in their tracks by the sudden gush of love between a woman and a man.

11. Shiva Rescues the Universe

Fortunately for the rest of the universe, though frozen in place, Chandri the moon goddess was positioned so her rays shone into the room. She pleaded with the prince to rise from the window ledge and look away from Damayanti. Certain jealous deities without a sense of humor, namely, Kala the god of time might search for the culprits who had stopped time. Chandri promised not to name names if Nala looked away. Besides who would attribute such a deed to humans?

Chandri assured the couple that after the wedding they would hold one another as long as they wished. But not now. Not with the honor of Bhima and Bhavani and the assembled glittering members of royalty who had traveled such great distances. Not to mention the gods. Now they must look away. Nala had to leave immediately and rejoin Virasen. Or there would be no story to tell future generations about the love between Nala and Damayanti. No swayamvara. No wedding. No unveiling the secret of enduring love.

The pleas of the moon goddess made no impact. Across the bedchamber Nala and Damayanti stared into a love stretching to forever. Such was their longing to hold one another that the light from their hearts continued to grow even brighter around them like a sun poised to burst into supernova.

Under such circumstances Chandri could think of only one deity capable of intervening. The question was ... would he bother?

Gliding down one of her frozen moonbeams arrived Shiva. The blue-throated yogi of matted hair and the god of change ... destruction and transformation were Shiva's domain ... he did not create the universe ... Brahma did, but really it was mostly Saraswati behind the scenes... and Shiva did not sustain the universe ... Vishnu handled this task along with the feminine opulence of his beloved Lakshmi ... what Shiva presided over was the frontier of change. The living fabric of the universe was woven by a trinity of Brahma, Vishnu and Shiva.

Shiva observed the universe flowing. For this short time, however, the flow stopped which disturbed the originator of yoga from his meditation. If every sentient being in the universe was destroyed or paralyzed indefinitely. including the gods, Shiva did not care in the slightest. For he was attached to nothing. His focus in meditation was to embrace his cosmic beloved Shakti. Yet Shiva was lured to the Vidabhar palace by an emotion he had not felt for thousands of years. Namely, curiosity. Whose love could trump his considerable reserves accumulated through eons of one-pointed concentration? Perhaps he could learn a thing or two from these mortal lovers.

So the three of them: Nala, Damayanti and Shiva sat motionless. If it was possible, Chandri became even more alarmed because the light surrounding them ramped up to another level of brillance. Without speaking a word Shiva's presence caused Nala and Damayanti to look to him. A question arose in their minds simultaneously. While it was true the prince and princess could not embrace for twenty-four hours without bringing disgrace to their families, how long had Shiva been waiting for his Shakti? This single thought broke the spell of energy. And the entire universe could suddenly inhale again and get about its business.

Shiva sighed and looked first at the princess. Was it sadness she saw in the eyes of the great being? Or was it cosmic bliss? In spite of their physical separation, were the two great yogis in constant embrace? Shiva and Shakti. Whether it was reality or myth, Damayanti felt the account of Shiva and Shakti's love was the most romantic story ever told. She could not be certain but the princess thought she spotted a wry smile at the corners of Shiva's lips. It was unnecessary to speak words to communicate with Shiva.

"Yes. And no. It's a paradox," explained Shiva. "Our love yearns for a semblance of embodiment. So we look to you." Now she was sure. Shiva was smiling at her. Then he turned to Nala, saying, "And you. Where we reside ... in regions beyond time and space ... humans in every culture have come up with their own names to describe this place ... that is everywhere ... here our embrace is eternal. Come." He motioned for them to get closer.

"Look into my eyes. You will see her. Am I right?"

Damayanti and Nala approached the great ascetic. In the blackness of his pupils were two beings Shiva and Shakti locked in meditative embrace. It was true. Around them were galaxies of light pulsating to the rhythm of the cosmos. It was a dazzling glimpse into the mystery of two beloveds. Fascinated neither the prince nor princess wanted to look away. Here was the love to which all others aspired but inevitably failed. With shame and fascination the young couple blushed in the private parts of their bodies. Each felt heat pouring from the other. They dared not gaze at each other.

"Shiva, you possess a physical body we can see and touch." Nala broke the reverie testing his premise by reaching out. Sure enough, the skin of Lord Shiva's foot felt tender and real. "Who is Shakti? Where is her body?"

Damayanti made the choice to look deeper into the lord's eyes. The answer to Nala's question must be right here, she thought. Because she did not believe it could be conveyed in words ... at least not the linear words of language ... while Nala made his attempt to understand the love of Shiva and Shakti ... Damayanti put herself in the place of Shakti visualizing herself in the embrace of the lord. And she recited the mantra.

Om Shakti Om ... Om Shiva Om

"For love to endure," said Shiva, "One must let it go."

"What does letting go of love have to do with finding Shakti?" asked the prince. "And why would I ever let go of love?"

"One day, Nishada prince, it will make sense."

"Princess!" snapped Shiva. He blinked to disrupt Damayanti's attention. *Was she still in a human body? Couldn't she go back to his embrace a short while longer?* In her heart the princess was getting her answer as she stared into the rapture of those eyes. *Shakti was closer to Shiva than any beloved could be with her body contained in the body of the universe. Her goddess body was too vast for the mind to see or touch. But not so large for the heart.* Finally it was words that brought Damayanti back to her human reality. Shiva recognized the difficulty she was experiencing fitting herself back into the mind-body package everyone identified as the beautiful Vidabhar princess. So he spoke slowly giving emphasis to each syllable.

"The journey to enduring love will not always be easy. You may wait years for a single gateway to open. And when it does, the love will not look as beautiful as it does tonight. People you trust will betray you." His words had the desired effect. She was back in her body. And Shiva kept talking. "One day your beloved will learn how to answer his own questions.

Countless beings are watching and waiting to see how the two of you walk this quest."

"Shiva, be my guru!" pleaded Nala. He bowed forward placing his forehead in supplication on Shiva's knee. All his life Nala had dreamed of this chance that might never come again. Realizing that as of tomorrow he would no longer be a lone warrior the prince rushed to add, "Be our guru!" Many times his father had stated the single greatest gift in a human life was to receive the guidance of an enlightened guru. "Guide us to the secret of enduring love."

"The princess already has a guru. And you have not proven yourself worthy of one."

"Show me how to become worthy."

"Do not test my patience!" admonished Shiva. "Ask Damayanti your questions. She will be the first one to initiate you."

Nala spoke quickly sensing Shiva would depart at any moment. "Please, Shiva, bestow your blessing on our union!"

"You may have it. If both of you wish it," said Shiva. "But ... think first. My blessing is not for everyone."

Whether to receive Lord Shiva's blessing or not? Aside from his hut atop the lofty Himalayan peak of Kailash, the next most likely place to find Shiva was meditating among the blaze of dead bodies wrapped in white cotton set atop pyres at burning ghats along Ganga. Some Brahman priests attributed Shiva's tranquility among the dead to some silly nonsense about him casting dark spells collecting the energies of lost souls. Many people were frightened of Shiva. But not Nala and not Damayanti. As the first decision they would make together as a couple, the prince and princess looked into each other's eyes. Each waited to see who would speak first. But words proved unnecessary. At the same time the princess and prince nodded their heads and turned to present themselves.

Shiva brushed three fingers across Damayanti's forehead leaving streaks of his vibuti ash that transported the princess into a swift intoxicating peace overriding the currents of her mind. The lord of destruction did the same to Nala. Then he joined the hands of the royal couple. They felt their bodies expand and merge into one ... birthing a third entity distinct from Damayanti or Nala ... was it Shiva? ... or was it the vessel of their relationship? Within this vortex of energies the young beloveds discovered the bliss of swirling into one another. Yielding to Nala's masculine presence, the princess felt herself flooded with energies rising up the first gateway. At first it felt glorious. Then the pressure began to build. When she heard the scream it did not register as her own voice. Was it a cry in agony or ecstasy? Situated three finger widths below the navel, her second gateway was burning from the heat of Shiva's blessing. All the pores of her being flared open. The princess strung out her inhales and exhales using techniques practiced so many times. Despite the intense pressure rising up her spine, the second gateway refused to open. Neither of them had ever felt more alive or in love.

What fascinated Damayanti was that she saw herself as multiple beings all in one. She was the yogi yielding impurities from body and mind to Shakti ... she was the woman being ravished by her beloved Nala ... she was the Goddess Shakti herself pulsating inside every particle of matter throughout the cosmos and merging with her Lord Shiva ... she was the eternal witness observing the entire event in multiplicity as though this awakening were happening to some other woman. Her robe became drenched in sweat as she laughed repeatedly like a mad woman. Was this her physical body? Every moment the princess thought it could not possibly get more ecstatic. Then a new wave of energies flooded through her. Was Nala still there? She could not tell anymore where her luminous body stopped and his luminous body started.

The voice of Shiva resounded through every cell in her body. "Now and forever the two of you are joined. With this blessing, no one can separate you. Not even the two of you."

As quickly as he arrived Shiva departed on a moonbeam. Before Nala and Damayanti could celebrate their great fortune, Chandri whisked the prince out the door along with the telepathic warning, "In two minutes Indra's spell will dissolve. So if you want to see Damayanti tomorrow, run! Don't walk."

Quietly Chandri shut the door and crossed the room. She slowed her movements so as not to disturb the highly sensitive state of the princess. Energetic awakenings of this sort required time to integrate. The moon goddess guided Damayanti into bed to ease her luminous body back into some semblance of physicality. The thing with this succession of energetic awakenings was that each time Damayanti returned to a normal state of consciousness, she did so with a larger luminous body. Tears flowed down the face of the princess. It took a long time for Damayanti to care enough to actually inhabit this body.

"I thought the gods were crazy. But you humans are too much," chided Chandri. "What's with this love thing? Princess, I thought the two of you were going to blow up the entire universe."

The surest way to bring the princess back into the body was to bait her with the prospect of some serious girl-talk. Chandri wanted to know which god Damayanti thought was a stunner. Barely moving her lips, the princess asked if the moon goddess thought Nala was handsome. Questions and answers started ping-ponging back and forth. Soon Damayanti had returned to her normal self. She confessed that until about an hour ago she had been feeling like the loneliest girl on the planet. Now she was desperate to broadcast far and wide, 'I am in love with Nala! And he is in love with me!' Damayanti declared she could not go through with the charade. The first thing tomorrow the princess was going to tell her mother and father to call off the tournaments and the swayamvara. Just announce Nala as her future husband. Damayanti was working up a decent rant when Chandri cut her off.

"Princess, stop! This is more lunacy than I can take in one night. Do you have any idea how much testosterone is flying around out there? If these men don't get what they think is a fair shake at strutting their stuff in front of yours truly tomorrow, they will rip up this kingdom and everyone in it into so many tiny pieces nobody will ever know that a place called Vidabhar existed."

With the departure of Shiva and the Nishada prince, Chandri had a hunch that Damayanti's emotional pendulum might swing the other way. Now the moon goddess told Damayanti to listen up and issued marching orders. Tomorrow the princess would go through with the swayamvara. And she would smile for every one of those kings and gods who moved heaven and earth to get here. And she would not under any circumstances tip her hand until she put the lotus garland around Nala's neck. Chandri asked Damayanti if she understood the importance of doing everything according to proper form.

When Damayanti turned stone silent, Chandri tried a different approach. She softened her voice and explained that her destiny awaited her tomorrow. Damayanti could build goodwill among all these powerful men and make them into future allies. Or she could offend and make enemies out of the entire lot of them. Chandri explained that males of every ilk had fragile egos ... even among the gods ... wise women and goddesses alike learned to steer the male psyche in ways that aligned with the cosmic order. Preferably without the men or gods even knowing it was happening.

"How many suitors are out there?" asked Damayanti.

"Three hundred and thirty-seven including four gods. You shattered the old record of two hundred and eighty-five set by Princess Amba and her two older sisters. Over the last three days Bhima and his ministers have been very busy while you have been sequestered up here. It's not like there's pressure anymore. You snagged your man. So have some fun. Whoop it up. Put on a show. Just imagine how many girls would love to have all these studs competing for their attention. Like every girl and goddess on the planet. This is when you nod your head and say, 'Yes, moon goddess. Great advice. For a second, I might have put everyone's life and honor at risk. Thank you for illuminating my pathway.'"

Damayanti pulled the covers over her head. "No pressure!" she whined. "You try facing all those kings and gods. I'm not going to do it. Even Indra is pressuring me to marry a god."

"So who cares what Indra thinks?"

"Oh, yeah! He's *just* the lord of heaven."

"Yeah, and I'm the goddess of the moon. But I can't tell you who to marry. And neither can he."

The princess was afraid she wouldn't make it all the way to Nala. Since returning from her first contact with Nala at the hunter pond, she had been tormenting herself with a fantasy of walking down the long suitor line where a hunchback cripple stole her love. Just like her mother with the gemstone on the hilt of the sword, Damayanti saw her own mind being captured by the deformity of the cripple's body. It made her feel sick and scared.

"When I see all those hungry eyes tomorrow, I'm terrified I'll mess it up and lose Nala."

The princess demanded Chandri wake up her father now and call off the swayamvara. Weren't there plenty of days and nights when Chandri didn't show up? New moons and long stretches when she hid behind clouds. So why should Damayanti show up tomorrow?

"It's true. Even goddesses hide from time to time. But here's the thing. When it is my time to shine, I do it. These are the moments of destiny that define a woman's life. And tomorrow marks your time."

"Let's just skip the swayamvara and go straight to the wedding ceremony. Won't it be lovely? That's where I'll shine!"

Chandri told the princess that tomorrow when she walked the long line of heavy-hitting suitors, the future of love would be walking with her. Generations of girls and boys, men and women everywhere will be looking to you. Not for your beauty or wealth or noble authority. They will be looking for your wisdom in the arena of love. What sort of beloved will the princess choose? Will she pick the richest man on earth? Or the best warrior? Or will she go for a god over a human? Don't cheat them out of the drama. Let all the world watch a woman select the man of her heart. And let the scribes and bards tell and retell the story in every language of what happens when human hearts collide.

It had been a long journey toward enduring love. Seeing what Damayanti needed more than anything else was a good cry, Chandri took the overwrought princess in her arms. Damayanti wept without understanding why. Was it joy in seeing Nala before the swayamvara? Relief Nala felt the same way about her? Fear of messing up what looked like it could never get better? Or was she just exhausted?

Chandri's divine gift as the lunar goddess opened up the flow of emotions for anyone within her touch. So she cradled the princess. And whispered a moon song in her ear over and over even after slumber had melted Damayanti's last defenses.

Enduring love is initiated by the feminine.
Open your gateways to receive the light
From All That Is. Sweet princess,
We, sisters of Shakti,
Embrace you as one of us.
In celebration we sing in your voice
In crisis we hold energy in your heart
In meditation we dwell inside the rainbow shaft
Awakening through you in every sister
Our initiation is for life.
This is how we as sisters live the life of enduring love.

Om Shakti Om ... Om Shiva Om
Om Shakti Om ... Om Shiva Om
Om Shakti Om ... Om Shiva Om

12. Morning Rituals

Before dawn the foreman of the almond grove and his wife climbed out of bed. In the darkness they roused their three daughters and dressed. From the mud hut they hurried toward the river. The night was quickly passing as Chandri's rival Surya god of the sun raced around the backside of the earth to catch the moon in his sizzling embrace. Ever the coy goddess, Chandri kept just far enough ahead to reflect a sliver of Surya's light that the married couple and their drowsy children used to make their way down to the ghat.

In the dark eternal stillness unique to this time between the end of night and beginning of day, the foreman held out a tiny ghee lamp. It took his wife a half dozen strikes of the flint to ignite the wick. Then the foreman chanted the mantra his father had chanted by this ghat and his grandfather before him. From oldest to youngest each daughter nimbly stooped low to set a burning wick atop a banana leaf on the water and cast away their offering. Then the man, woman and three girls watched as a flotilla of tiny lights was carried downstream. Up and down the riverbank other families had come to the river with the same petition.

Everyone was looking for an omen. If the candles were extinguished or dispersed in the current, it portended ill. Through the final moments of night the ghee wicks sparkled in a beautiful procession straight down the middle of the stream as far as anyone could see. The first rays of the day confirmed what the foreman, his wife, their three girls and so many others felt in their hearts. Gazing at the river all of them were happy to be alive.

Across the Vedic subcontinent conch shells blasted in succession. Atop parapets, mountain lookouts, temples, bazaars and roadside altars, humble men and women of every age and caste chanted prayers. This morning the blessings were steered in the singular direction of the continent's favorite princess and her swayamvara.

Three weeks ago when Bhima ordered his messengers to fan out in all directions to announce invitations, Vishwakarman the God of Architects arrived unannounced landing his golden chariot with its million flying wheels and levers in the royal courtyard. Strolling up to the throne Vishwakarman pointed at Bhima's top general commanding him to take four legions of the Vidabhar army out to clear the finest teak trees from the king's forest. Vishwakarman ordered the remaining legion to follow his apprentices out to the job site to serve as laborers. Dreaded for his unpredictable temperament and revered for anything his hands produced, Vishwakarman was the architect who had designed and constructed all the magnificent celestial edifices. In fact, if anyone tried to build anything in heaven without checking with Vishwakarman first, well, there'd be hell to pay. And no one ... I mean, no one ... told Vishwakarman what they wanted him to construct. Not Brahma. Not Vishnu. Not even Shiva. Of course as the yogi ascetic, Shiva owned nothing made from Vishwakarman's hands in his Himalayan abode. Anyway Bhima sat numb in silence observing this most eccentric genius of the gods at work.

The enormous lotus-shaped amphitheater was erected with moving staircases, fountains at every corner issuing streams of divine nectar and teams of cherubic sprites serving banquets of delicious treats so everyone in Vidabhar could celebrate the event in style. A complex lattice was rigged up by Vishwarkarman to support colorful silk banners identifying the kingdoms in attendance as well as serving the practical function of rotating in synch with the sun's trajectory to keep the faces of spectators in shade throughout the day. From the rich soils of the Indus valley hundreds of miles south, an entire field of the lushest green grass was uprooted in one piece and transported by Vishwakarman.

Beyond Vidabhar in every capital across the subcontinent Vishwakarman had enlisted an all-star cast of the greatest saints, starting with Parvata and Narada, to use their yogic minds to project streaming images from the swayamvara onto a fantastic network of shimmering screens. Ordinary people in faraway kingdoms were preparing to witness the much anticipated event. Up to the minute before the doors were opened Vishwakarman attended to finishing the final details. Each seat came with a scroll listing bios of all the suitors as well a detailed tournament schedule. Hundreds of black panel screens of Vishwakarman's design had been distributed to his exact specifications throughout the

Under the shade of her favorite banana tree Damayanti admired a newly opened white lotus blossom on the palm of her hand. She closed her eyes and kept the image of the lotus in her mind. Then she took in a long slow breath. And she recited the mantra.

Om Shakti Om ... Om Shiva Om

Without change in her facial expression she merged with Goddess Shakti. The rainbow shaft ignited in her pelvic floor. Her finely trained yogic mind infused the flower in her hand. Like the girls on the amphitheater field she plunged the wooden needle through the stamen and pulled it out the other side. From a basket at her feet she selected another lotus blossom.

Damayanti felt at peace in the silent recitation of the mantra. She picked up each white flower as though the gesture mattered more than anything she had ever done. In this way the princess was stringing the garland that would determine the destiny of her life.

"Is this the girl who sank pouting to the bottom of the lake?"

Damayanti had no idea how long Great Swan had been watching. Extending her long slender neck the swan flapped her wings showering droplets of lake water over the princess. But Damayanti appeared not to notice. She completed working with the flower and added it to the others on the string. Then she looked up.

“Is it okay for me to take a rest before the garland is complete?”

“No. Just wanted to see if I could distract you.” Great Swan sat beside the princess. Smacking her beak together she preened herself picking out impurities from the tiny crevices between the downy plumage of her white feathers.

One flower after another Damayanti infused rainbow light into the garland. Since the evening tryst with the prince and Lord Shiva she had felt the cosmic pulse of Shakti. Everything was situated in its right place and time. There was no need to hurry. All was interconnected in a fabric of life that she recognized in the way the petals were connected to the stamen and stem. After she cinched the thread holding the last of the lotus flowers, Damayanti beamed with pride. She was tying the final knot in her preparations for a new life. Grown from the mud at the bottom of the lake, these lotus blossoms had been handpicked by the princess and her handmaids.

When she looked up, the princess was surprised by a flock of swans twice the size of the one she had flown with to find Nala. In awe she knelt down on the grass. Had the flock been here the entire time? Or did they mill into the garden in pairs? Damayanti marveled at the mysteries left unanswered by life. Perhaps one day the princess might understand how these swans glided so effortlessly. Scooping up the string of flowers Damayanti rose to her feet. One by one she surveyed the individual faces of sister swans whom she knew so intimately seated next to their mates.

"Clan of swans," So saying Damayanti lofted the prized object of men's desire. "Will you bless my garland?"

A high-pitched cacophony of shrill honks and hoots blasted out approval. In return Damayanti motioned as if she were going to toss the garland out to the flock. Instead she bent down and draped the white flower garland around her guru's long regal neck. Here was where the princess felt most at home. Not among the members of her own race. But among these elegant pensive birds in her father's garden surrounded by the trees and plants she loved.

On her knees Damayanti inched forward left and right in tiny baby steps to get as close as possible without knocking her guru over. "Great Swan," said the princess suddenly feeling a quiver of forlornness in her lips. "Always let me remain your disciple."

Great Swan had given this girl tools to open her first gateway. She had shown the patience of a guru coaxing the princess back from the deeply ingrained patterns of distraction inherent in the untrained mind. Poised to stride into a role few women had glimpsed, Damayanti felt that she could remain here beside her teacher. The princess rested her head on Great Swan's familiar webbed feet. After working so diligently to make progress together she did not want to lose her guru just to become some man's wife.

The gift of the guru happened in an energetic transfer more potent than any spoken words. On this significant morning surrounded by the flock, the princess received all she needed at Great Swan's feet.

Here was the treasured nuptial blessing Damayanti had been pining for since childhood. Her guru's blessing. And she felt it. The cells in her body began to hum with the voice of many-as-one reciting the mantra Great

Swan had given her. It was the same mantra Great Swan had been given by her guru.

Om Shakti Om ... Om Shiva Om

One after another the princess had eschewed the well-laid campaigns of her mother. Instead she had spent the years of her youth becoming part of a sisterhood lineage of great yogis. She wondered if it would be asking too much for Great Swan and Hansaram to move with her to Nishada. Surely there had to be a quiet lake near the palace just like here in Vidabhar. Or there was always the pond where Nala, Virasen and Pushkar had been hunting. She was about to pour out her concerns when she became distracted.

For the first time in her practice the princess discerned new voices intruding into the voice of many-as-one. Her prostrate body tensed with indignation. Who dared trespass on our sisterhood? Polluting the sweet purity of her alto sisters was an overbearing din of male guttural vibration.

"I am ready to stand beside Nala. I just don't want to lose my connection to you and the sisterhood. Men are so loud and they are always demanding the center of attention."

Great Swan leaned forward over Damayanti's body and blew a series of long reedy notes forming the familiar sounds.

Om Shakti Om ... Om Shiva Om

Three times she tapped her beak on a specific point along the sacral spine of the princess. Great Swan was breaking up something stuck at the back of Damayanti's second gateway. "Does it look as though I have lost my connection' " asked the swan, "after all these years of treading water alongside my mate?"

In the same place three fingers widths below her navel the princess felt a burning discomfort like the one she had experienced last night with Lord Shiva. The sensations fit what Great Swan described as Shakti knocking at the second gateway. Today there would be enormous pressure on Damayanti to keep to a strict schedule. The princess doubted it was possible to fit a spiritual awakening into the swayamvara.

"In the months and years ahead, remember to trust Shakti. Always make time to practice. From this day forward, I pass on to you, the duty of teaching all I have taught you."

Damayanti did not catch the significance of these last words. She was too absorbed in what was happening in her body. The guru laughed and brushed her beak through Damayanti's beautiful long hair. "This afternoon when you are tested, relax," whispered Great Swan. 'This is what you've trained for. To select the man worthy of your love."

Henceforth the princess would hear the voice of many-as-one as a blend of female and male voices. This addition of male voices into what had previously been their feminine sanctuary was Great Swan's wedding gift.

Among swan clans the ritual of a female selecting her mate was treated as the pivotal event for the wellbeing of the flock. As long as the females choose wisely, the swans would prosper. Even though their gift was presented to the princess in the garden, it was intended for both Damayanti and her husband-to-be. After this day it would become Damayanti's dharma to hold the gateways of initiation open for her mate and others in his kingdom seeking the ways of the path. This duty was the payment Great Swan as the guru would exact from her disciple Damayanti for the years of instruction.

As the energies tapered down, Damayanti asked her guru if she was making the right choice in selecting Nala of Nishada. While she waited for a reply, it suddenly got quiet. The princess lifted her head to discover Great Swan and the flock had gone.

Damayanti lifted the garland off the ground and put it around her own neck. Then she scrambled to her feet and hurried back along the hedged path to the palace. She heard the voice of many-as-one assure her that the sisterhood would always stand beside her. Even when she was unaware of their presence, as she had been while threading the garland, they would always remain close. This sisterhood of Goddess Shakti initiated by the feminine was emerging for her now as the blended level of female and male energies. As the palace handmaids washed her body and dressed her one last time, Damayanti felt that no other training could have prepared her for what lay ahead.

At the riverbank Nala petitioned in salutation to the river goddess Godavari. With hands in prayer he requested permission to gather her peaceful flowing waters. Godavari smiled at the handsome prince and beckoned him to wade in. As he bent low to fill the bowl, the goddess whispered auspicious omens for the swayamvara. She confided if things didn't go his way to come back to her for consolation.

Side by side Nala and Virasen had slept without mention of Indra's favor. The king felt his son's exuberance but dared not ask for details. Nala brushed blades of grass off his father's foot before immersing it in the chilly water. It felt strange to Nala to keep his love for Damayanti secret from his father. Never had he hidden anything from Virasen. As his wet hands vigorously squeezed and caressed the sole of his father's foot, Nala realized that this stance of self-restraint must be one of the awkward stages of stepping into manhood. He hoped he would never grow used to it.

"What happened back at the pond," confided Nala, "had nothing to do with Goddess Shakti." So much for stances of self-restraint. The act of washing dust from this man's feet gave Nala more satisfaction than all the victories in horseraces for which he was renowned.

"How do you know?" asked Virasen leaning forward. In effect admitting his hunger to be admitted into the divine drama.

"When I delivered Indra's message," replied Nala dipping his hands into the bottom of the bowl where he rubbed away knots of tension from the sole of Virasen's foot. "The princess confided it was she who sent the light arcing into my chest. And it was as great a surprise to her as it was to you and me."

"Then why we didn't see her?" asked the Nishada lord. "Now more than ever I'm convinced the princess is Goddess Shakti incarnated as a human."

Much as Nala would welcome having Damayanti and Goddess Shakti wrapped up in one woman's body, the prince felt obliged to burst his father's bubble. "Her guru, is one of the white swans possessing the art of cloaking themselves. As part of her yoga training, they adopted the princess as a member of their flock."

Suddenly the young man regretted venturing down this path. He lifted one foot out of the bowl and crossed back to the river for fresh water. Then he followed the same procedure of brushing debris off Virasen's other foot before lowering it into the bowl. To match the shock of the chilly water Nala massaged furiously. Why his father kept insisting on this connection with a formless goddess was beyond him. He wondered if perhaps an inherent part of old age required forcing meaning into everyday life. While the land of Nishada had never prospered like their more enterprising neighboring kingdoms, Virasen had elevated his status among the warrior legions of gandharvas with his bravery in battle against the rakshasa demons. So it just wasn't like Virasen to be getting all touchy-feely about this Goddess Shakti stuff.

Eventually Virasen broke the silence by blurting out. "In matters of love, females possess a sense that make them more natural wayshowers."

Oh God, wondered Nala, what's gonna come out of my dad's mouth next? The prince was all for being shown the way of love by Damayanti. He just couldn't stand hearing his father tell him about it. Nala pulled Virasen's other foot out of the bowl. Resting one foot on his own thigh the prince used his long black locks to dry his father's other foot. Then Nala rubbed sandalwood oil to scent Virasen's newly washed skin.

Virasen confided that an explanation was in order for his erratic behavior at the pond. Since that dusky day neither of them had broached the subject. For a long time the king had held a secret waiting to be revealed to his elder son. After Indra's odd request yesterday and Nala's sudden rise to the head of the pack as the inside favorite to win the prized lotus garland, it occurred to Virasen that the time was now or never. In an awkward tone he recounted a series of farfetched events.

Back in his days as a prince while training alone on the archery field Virasen heard a seductive voice whisper, 'You have been stalking me in your dreams. Now I am here. Are you ready for love?' In celebrations after Indra's conquests Virasen had gotten into his share of frolicking escapades with soma inebriated apsaras. So he had suspicions as to who was behind this interruption in his training. The young Virasen demanded the speaker show her identify. The voice replied, 'I am Goddess Shakti permeating every particle of creation.'

Instantly Virasen narrowed the field down to Urvasi as the only apsara audacious enough to trot out Goddess Shakti's name in jest. Early in the morning before going into battle Urvasi had incited the bold prince to belt out bawdy ballads in the gandharvas quarters. In his heart he had harbored a secret dream that Indra would hook the two of them up. The brave prince and the flirtatious apsara. So the message about stalking her in his dreams had some truth in it. For this reason the prince decided to play along. Maybe this was how apsaras conducted foreplay. He asked, 'How can I be ready for love with someone I can't even see?'

"Now can I ask you two things?" asked Nala. In the regiment of jogging Nala was confident he could bring back the father that he knew. "One, tell me about my mother's swayamvara and how she choose you. And, two, please grant me your blessing in winning Damayanti's lotus garland."

Like the many noblemen spanning great distances to gather here, Virasen described how he had journeyed almost a month to attend Uttani's swayamvara. While the Brahmin princess, as she was known, didn't attract the sort of madness that surrounded Damayanti's swayamvara ... after all, no woman ever had ... Uttani's beauty and purity of devotion attracted close to one hundred suitors. At previous swayamvaras Virasen's efforts had been put to shame by a band of brother princes who were collecting as many wives as they could with their exceptional skills. All year Virasen had been preparing to defeat these brothers.

Before the crack of dawn each morning on his journey the young king practiced a different martial art. So great was Virasen's focus of mind and body that Indra came down from heaven to praise his friend's newfound prowess. After exchanging pleasantries Indra announced that he would turn out to see how Virasen fared with the Brahmin princess. But what he really meant was that he wanted to see how Virasen fared against the band of brother princes. Indra was a warrior god. And like all warriors, nothing got his juices flowing like watching a program of really good fights. As usual Indra had brought along his retinue of gandharvas and apsaras. Now Urvasi had not quite gotten over her thing for Virasen. So when she leaned over the rail of Indra's golden chariot to offer the warrior king a lift, eyebrows were raised. What would Virasen do? Climb aboard and play with the seductive apsara? Or stick to his practice?

The gods were always coming up with inventive ways to present transformational crossroad moments in a man's life. Virasen and Urvasi were gazing hard into each other's eyes. But the young king waited too long for the impetuous Urvasi. She shoved Matali aside with her voluptuous hips. Grabbing the steering wheel Urvasi hit the gas pedal. Or whatever device it was that propelled the enormous chariot. It looped high in the sky and nosedived straight down on a crash course with the Nishada lord and the earth. The only sound anyone heard was Urvasi's screaming laughter. Indra stopped the chariot a few meters from the frozen prince. Then Virasen joined the apsara's laughter. Indra called out a farewell to Virasen as Matali got back behind the wheel and drove the chariot up into the sky.

At the swayamvara none of the candidates had the stomach to fight with Virasen. None except the band of brothers. One at a time the Nishada nobleman stunned Uttani and the spectators with his spectacular victories. After the tournament Uttani walked down the swayamvara line paying homage to each suitor by saying a kind word or two. Meanwhile Virasen felt a stabbing pain in his chest that he could not explain. Not once in the tournament had he sustained a blow to his chest. Among the suitors it was a foregone conclusion that Virasen would win Uttani's garland. By taking a few minutes to check-in with each of them Uttani was insuring that there were no hard feelings.

To everyone's surprise, as Uttani and Virasen exchanged their first glance, Urvasi leapt out from her seat among the other apsaras. In her hands she clutched her own lotus garland. Charging at breakneck speed toward the Nishada prince, Urvasi set the Brahmin princess in motion as well. So a most unusual collision was shaping up before the spectators. Whose garland would be lassoed around Virasen's neck first?

Young Virasen was thrilled at the prospect of becoming Uttani's husband. But he had no idea what he ought to do. For a moment he envisioned a collision between Urvasi and Uttani. When the two beauties arrived at the same time, Virasen was sure the apsara would deck Uttani. Such was the silliness that raced through a man's mind as a reasonable way to resolve matters of love.

'Virasen, give me your love here. And join me in the heavens. I will bless you with immortality as your apsara bride.' Urvasi looked her ravishing best when her emotions were running high. So she was going to be very difficult to refuse. Since his arrival the Brahmin princess had shown kindness and carried herself with royal dignity whenever she was near Virasen. Touching the pain in his chest Virasen realized that he loved both Urvasi and Uttani. In choosing one of them, he would have to break his heart in half. Urvasi underscored the dilemma by shouting, 'Or spurn me for this human. Make a choice.'

As the two of them galloped along the riverbank the old king asked his son. "What would you have done if you had loved both an immortal apsara and a beautiful chaste Brahmin Princess? And you had to choose one?"

"I would have begged Urvasi and Uttani to petition my father's advice," replied Nala.

Belly-rolling laughter ricocheted off the stone walls of the ghat as the two men danced in joyous waves of being father and son. Once again their innocence had returned. As though the stakes of the swayamvara meant nothing to them, Virasen and Nala ran across the stream of men and women heading toward the amphitheater. Under the tree where they slept were the four steeds who would pull Nala's chariot. The prince went from one horse to the other running his fingers through their snow white coats and whispering in their ears. Already this morning he had walked them down to the river where they had quenched their thirst. He had fed and groomed these beasts who were his dearest friends. In a few minutes Nala would talk strategy with them for the race.

"For the rest of my days," said Nala, "I will thank you for the choice you made, father."

"Goddess Shakti wanted me to choose Uttani." Virasen explained that it was only as humans that the soul has the chance to evolve. Celestials already live with their seven gateways open. But here we were given the gift of discovering the secret of enduring love. As Nala massaged the hindquarters and shoulders of his steeds, Virasen described how Lord Indra and the others cheered when he dropped to one knee in front of Nala's mother. To her credit Uttani never held the embarrassment of Urvasi's behavior against the Nishada nobleman. She just smiled and put the garland around Virasen's neck.

"May I be blessed in matrimony as you were, father."

"Nala, I love you as much as life itself. Goddess Shakti wants Damayanti to choose you. So don't worry. Nala, remember the words you and I spoke down at the river. And the question you will ask Damayanti. There's only one more thing you need to hear. While I broke tradition in choosing Uttani ... instead of letting her choose me ... after that day I yielded to Uttani's wisdom in all the important matters of my life. Remember to keep your wife close to your heart. Make no important decisions without consulting Damayanti. She will be the backbone behind your throne. So, yes, of course you have my blessing."

Virasen grabbed the reins of two of the horses and hitched them to one of the lightweight chariots. Nala hitched the other pair of horses in front of the first pair. Stepping aboard the chariot Nala said, "Let's go to see the horse track inside Vishwakarman's amphitheater."

13. Procession of Races

Flapping enormous black wings Vibhishana king of the Rakshasas blotted out the sun in his descent over Vidabhar. Earlier this morning King Bhima's general had announced the order to stand-down at the expected arrival of a most unlikely visitor. Tremendous discipline was required to refrain. But to attack a sole unarmed demon invited as a guest to such an event would have constituted a serious breech of decorum. What's more as an immortal being, no missile or arrow could harm Vibhishana. So as he spiraled down toward earth, the senior veterans of the Vidabhar army fanned out to calm down their junior soldiers. To watch a demon of Vibhishana's stature land was an impressive site to behold. Coming in at a fantastic speed Vibhishana brilliantly suspended his body so that he gracefully landed on his feet. Without missing a beat the rakshasa lord retracted his wings so that he appeared indistinguishable from humans. In this manner the urbane lord walked past the leaders of humanity and heaven seated in the box seats.

"This event marks a truce between our races," said Vibhishana in a voice so resonant it could have easily carried throughout the amphitheater without Vishwakarman's brilliant acoustic design. "King Bhima," he continued, "while it may surprise you, every Rakshasa has been glued to the unfolding drama surrounding the beautiful princess. And so, like the other well-wishers in attendance, I have traveled from faraway Lanka to honor your daughter."

Although they had waged wars against the gods and humans for thousands of years, the rakshasa demons valued the purity of the vessel of marriage as much as anyone. Once conjugal virtues were discarded in blind pursuit of possession and conquest, it was understood among sage leaders of every race that life's meaning would dissolve. So while Vibhishana's demon scent raised fists to hilt among every warrior in attendance, his presence was received with guarded kindness. Even Indra refrained from scowling. This powerful ancient demon carried himself with agile dignity as he advanced to the throne.

"While Rakshasas produce nothing that humans trust, please hear these words. 'On whosoever this splendid princess bestows the garland, he shall remain forever free from dispute from our kind," announced Vibhishana turning first left and then right so that all could see him. Then he bowed to Bhima and turned to Damayanti. Vibhishana knelt on the earth without breaking eye contact with the princess. "Damayanti, accept a boon you may redeem when threatened by darkness. Princess, call my name Vibhishana. And I will hold back the night. On my honor you will remain safe to feel the sunrise on your face."

The corners of Damayanti's lips perked up as she nodded her head in ascent. Here her youthfulness snuck out. For no one but the most innocent child could possibly smile at a demon. And, lo and behold, in front of her father, mother and all assembled, Damayanti did just this unfathomable thing flashing her million-kilowatt smile.

Like a smitten schoolboy the Rakshasa king smiled back awkwardly and placed a single black rose on the earth.

"Last night I dreamed the garland was meant for me," said Vibhishana. If it was possible for a demon to blush, the Rakshasa lord would have been turning three shades of crimson.

"I wonder how many others were awakened from their sleep by the scent of your lotus petals. Perhaps one day demons and humans will regularly celebrate nuptial union instead of battling for supremacy over one another. Hail to you, sweetest of humans, Princess Damayanti. May you show us the way to enduring love."

Apparently not even a demon could resist Damayanti's charms. Vibhishana retreated to the highest perch at the opposite end of the amphitheater to observe the happenings of the day.

In this highly unorthodox fashion commenced the procession of races. Since everyone wished to pay homage to the Vidabhar princess, this procession was suggested by Great Swan as a way to inaugurate the day. Rising from seats in various sections of the amphitheater was a steady stream of representatives from all the races of animals, deities and humans in attendance. Ganesha the Elephant God jumped to the head of the pack followed by a quickly forming queue. Jambavan king of the bears pulled out a pen so Damayanti could autograph his program. Chatting gaily side by side were two dear old friends Sugriva king of the monkeys and Hanuman the golden monkey famed for his eternal service to Ram. Next was Karkotaka the Naga king of the snakes possessing the head and arms of a human joined with the neck and trunk of a serpent. As a parade of rishis, mahatmas, saints and sadhus wearing orange robes stopped one by one to bless the princess, a cry of joy erupted throughout the crowd. All faces turned up to spot Lord Vishnu flying into the amphitheater atop his beloved eagle Garuda. Fed the greenest grass by Brahman priests, Nandi the bull selected a shaded spot to watch the festivities. Arm-in-arm Tapasvini glittered brightly as the supermodel star of the apsaras walking alongside Chitraratha the gandharva general who stood towering with pride and bulging muscles. Goddess Saraswati flew in on her white swan.

The amphitheater crowd was amped up to the max to see so many luminaries of the very highest order gathered in one place. This swayamvara was that rare instance of a highly anticipated event where the reality more than lived up to the hype. At least so far. Everyone was charged up to see who would come out with the victorious lotus garland. All eyes turned to the playing field.

Damayanti broke her gaze away and sidestepped to touch the king's feet where she let out a sigh of relief. Being in close proximity to her father always relaxed the princess. She brought her hands together over her heart. But the fiercely stoic King Bhima refused to look directly into the eyes of his daughter. At this moment when every nuance and gesture was scrutinized by so many spectators, another princess would have been distraught with concern. What had she done to incur her father's disapproval? Toning down the wattage of her million-watt smile, she looked into his soul and saw certain things. One, he was repeating his mantra. Just as she was doing. And two, she recognized the terror behind his noble disposition as something she had seen in so many men during her travels with the clan of white swans. Put simply, Bhima was scared that if he showed a hint of vulnerability, he'd quickly start blubbering in ways unbecoming to a king. So he clenched his hands into fists and scrunched his eyes to hold back the tears.

More than anyone else in Vidabhar it was King Bhima who would miss Damayanti. In these last years the two of them had become fellow yogis. Of course they had always been father and daughter. But now they had also become dearest friends. Together they shared a glorious vision no one else had glimpsed. As Great Swan's only disciples, both of them had been embraced by her enduring love. And, in return, they had given their imperfect love. Both had received their guru's teachings. And both had practiced these teachings in the world. Even if no one else had a clue they were doing so, both father and daughter knew the other was toiling in dedicated fashion to obtain the secret of enduring love. Now they would be practicing their guru's path with a great distance between them. So it was no wonder Bhima had not pushed as hard as Bhavani for their daughter to name the day which had finally come. For all his supreme effort the king failed to hold back his emotions. Three searing hot tears ignited like flames shooting out from Bhima's tear ducts.

Fortunately Damayanti had already moved onto yet one more throne which Bhima had set higher than his own. This perch belonged to Great Swan. Here it was Damayanti's turn to be overwhelmed by emotion. But she made no attempt to hold anything back. As awkward as it was to pranam in a wedding dress, no level of royal protocol or discomfort was going to keep Damayanti from lowering her forehead onto her guru's feet. Here she shed tears that flowed like a human monsoon down the marble steps. Here the princess was not motivated by an agenda of showing the world how grateful she was to her guru. Nor she did care whether anyone approved or disapproved of how much she adored her guru. With her forehead pinned to those familiar webbed feet she felt the flow of love that had sustained her through the countless doubts and distractions of her mind. This was her guru's energy. And it was this transmission the princess would miss most dearly when she moved away from the palace lake.

The only reason she resumed the swayamvara was because the transmission ended. It was her time to grow up. And as much as she wanted to stay right there at this altar, Damayanti knew the second gateway would never open if she remained at her guru's feet. So the princess rose and removed the lotus garland that King Bhima had earlier draped around Great Swan's neck. Then she stepped down to the field to face her destiny.

Stretching from one end of the field and back three times, the assembly of men standing before the princess looked more like a gauntlet than a pathway to love. Only now that she was down here on the field did it sink into her consciousness how many men had traveled great distances to win her heart. Damayanti could not fathom what had motivated these men. Almost without exception she recognized none of their faces. In her cloaked travels with the clan of white swans the princess did cross paths with a few of them. From the eastern realm she remembered a mining king famed for his land's raven blood rubies. There was a long bearded emperor from the snowy far north region beyond the Himalayas. Of course she spotted Mohanna. Even with these men whom she had observed up close, it struck her that none of them had ever seen her. What odd creatures, she thought, these men had battled one another all day long in front of millions of spectators when their odds of victory were so slim.

The princess strode down the first line with eyes for one man but trying not to make it too obvious. These exhausted men looked much more like a battery of boys desperate to be caressed by their mothers than the famous kings and warriors feared throughout the world. Approaching the corner at the end of the first line she finally realized the power of being a woman. So this was what her mother had been talking about all these years. All day these men had wielded swords, battleaxes and maces to prove their worth. But in the final decisive moment, where her power trumped all these men combined, the only weapon the princess carried was a string of white flowers.

As she stared down the parade of faces along the second line, Damayanti felt an unbearable burden. How could she choose just one man and disappoint so many others? Damayanti was dumbfounded how her mother could have wasted her entire married life obsessing about a return to this crossroad. She could see no beauty here. Nor did she feel love. This power fed off the desperation that these men concealed in their hearts. It was cold and cruel.

Damayanti wished she could discard this power. Then she thought of what Chandri said about girls and boys everywhere looking to the princess and this swayamvara for guidance in the ways of love. So she did just that. The princess discarded the illusion that she held any power over these men. They had chosen their journey. And she was choosing hers.

In front of the next man in the line Damayanti stopped and turned to face him. With her winningest smile she extended the garland opening her palms in the direction of the man's heart. All the while she silently recited the mantra. Then she turned to the next man in the line and did it again. She was not going to rush through this ordeal.

From the royal box the princess had descended the crystal stairway with the aim of loving one man, only to discover that in order to do so, she must love each and every one of them. These were the teachings Great Swan had instilled in her disciple. The men standing on the second line were gawking at the princess perplexed by her sudden change of actions. So too were the other men on the field. As was Damayanti's mother. And the spectators scattered across India far and wide.

From the Vidabhar throne Bhima arose and extended his open palms just as his daughter was doing. In unison the entire amphitheater of spectators, including the gods and goddesses, stood up and opened their palms. This swayamvara had been billed as a celebration of enduring love. Every morning and evening of practice had prepared the princess to discern which way she would walk at this crossroad moment of her life. Now Damayanti was proving to be a princess who led by the example of following her own inner guidance.

Just what these men would do with this love was anyone's guess. This was not Damayanti's concern. Or Bhima's. Or the million others who stood with open palms. Each man would decide how to contain or dissipate the mantle of energy behind the love. And how to let the love awaken their capacity to face the crossroad for themselves.

At the beginning of the third line of men Damayanti's heart jumped. There standing in front of her was Nala. Stumbling to make sense of what she was seeing, the princess almost dropped the garland. A hush passed through the crowd that stretched across a continent. Here was the moment everyone had been waiting years to witness. Was the princess about to hoist her lotus garland? Or drop it to the earth?

Damayanti turned to Great Swan. But her guru's eyes were closed in meditation. Bhima and Bhavani were waving for her to do it. Put the garland around the neck of the man you love. But where there should have been Nala, the princess seemed lost in a fog because there wasn't just one Nala. There were five Nalas each gazing with the same adoring expression on their faces. No one else appeared to notice the oddity of five identical princes of Nishada. What illusion was happening here? Was it the orchid from Maya's garden playing tricks on her? She yanked the flower from her hair and crushed the fragile enchanted petals into the earth. But nothing changed.

What was the bewildered princess supposed to do? So much planning had gone into the ceremony. But nothing had prepared her for this dilemma. Damayanti walked up to the first Nala and extended her open palms over his heart. Then she closed her eyes and recited the mantra.

Om Shakti Om ... Om Shiva Om

When the princess peered into Nala's soul, she was enveloped in the flames of a tremendous love. Here in this man was everything she had dreamed that love could be. Surely he was her perfect beloved. Her Hansaram perfectly matched to fit into her life. But Damayanti remained uncertain. Should she drape the garland around his neck? Or move onto the next Nala to see if she felt even more love? If she didn't, why couldn't she go back to the first Nala?

Tensions mounted as the princess sidestepped to Nala Number 2 where she performed the same act of extending her palms and closing her eyes. Again she was washed in a tremendous love more remarkable than anything she had felt before. How could she doubt that this man was the answer to her soul's deepest yearning? Again she remained uncertain. As Bhavani had told her so many times, a princess only gets one chance to lower her lotus garland. So she had to get this right. With the next Nala, she was sent into a deeper state of intoxicating bliss.

What Damayanti could not see that everyone else could were the faces of four gods. In reality the first Nala was Agni decked out flamboyantly in long flaming red fiery robes made especially for the great event. Next was Varuna expelling his intoxicating blue mist. At present she was standing in front of Yama who was backing up his boast shouted in Indra's palace by looking every bit the dapper stud of the gods. Despite the mesmerizing power of this divine spell, if the princess had looked closely she would have noticed clues. Even though they had been standing outside exposed to the equatorial heat, none of these Nalas had perspired a drop of sweat. Nor did their feet touch the earth. But who could blame the princess for failing to spy such details when the pressure to make the right decision was so great?

Everyone was transfixed as Damayanti sidestepped to the instigator of this test. In his heart Lord Indra held the affection that a father feels for his daughter. Though he had pretended to know nothing about this swayamvara, Indra had been keeping a protective eye out for the Vidabhar princess since her earliest days as a girl on earth. So it was fitting that he should be the one standing between Damayanti and the man she envisioned as her perfect beloved. Being immersed in the luminous mantle of a single god was the sort of occurrence that would forever alter the consciousness of any ordinary human's life. Here Damayanti was simultaneously swimming in the souls of four gods. By now everyone realized the formidable nature of the challenge. For in the eyes of the spectators the gods had begun flashing between their true form and their Nala disguise. It didn't take long to figure out the mischief being played on the princess.

What crazy thoughts must be screaming through the mind of Damayanti? This was the trillion rupee question everyone was asking themselves. Even Nala. For he too was mesmerized by the shapeshifting of the gods that she could not see. And the answer was: there was no screaming. The princess was floating in cosmic oceanic currents of the godhead. In her mind was stillness. And the mantra.

Om Shakti Om ... Om Shiva Om

The princess let go of all concerns about getting it right. The sisterhood enveloped the energies of the four gods. And a wisdom emerged in the princess that was so deep she acted without recognizing the presence of thought. This was the feminine essence which Great Swan had demonstrated in actions and teachings.

Standing in front of the final Nala, the princess extended her open palms over his heart. Before she could close her eyes and recite the mantra, the rainbow shaft of light spiked up Damayanti's spine. She felt the energies pass easily through the first gate. Since the incident by the Nishada pond she had been feeling an intense burn in a particular point along her spine which she had measured as three finger widths below her navel. Now the light smashed through this barrier. So much energy flowed that her vision expanded into Nala's heart clearly seeing all his dreams, fears, inadequacies and strengths. Then she looked into his soul, where despite his human flaws, all her questions were answered.

With an entire continent of romantics weeping for joy, Damayanti raised her lotus scented garland. Nala bowed down to one knee. And the most beautiful princess that anyone had ever seen draped the white flower garland around the neck of the Nishada prince.

The four imposters shapeshifted back into Agni, Varuna, Yama and Indra. One at a time the gods pressed their hands together over their hearts and bowed to the princess. Then in unison the gods shouted out, "Hail to Damayanti! And hail to Nala! May the story of their love endure through the ages!"

Lord Indra stepped forward to bring the Vidabhar princess and the Nishada prince together. Before actually doing it, he whispered close to Damayanti's ear. "Congratulations for opening the second gateway. All of us in heaven are rooting for the two of you." With the blessing of the gods and the entire planet, Damayanti and Nala joined as one in their first embrace.

Gods and goddesses, women and men, demons and celestials, animals and even the plant devas rushed forward to congratulate the princess for passing what instantly became known as *Indra's test*. A procession of apsaras and gandharvas swam through the air above the amphitheater showering the field with rose petals. Like geysers, the rainbow shafts of light continued to gush up from the nuptial couple expanding over everyone on the field including Bhavani, Bhima and Great Swan. The light fanned out to the rishis and yogis who had not stopped meditating for even a blinking peek of the beautiful princess and her wedding ceremony. Spilling over the entire amphitheater, the love light then mushroomed out to envelop every sentient being with an open heart. Throughout the six corners of the universe wedding celebrations commenced that lasted for weeks.

"Boys," sang out Chandri from her vantage of waning light climbing over the blackening horizon of the evening sky, "You better get home soon. Or the Big Guy might make you unemployed immortals."

In a flash Indra and the others piled onboard the enormous all-purpose party warrior chariot. The band was already warming up. All the celestials commenced with some seriously outrageous dance moves. Somewhere between the outer reaches of the atmosphere and the gateway of heaven Matali tipped Indra off to a lone dark cloud blowing in the opposite direction of the wind.

Crisscrossing Indra's heavenly vessel, the fast-moving cloud was heading down toward earth. Matali looped back directly in the path of the suspicious cloud. Indra raised a hand and the music stopped. In his most intimidating thunder-filled voice Lord Indra demanded whoever was hiding inside one of his clouds to show himself. As the lord of clouds Indra took it as a personal affront whenever anyone used clouds to cloak their identity.

"No time for nonsense," shouted a nasally high-pitched voice. The renegade cloud steered around the chariot picking up speed. "I'm racing down to earth to win Damayanti's lotus garland."

Matali easily matched the cloud's pace. Without a second's hesitation Indra blew away the condensed vapor revealing a grotesquely deformed hunchback. "Kala!" shouted Indra. "You're too late!"

"Late?" exclaimed the reclusive deity. "Impossible!"

"Who made this bonehead the god of time?" quipped Agni. "Tell me, Kala. How do you always manage to be late for the events no one else would ever dream of missing?"

To soften the suddenly acrimonious mood Yama flashed a rare smile before saying, "Brother, we put our best effort forward to win the heart of the princess." Acting as an ambassador on behalf of this universally reviled hunchback, the god of death stepped between Kala and the others. "But Damayanti saw through our guise," continued Yama, "and slipped the lotus garland around Nala's neck. Then a rainbow shaft of light enveloped the two of them. And we sang out our blessings."

Yama's fondness for Kala stemmed from their uniquely shared vantage in the life of every sentient being. With the cinch of his noose the god of death marked the end of every mortal's life. But there was a little known loophole in Yama's unimpeachable reputation. Death wasn't official until someone marked an entry in the book of time. And that someone was Kala. Without the entry it was always possible for rebellious spirits to slip out of Yama's noose and return to their recently departed bodies. For the record, it didn't happen often. And you will never hear Yama admit the existence of such aberrations. But you know how it works with paperwork. Mistakes get made. Mortals defy the gods and then crow about it from mountaintops thumping their chests. Bards gain acclaim telling their stories and these humans attain a kind of poetic immortality. In the end though Yama always gets the final say. That is, after Kala does his job.

Here though Yama had his work cut out for him. Both gods Indra and Kala were provocateurs with famously foul-mouthed tempers.

"Too bad you missed the swayamvara, Kala," said Yama. "Those kids are truly made for each other."

Picking up on the lord of death's attempt to pacify the situation Varuna added in a dreamy voice, "Perfect beloveds poised to tip the scales back to balance for all human couplings."

The vengeful cloud grew even darker than before around the god of time's energy field. Grotesque wrinkles on Kala's face hardened as Varuna's words struck like blows to the head. Kala made it clear he wasn't forecasting any happy endings.

"It means less than nothing for a man and woman to portray themselves as paragons of enduring love. When the sun and stars sparkle in his favor, even the most pathetic laggard shines like a mahatma," declared the defiant god. "Let clouds cover the sun for just a moment and watch how Nala will gamble away, betray and abandon his princess. Afterward he will deny he ever knew love. This is the track record for the best of humanity. Same as it's ever been."

Malice dripped from Kala's words like acid raindrops falling from the sky. While Kala would never be described as an affable sort of deity, Yama was flummoxed as to why his brother kept ratcheting up hostilities on such a universally glorious day. He took a moment to examine the threads of cause and effect for his colleague. What Yama observed was a history of enmity with Indra tracing back to an ancient dispute the details of which were covered over by Lord Brahma's seal. Yama guessed that the dispute had something to do with a quarrel over an apsara or a goddess.

"Indra, let's see how your chosen number one specimen of manhood behaves after I strip off his pretty-boy veneer," taunted Kala. "Wanna bet he isn't reading the Vedas or performing pujas to the Gods when I'm done with him?"

"No one chose him save Damayanti," replied Indra.

"I see your fingerprints in all of this lovemaking. And it makes me sick."

17. New Life ... Old Challenges

The fierce rays of the midday sun pierced the razor thin molecules of Himalayan air mixing with the parched trail dust into the mare's lubricious sweat. After the long jagged ascent to the exposed mountain pass connecting the Asian realms of east and west, the ripe equine scent flared through the prince's nervous system with a fury he channeled into driving his mount and men to pick up the pace. Four years had passed like the steady fulfillment of a dream hatched back inside Vishwakarman's amphitheater. Once again Nala was journeying home from another successful caravan. He was the husband of the most beautiful woman on the planet as well as the recent father of two beautiful little girls Samadhi and Sumitra. Despite all his dreams coming true, Nala remained inconsolable.

The Nishada nobleman clenched the moist leather reins close to his gut. With these hands that he used to caress the skin of his beloved, Nala itched to tear down all they were creating. And he was clueless as to why. Were these familiar appendages plotting his demise? Wherever he traveled, the prince felt a violent compulsion to slay some terrible demon. Known for their innate ability to conjure magical illusions, rakshasa demons could disguise their flesh-eating form in anyone of a million shapely bodies. Was there a rakshasa hiding inside the prince driving him toward an unavoidable destination just as the prince was driving this caravan toward Nishada? Or was the demon waiting in ambush somewhere on the road ahead? Despite his near constant supplications to Shakti and Shiva for guidance, Nala felt exhausted and alone in his paranoid struggle.

As the heir to a prosperous kingdom ... the stud prince who snagged the choicest princess ... to whom could Nala turn? Who would possibly understand a secret desire to destroy perfect harmony? What kept digging like a burr under the saddle of his mind was the thought that before marrying Damayanti, he never suffered such isolation. No matter how insurmountable or trivial the concern, the prince had always sought out the guidance of his father. Virasen willingly played the role of the guru Nala never had. If only the prince could trace back his suffering to a source, he was certain he could dispel this mysterious obsession of placing the next wager on which to stake his father's kingdom.

Today was no different. Somehow he had managed to hold himself in check. Ahead the citizens of Nishada were abuzz in preparations for the swayamvara anniversary celebration awaiting his return. And so, despite the maddening conversation going on in his head, the prince rode on. And he reminisced about events since he had lost the horserace and won the garland of Damayanti's heart.

As wife and husband, Damayanti and Nala flourished. Less than a year after the swayamvara the princess gave birth to Sumitra. And Samadhi quickly followed after her sister. At dawn on her first day in Nishada the most important action Damayanti took in her new home involved walking down from the palace into the sorely neglected garden. That day she cleared out weeds and brush. And she spoke with species after species of plants and trees negotiating among the devas as to which plants would remain in the new royal garden. The princess knelt down and introduced herself to each deva associated with each plant. In a language as natural to her as any native human tongue Damayanti commenced to make dozens of alliances in the plant kingdom. Out of the nearby jungle a herd of elephants came forward to help the princess with her task. She rewarded her new friends with mangos fed from her hand.

Within the hierarchy of the Nishada royal family Damayanti established herself by doing what Great Swan and her father had always taught. She led by example. In short order Damayanti transformed the tired palace grounds into a lush beautiful garden where she initiated a practice of meditating each morning and night.

King Virasen and Queen Uttani joined in planting flowers and saplings Damayanti had brought from Bhima's palace grounds. Together the three of them filled in fertile soil around the cherished banana tree which Damayanti uprooted herself back in Vidabhar and brought to provide shade over her new garden altar. This tree and its fruit would remind the princess of her guru and the lineage of the sisterhood. Kneeling on the dark earth Queen Uttani examined her new daughter's long slender hands. Calluses built on Damayanti's palm knuckles told Uttani that her daughter was a woman of action. Now the newly acquainted mother and daughter gazed into each other's eyes and sighed with relief. Both of them were pleased with what they observed in the other. Meanwhile Virasen ordered the gardeners to prepare the soil for the next plants.

The news of her son's triumph in bringing home the Vidabhar princess had thrilled the queen. Now she traced her fingers along the tender shallow lines of youth in the palm of Damayanti's hands. Amid the spectacle happening before her eyes, Uttani shed a tear over the realization that she finally had a daughter. And not just any daughter. It turned out the bards were right. Damayanti did give away whatever she possessed ... beauty, wisdom, compassion and love ... so freely everything returned to her multiplied in divine profusion. The garden was proof enough but Damayanti had more ambitious plans. She was the embodiment of what Uttani always yearned for in a daughter.

Beyond the outer gates of the palace and the city Nala took his beloved on a tour. Astride a lightweight chariot the prince guided favorite steeds into ancient forests and forded crystal clear rivers. Set in the western foothills between the impregnable matrix of the Himalayas and the verdant Indus valley plateau, Nishada was a kingdom of largely uninhabited wilderness. Each day Nala beamed with pride as he showed Damayanti the vast tracts of land at their disposal. On these trysts Nala left his bow and quiver back at the palace.

So much love gushed between the royal newlyweds that wild animals sported with them. In Nala's arms Damayanti felt her first and second gateways open effortlessly to the awakening of enduring love. Reminiscent of the swayamvara eve and day Damayanti firmly believed that her years of yoga under the instruction of Great Swan were yielding a divine nectar which tasted so sweet in Nala's lips.

During these mornings when they rode out together, Damayanti wanted so much to tell her husband about the insights still fresh from her meditations in the garden. But she held her tongue. Great Swan had taught the princess to wait. She was only allowed to speak of the practice when asked. And Nala was not asking.

The veils separating the realms of spirit and human desire were dropping. Each day Damayanti was discovering her place in the center of an ever-swirling tidal flow of energies. In response to her new surroundings the princess was putting greater trust in the mantra.

Om Shakti Om ... Om Shiva Om

Channeling these energies into decisive actions was becoming second nature to Damayanti. With Great Swan back in Vidabhar and her other sister swans flown off to lakes and rivers scattered across the great ancient land, the princess was bursting at the seams to share her secrets with someone. At night after everyone else had gone to sleep, Damayanti often walked over to her bedchamber window where she called out to the moon. But Chandri wasn't answering. And Shiva wasn't gliding down any moonbeams. So the princess would climb back into bed and whisper into her beloved's ear. Talking could not be a violation if no one was listening. In this way she fell into slumber until her internal clock awoke her before the first light of dawn for meditation.

In one of the verdant uncultivated hillside fields Damayanti tried to teach Nala how to converse with the devas. Both the prince and princess were eager to locate the best places to plant the seeds of rice, legumes and vegetables that they brought back from Vidabhar. In the event their first crop failed it was exceedingly unlikely they would get a second supply. So they knew they had to get this right. While the prince did not come out and say so, it was clear enough from his half-hearted effort that he possessed little interest in adopting his wife's ways. So Nala flashed a boyish grin and took ten steps back from Damayanti. The prince sat down in crosslegged padmasana and dutifully watched his beloved. One by one she closed her eyes and reached blind to touch the plants. For her the caress was a sacred act. She started by making contact with the bark of an old pomegranate tree. Then she repeated the gesture with plants large and small. In this way Damayanti gleaned the wisdom of the earth.

After several hours Damayanti turned to Nala. She had finished her mission. The princess was pleased because she knew this field would yield a bounty of jasmine, green beans & oranges. Nala stood up and walked back and forth before selecting a spot where he commenced to bending over tall fronds of lavender. Then he lifted the princess into his powerful arms and laid her down on the soft scented flowerbed. The act of lovemaking might have been Nala's way of masking his own insecurity. When the princess peered into her beloved's soul, she saw how frightened Nala was at the prospect of appearing inept where Damayanti was on the cusp of attaining mastery. And she also saw that she needed to be patient.

It was not her place to change Nala. Her place was to love him. And in her expression of love she trusted Nala would find his own way to open the seven gateways. She trusted the wisdom of Goddess Shakti who had burning shaft of light that had brought them together back at the pond and during the swayamvara.

When she tried to talk about the rainbow shaft that had passed between them during those magical moments, Nala cut her off. It was as though he was terrified to hold the scepter of power that had been awakened by their love. To the princess this behavior seemed odd. Why had Nala pledged so many promises of love and devotion back in her bedchamber on the swayamvara eve only to act as though none of it had ever happened?

From her guru Damayanti had learned that the best thing to do in such a situation was to be the love you wanted to receive in the world. So she practiced her meditation twice a day. And she welcomed Nala's embraces. She encouraged her husband to build the kingdom's wealth harnessing the power of the Shakti energy in the plants and trees and domesticated animals. And she prayed that Nala would admit her into his world of illusions, dreams and fears. As she had admitted to Great Swan.

So here was this older version of her husband answering her prayer. Whatever doubts Damayanti had as to her ability to guide the king were nullified by the ardence of his plea. Thinking back to the morning ritual of stringing her lotus garland underneath the banana tree in the palace garden before the swayamvara, she remembered that part of Great Swan's wedding gift included the words. *From this day forward, I pass on to you, the duty of teaching all I have taught you.*

The princess accepted King Virasen as her first disciple. She instructed him to close his eyes and sit crosslegged with his sit bones grounded and his spine straight. Damayanti proceeded to guide the king in the ways of proper breath.

True to his word Virasen practiced yoga meditation according to Damayanti's strict schedule. In most kingdoms when the king starts something new, other members of the royal family and court want to do whatever the king is doing. Especially if they notice the king is a whole lot more centered and peaceful throughout the day. Virasen felt as though all his life he had been breathing with one lung. Now whenever he closed his eyes to meditate, he suddenly felt as though he had been given a second lung. His breaths extended into much longer cycles of deeper inner peace than he had known. To the best of his ability he incorporated the nuances of Damayanti's instructions. Three weeks later Virasen was initiated into the mantra.

Om Shakti Om ... Om Shiva Om

The next person to show up early one morning sitting in front of Damayanti was Queen Uttani. While the lives of Virasen, Nala and Pushkar had revolved around the cycles of fighting in military campaigns, preparations for the next military campaign and ruling over the people of Nishada, Uttani had dedicated herself to the worship of Lord Shiva. So the morning and evening schedule of meditation came effortlessly to the queen. Incorporating yoga postures to prepare her body for the stillness of seated meditation was a welcome addition to her practice.

On the day she took initiation Uttani felt so much joy. While she had recited prayers to Shiva and the other gods all her life, Uttani had never used a mantra. It was so much simpler than a prayer. When she discovered that Great Swan's mantra invoked Lord Shiva, Uttani wanted to scream out to her husband that her life was complete. The mantra felt like a direct pipeline between herself and Shiva.

From the first time she recited the mantra Uttani envisioned herself as Goddess Shakti and Virasen as Lord Shiva. Practicing each morning and night next to her husband fueled her vision. Now instead of Virasen spending hours training with their sons, he went on long walks each day with Uttani. They had little need to talk or hold hands. Together they felt a shared intimacy that was the weaving of their lives into one another. On these walks they recited the mantra which acted as a silent confirmation of their love and the choice they had made years ago to spend their lives together. This elder stage of life that forced her husband to slow down shined as the best days of Queen Uttani's life.

Uttani confided these inner workings of her mind to Damayanti as any disciple would do with her guru. Over the course of her instructions Damayanti coaxed the queen to observe the mind's tendency to associate images with the mantra ... and to keep coming back ... stripping all the images away ... even the most beautiful ones of Virasen and herself ... in order to return ... back to the pure mantra.

Om Shakti Om ... Om Shiva Om

Soon it became part of Damayanti's morning ritual to discover which new face was waiting there when she opened her eyes. The garden became crowded with disciples and an assortment of wild animals including a black panther, a family of monkeys, a herd of elephants and flocks of

18. Sumitra's Smile

"Daddy, why are you hiding in bed while Mommy and everyone else is in the garden?"

The morning started like so many others with Nala indulging in slumber and four-year old Sumitra pulling back the covers and climbing into bed. The girl clung to her father with the primal grip of innocence. She was the only one Nala allowed past his wall of fear.

"Cuz Daddy needs extra sleep from his long journey carrying wagonloads of amla to foreign lands."

With an impetuous brilliance unmasking any and all paternal facades Sumitra beamed one of her million-watt smiles at her daddy.

"But you are not asleep anymore," she declared. "Why can't we go down to the garden together? The steps are too big for me. You can carry me. And I will protect you from Mommy."

Quite simply, this was all it took. In that moment Nala realized if a child so young could see he was hiding from his wife, what must the rest of the kingdom be thinking? It was time to face facts. With the rest of the royal court seated in meditation, the prince lifted his daughter into his arms, and off they went through the empty palace. Down at the garden no patch of earth was unoccupied except the grass mat directly in front of Damayanti reserved for newcomers.

Nala motioned for Sumitra to be absolutely quiet. The air in the garden was charged with an electric current heightening the child's sense of touch and smell. In stealth Nala stepped around the closely seated statuesque bodies. And the young girl basked in the intoxicating scent of sweet tulsi carried in the morning breeze. As her father lowered her toward the grass mat, Sumitra felt a sticky traction in the pores of his skin making it impossible to let him go. Nala seemed to grasp her dilemma. In a clockwise downward spiral he pirouetted onto the grass mat and snuggled Sumitra onto his lap in a single awkward-but-effective motion.

When Damayanti opened her eyes, she blinked several times before letting out a cry of surprise. Everyone else shifted their attention from meditation to what was happening between their prince and princess.

"Teach me the secret of enduring love," petitioned Nala. Sumitra ran into her mother's arms sobbing without understanding why. It took a minute for Damayanti to collect herself. She took several deep breaths and imagined it was Great Swan speaking through her lips.

"The secret is simple. All we have to do is realize the love already dwells within us. All the love any of us can ever give to the perfect beloved. All the love we can ever receive from the perfect beloved. This love already exists in me. And in you. And in everyone. Pretty simple, huh?"

"So why it is a secret?" asked Nala. He seemed genuinely curious.

"Because no one believes it. Everyone keeps looking for love outside themselves. So what starts out as a simple axiom becomes an impenetrable secret. And we develop seemingly powerful minds that get us further and further away from enduring love. Then we have to unlock seven gateways ... that used to be open all the time ... like they are for Sumitra ... before we can discover this simple secret."

"Isn't there a shortcut?" asked the prince. This tendency to seek the shortest distance between two points was the part of Nala's nature which drove him to ride horses with such blazing speed. Likewise it was this same tendency that blinded the prince to his weakness of gambling. He was always trying to get ahead by finding the shortcut.

"Yes, it is called spiritual practice. Let's close our eyes and meditate." While everyone else returned to an extra session of practice, Damayanti quietly whispered the introductory instructions to her husband and daughter that she had given to Virasen, Uttani and the others seated around them in the palace garden. So began the meditation practice of Nala and Sumitra in the palace garden.

19. Clay Swan

Weeks later Damayanti rested her forehead on the webbed feet of Great Swan. At the centerpiece of the garden altar the princess had fashioned a clay replica from memory. In the sixth year of her marriage the princess initiated her one thousandth disciple into the mantra. As she took a moment for herself, Damayanti felt so privileged to have had Great Swan almost completely to herself throughout her adolescence. One guru. Only two disciples. Damayanti and Bhima. Now everything had become complicated with the endless string of requests to lead initiations for entire villages scattered across the kingdom.

Each time a seeker arrived with questions about Goddess Shakti's gateways or the two-headed serpent Kundalini, the princess absorbed her guru's lessons at a deeper level. The first level of learning from the guru happened through direct practice. The second level of learning from the guru occurred through applying lessons gleaned from the practice in daily life. The third level of learning from the guru occurred through teaching others the direct practice and its applications in daily life.

When the princess learned to sit with a straight spine and a long steady breath on the garden bench beside Great Swan, she never gave a moment's thought to the notion that one day she would become a guru to a single disciple as Great Swan had done with her. Much less to a thousand disciples in Nishada. Even now if she thought about the responsibilities she carried as her guru's emissary, sometimes it felt like an impossible weight. So she tried not to think more than one day or two ahead about the tasks of her life.

The art of living in the moment was part of the animal wisdom Great Swan imparted to Damayanti. But lately the number of requests coming from other kingdoms left the princess perplexed. Should she keep turning down these seekers in order to tend to her girls, husband, family and her existing flock of disciples? The words of her guru had been plain enough.

From this day forward, I pass on to you,
the duty of teaching humans all I have taught you.

Was there a limit as to how many humans Great Swan had meant and how far the princess was to travel? Or was it possible Great Swan would fly in formation with the flock of swans to Nishada some day and lift the burden of all these disciples away from her? Perhaps Great Swan was missing Damayanti as much as Damayanti was missing her. After all the two of them had lived within earshot of each other since Damayanti's earliest memories. Nothing would please the princess more than to resume her life as a disciple at her guru's feet.

Whenever the hard tug of running back to the Vidabhar palace lake threatened to pull the princess off-kilter, Damayanti came to the altar under the banana tree grafted from her favorite tree back in Vidabhar. Here she whimpered confessions of needing a guru's love ... here she prayed for the awakening of so many confused souls ... here she cried tears of frustration at the aching burn in the middle of her belly that she knew was the pressure building outside the third gateway fastened shut inside herself ... here she sobbed in joy for the wonderful life constantly unfolding from a swan's decision to teach a human the simple secret of love.

Om Shakti Om ... Om Shiva Om

20. Dharma Platoon

While it was the goal for every king, minister and merchant competing for an advantage to keep his wits about him, one reason the prince had recently come back to Nishada with impressive treasures was the growing strength of his negotiating skills. While other men invariably dulled their senses in the entertainments associated with affluence, Nala had surrounded himself with a team of six trusted men whose task was to keep the prince clear in his head and on schedule.

Each night two of these Nishada warriors were instructed to interrupt any gathering which threatened to run into their meditation timeslot. Regardless of who it was ... a king ... a courtesan ... a warlord ... a caravan leader ... their biggest customer the emperor of Persia ... even Lord Shiva himself ... each member of the team understood that the priority was to rejoin their kinsmen. Meditating at the appointed time was their way of connecting back home. This first pair of men were known as the timekeepers.

The middle pair were the food watchers. Eating too close to meditation lead to torpor. Each day these men arranged simple ascetic meals after morning and evening meditations. The final pair of men kept an eye out for any miscellaneous interference. In particular the king decreed that the lives of these men hinged on keeping gambling out of the prince's line of vision. This final pair was empowered to perform any action necessary to prevent games of chance. Their other main responsibilities were selecting accommodations suitable to sitting in silence for morning and evening meditation.

Virasen selected only married men for these trade missions to make it easier to enforce the king's credo forbidding womanizing. Nala refrained from smoking at the hookah and drinking alcohol. In some cultures it was difficult to trade without participating in the acts of sharing food, smoke and drink. Among strangers the first thing Nala's men established was that their religion required abstinence and silent prayer to their god at sunrise and sunset on an empty stomach. Along the trade routes, where so many different cultures crossed paths, the one taboo no one questioned was the oddity of another man's religion. As long as Nala and their men did not proselytize their rituals, they would be left to their own devices. So the last of Virasen's strict rules decreed that any mention of Great Swan's practice would be punished by death. As a result the men developed their own language to communicate with as few words as possible.

During these years of trade missions Nala had replaced one team member for incompetence. Another man fell in love with a Persian woman and settled down among the smooth-talking foreigners residing at the confluence of the Tigris and Euphrates rivers. Otherwise his trade team had remained intact. Together these men were constantly upgrading their standard of service to the prince. Each of them had been drilled in the unforgiving military discipline established by Virasen. Just as their forefathers had been trained by previous Nishada Kings. As soldiers they recognized that it was their duty to boost the prince into becoming a force of reckoning on the stages of commerce and diplomacy.

The hothead prince had traded-in his warrior strut for business skills that parleyed well in negotiating fruit and spice contracts for the consortium of Vedic Kingdoms in the western realm exporting outside the region. When noblemen gathered at banquets and weddings Nala was now becoming a big wheel feted in places of honor. Nala's priorities had become simple. His wife and daughters ... his parents and brother ... the Nishida Kingdom ... but above everyone he had learned a new priority. The practice. This was what Great Swan had taught Damayanti. And what Damayanti taught Nala. By keeping his priorities straight, the prince felt his love for Damayanti renewing itself. More than any member of the trade team this discipline stilled the demon voice inside Nala's heart. As far as he was concerned, the princess was his beacon guiding him and his team back home twice a day while they were on the road for months at a time.

Within the royal hierarchy Virasen had laid out a clear chain of command. Damayanti was in charge of growing. Nala was in charge of selling. Pushkar transported the goods: amla and other fruits ... spices including tulsi, cardamom, pepper, mace and cumin ... all of which Damayanti was constantly working to improve. It was an arrangement that suited the personalities involved and opened the gateways of abundance in Nishada.

21. Saffron Hills

In her busy life Damayanti found balance by burying her hands in the earth. It was as though mother earth were spoon-feeding the princess through the pores of her skin energy every bit as vital as her twice a day meditations. Touching the earth and talking to the plant devas grounded the princess by giving her the strengths that came from healthy roots. Slowly over years the practices of yoga and gardening had become so embedded in her daily life that she could not fathom ever going through an entire day without them. Fortunately Damayanti had structured her life in ways making it easy to return to the earth and the meditation garden.

Her team of Vidabhar foremen had adapted to their new climate and crops so well that they had been anticipating Damayanti's wishes. New methods of repelling pests and saving steps in getting the fruit from the trees into Pushkar's crates were among the innovations they presented as tokens of love to their princess. Her school of women healers had joined Damayanti in her daily art of conversing with the different strains of herbs. More so than speaking the language of the plant devas what these women learned from their princess was how to listen. The herb devas had so much to say. By slowing down to the rhythms of these plants, the women learned how to improve their potency and taste.

The gardens and groves of Nishada had become enchanted places to sit and reflect. Lately Damayanti had begun to drift off in afternoon slumbers under her favorite banana tree. In her dreams she conversed intimately with devas throughout the plant kingdom including the individual species of many trees, shrubs, vegetables and herbs. These dreamtime communiqués were one of the unique ways the princess grew alliances that resulted in stunning gardens, higher crop yields and greater balance in the co-existence between humans and plants.

Recently a strange herb which grew far away in the higher elevation of the northwest hills had been seeking a private darshan with the Nishada princess. On a daily basis he was squeezing out his fellow compatriots and seizing control of this special time in her day. It got to the point where he was repeating the same detailed instructions for how to prepare the Nishada fields for his seeds. Through the grapevine of devas, the herb had heard about the splendor of the Nishada gardens. Every afternoon the princess was being guided out to the garden under the banana tree where sleep came over her. This herb exuded a powerful energy more seductive than any she had encountered in the plant kingdom. And he kept lobbying for the princess to listen closely so that his herb could one day grow in Nishada. The deva whispered his wish to be close to the princess. And no one else. This pact was to be their secret.

Her problem was she doubted the accuracy of what she was hearing. The herb summoning her to these afternoon dream sessions was notoriously difficult to cultivate. As the king of all herbs, saffron with its long thin fragile orange stamen required tremendous care to harvest. Sought after in far away kingdoms for its unique nutty fragrance, saffron had the reputation as the most expensive spice in the world. Each time she rested her head on the earth underneath the banana tree, the princess felt powerless to repel this presence. Was she really being duped by a nefarious spirit seeking to lead her down some dark inescapable pathway?

While it was true that plant devas gravitated toward secretive alliances to advance their growth into new patches of fertile soil, the princess asked herself the same question each time she arose from these afternoon naps. Was he really the saffron deva? Damayanti could not afford to get dragged into a series of fruitless distractions. She was already a woman with too many balls in the air.

Despite her concerns each day after her midday meal Damayanti kept returning to the sanctuary of the shady banana tree. And each day she closed her eyes and curled her body to the contours of the earth. The princess let sleep take her into the dream realm. What brought Damayanti back again and again was the burning sensation she kept feeling in her mid belly just below her ribs. The saffron deva, or whoever he might be, was applying constant pressure to the door of Damayanti's third gateway. Throughout their time together the princess felt a powerful surge of cosmic energy building inside her. And she was absolutely conscious of everything happening to her. As though she was not really sleeping ... but instead dreaming while awake ... in fact more awake than she was during her normal life.

"How did you find me?"

"Your kidding, right?" scoffed the saffron deva. "Don't be modest. Everyone in the plant world knows about the ravishing Princess Damayanti. Even an herb growing in the remotest places."

While she tried her best to conceal it, the princess was flattered that this king of the herbal realm was paying so much attention to her. But still, was he really who he claimed to be? Damayanti still had doubts. "Why me?" she asked. "Besides this beauty mumbo-jumbo poetry, there must be another reason you keep intruding on my afternoon slumbers."

"Isn't beauty enough?" said the deva laughing uproariously. Damayanti was tickled by his irreverent sense of humor. She didn't get to share this sort of repartee with anyone else. "That's easy. You are stunningly beautiful. And you cherish my sisters and brothers in the plant world like few humans on this planet. So, princess, you have captured my heart. From this day forward I am at your service."

Damayanti felt a warm surge of energy flooding through her belly again. With every thought of the saffron deva this flush of energy washed against the seal of her third gateway with a pressure building in strength. If only she could trust this new intruder into her dreamtime sanctuary.

"Who sent you?"

"Do I look like the sort of herb who needs permission to reach out to a friend of the plant realm?"

These verbal jousts of pushing back and forth between the two of them reminded her of a playful side to her nature that just didn't have a place for her anymore.

"I'm serious. I know someone sent you. Tell me who? Or I won't meet you here anymore."

"Too serious, my pretty princess. What happened to the girl whose days were spent watching white swans frolic on the palace lake?"

The saffron deva had pegged her all too accurately. Somehow the momentum of human affairs had steered Damayanti away from a spontaneous part of herself crying out to play. She just needed something more from him if these afternoon soirées were going to continue.

"You have to leave right now. I can't talk with you anymore."

"Damayanti, you have to laugh more. If you get too somber, it's not good for opening your inner gateways."

"Leave now! And what do you know about my inner gateways? Don't answer that!"

"Okay, you win. I was sent by Lord Shiva. I didn't want to tell you because I wanted you to think I was visiting you purely of my own volition."

"Really? You actually expect me to believe the lord of destruction ... the great ascetic yogi gives a hoot about my gardening habits. I don't think so. Now get out of my dream. And don't come back!"As the words came from her lips Damayanti felt a spasm of pain in her belly as though she was hurting herself by shutting the door on this provocateur of the plant realm. She would dread his absence. But the princess felt it was for the best. Especially if he was going to waste her time making up stories about Shiva.

"On your swayamvara eve you asked for Shiva's blessing. Well, it's taken him six years. He had to meditate on it. And no one rushes Shiva. But I'm your wedding gift. Shiva is giving me to you as a way of enhancing your passion for plants."

This response garnered the saffron deva instant credibility. Damayanti thought to herself. How could he know about receiving Shiva's blessing unless he had heard it from Shiva himself. Besides no deva would risk getting on the wrong side of dharma with the lord of destruction. What he was saying had to be true. So the princess drew in a long deep breath and let out a sigh. She decided it was okay for her to let down her guard and welcome the saffron deva as a friend and ally. Hopefully one whose crocus flowers would grow fertile in Nishada for a long time.

Besides Damayanti was exhausted from her many ministrations within her family and the kingdom. With the saffron deva she experienced an instant kinship. He was a potent herb grown from strong convictions producing subtle sumptuous effects on the tongue. In the kitchen saffron became her favorite herb. With the commencement of these afternoon slumbers Damayanti started requesting her meals be cooked with saffron daily. She felt invigorated by their connection and secretly yearned to have the herb close to her at all times.

"Princess, I have come to shower my affections on you by growing in the higher elevations of Nishada on the southern slopes which will henceforth be called the Saffron Hills. And, most importantly, Shiva sent me to help you coax open the third gateway."

Once again she felt energy surging through the first and second gateways. She smiled because she could feel the rainbow shaft warming her belly. These afternoon dreamtime encounters would be their special

Om Shakti Om ... Om Shiva Om

Her body flexed rigid with the surge of energies rising up her spine. This was not how the awakening was supposed to happen. Even as these thoughts crossed her mind, she heard the saffron deva laugh in a cackle that reminded Damayanti of her guru. He instructed her to relax and keep reciting the mantra.

Om Shakti Om ... Om Shiva Om

He would do the rest. So she yielded. It wasn't as though the princess had many options. Virasen had not brought the princess and Pushkar all this way north to refuse this deva just because he was known the world over for his aphrodisiac powers. The saffron deva mixed his aroma with her own scent in a slow steady rhythm that seemed to anticipate the slightest movement of the princess. As she inhaled deeply, she tasted a new third scent that was the commingling of herself with the saffron deva. The effect left her surrendering into a state of energetic intoxication.

Somewhere she knew what she was doing was wrong. She tried to close her body down. When the saffron deva asked why she was resisting, the princess cried, "The only seed that can enter my body must come from Nala."

The saffron deva was known for his fertility. The Vedic tales were filled with stories of gods and devas impregnating females with little more than a glance. What was happening between the saffron deva and Damayanti was definitely much more than just a glance.

"Rest assured, princess. My seed is for the earth. Not your womb." The deva gave his word that he had not brought the princess to his sacred mountain home in order to defile her. Their time together was to accelerate the opening of her third gateway. She recited the mantra.

Om Shakti Om ... Om Shiva Om

What happened next she didn't know. The princess lost consciousness for she knew not how long. When she awoke the first rays of the sun were shooting out over the horizon. Had she spent the entire night out here in this mountain field? Time seemed to be playing games with her. She jumped to her feet. Enlivened by the mountain air the princess moved her limbs into and out of yoga asanas. Her gut was burning right in the same place she had been stuck since her arrival as Nala's bride in Nishada. The third gateway revealed its location inside her solar plexus. Probing with her fingertips between the curvature marking the end of her ribcage and her navel she noticed that this morning the burn was different. She felt softer. More surrendered. More feminine. As though she had relinquished herself to a state of yielding into some stronger force of nature. And she felt positively electric and alive and like a goddess. What was she saying? How would she explain these nocturnal negotiations to Nala? To Virasen? Or Uttani? Then she recalled the explicit orders of the king to keep every detail of her project a secret until she harvested the saffron.

She smiled girlishly at the sky. No one would know what happened in this field but Shiva, Shakti and her serpent Kundalini. And this deva of a most devilish spice. In her furtive mind the princess concocted a girlish fantasy that the saffron deva was actually Lord Shiva. And that she might become his Goddess Shakti. Was she heading for trouble? She wondered what Great Swan would make of this new direction in her spiritual practice. She had heard a word used to describe this yoga. It was called tantra. And it was considered a high-risk high-reward path involving the pleasures of the body. One that could lead directly to Shakti-Shiva consciousness or complete ruin. But she told herself that she was working to open her third gateway and serve the Nishada kingdom by cultivating the highly sought after saffron herb. And nothing more. What she was doing could not possibly be tantra.

For the next six days the princess had no need of food. Most of the time she spent asleep learning the secret path of surrender to the saffron herb. And to her surprise he kept her appetites satisfied.

22. Tick Tock ... Tick Tock ... The Drama Thickens

From the hamlet Pushkar felt close to the snowy Himalayan mountaintops. So close he wanted to leap up and slap the rooftop of the world. Despite the spectacular vista Pushkar had little to explore. His orders had been succinct. Protect the princess. Travel without calling attention to yourself. Do not pester the princess. She is going on a meditation pilgrimage. Upon reaching the destination, stay nearby. Do not interfere. Damayanti needs undisturbed time to meditate. Across the valley Pushkar counted the white dots of distant shaggy goats grazing on the steep grassy slope. Even after their first day of travel, a thousand more times he wanted to probe the princess. Why are we going north? Why the secrecy? What were we setting out to accomplish that was valuable enough to justify the princess traveling in anonymity? The questions arose incessantly like the spokes of a wheel spinning in his head.

The sun traveled halfway across the sky with nothing happening. Then the young prince spied a line of yaks transporting burlap sacks of rice and other sundries up the steep dusty trail. No one was guiding the animals. With no sense for the passage of time the beasts of burden marched forward at a near-glacial pace. Clip-clop ... clip-clop ... clip-clop. As the arrival of the supply train was the most significant occurrence in his day, the Nishada counted and recounted twenty-two yaks. He tallied and re-tallied the worth of their cargo.

Far below he spotted a crippled Brahman priest waiting for the yak dust to settle. Clad in a soiled orange robe the old man was catching his breath. However slowly the yaks were traveling, when the Brahman resumed his journey on the trail, he made the cargo animals look like speed merchants.

Each time the hunchback Brahman placed his right foot on the earth, he leaned into a short bamboo cane flexing it beyond any reasonable point. Lifting his left foot the old man clenched his teeth as though he was digesting the painful price of forward movement. Then he paused before taking one easy gliding step. It was followed by another murderous one. Like clockwork he again paused ... then stepped forward with a graceful stride ... followed by a step fraught with struggle. In this fashion the Brahman made his way up the precipitous winding trail.

Unimpressed by the holy man's rate of progress Pushkar grew bored. To kill time he engaged in a mindless fantasy of tapping his thumb and index finger over and over while gauging the distance. The prince was calculating how long he'd need to wait before he could reliably fire an arrow that would shatter the cane in the precise moment the haggard man was leaning most heavily on it. With military precision Pushkar strung his bow and fitted an arrow. Thirty-nine steps was what he reckoned as he trained his arrowhead on the target.

It took restraint for Pushkar to keep from letting the arrow fly. He wanted to watch it soar through the air. To see if he could accomplish the feat. He was that bored. But the prince had not been raised to attack crippled Brahman priests. Before the old man had sense enough to see what he had been doing, Pushkar unstrong the bow and tucked the arrow back in his quiver. It was a long time before the priest made it up to the hamlet. While he was walking the Brahman could not speak either both because his heart was racing and because the pain was so great each time he leaned into his right foot.

"Hail to you," called out the priest who was wheezing between his words, "Mighty king of the Himalayas!" When he had caught his breath, the exhausted priest cried out in a frail cracking voice. "May a traveler stop for a moment to drink from your mountaintop spring?"

From a robe pocket the old man pulled out an earthenware pipe and expertly struck a flint. Without missing a beat he took a deep drag from the chillum. Pushkar was surprised how long the old man held the smoke in his lungs. Hadn't he just been wheezing a moment earlier? The priest held out the pipe to the prince.

"Traveler?" scoffed Pushkar ignoring the offering. "Where, oh where, could you be traveling from?" Pushkar made no attempt to conceal his contempt. "I'll wager you just wandered up the trail from those meditation caves in the valley where you've probably lived the last fifty years?"

"How much, young man?" asked the Brahman.

"How much what?" snapped Pushkar.

"How much will you wager?"

"More than anything you can match, old man. And, by the way, where might you be going?"

"Insolent prince, you don't know with whom you are speaking. The great celestial rishis turn to me for advice. My father is Brahma creator of the universe."

Pushkar reckoned the old man was soft in the head from too many drags on the chillum. Despite feeling as though he ought to take pity on someone, who was obviously suffering more in a hundred steps than Pushkar would in running a hundred miles, he could not resist another verbal jab. "So where are you going, son of god?"

"It's possible I've just arrived."

"Whoever you are, drink to your stomach's content," muttered Pushkar. He pointed to the stone trough and pivoted in the other direction. "But leave me alone."

The prince marched off to resume counting goats. He didn't go far. The hamlet was populated by one hut for the goatherder and another hut for the farmer. Only the goatherder's wife and four children were here. The goatherder was tending his flock. In less than a fortnight the farmer would lead every able-bodied woman, man and child within sixty miles converging here for the harvest.

In the morning and the evening the goatherder's wife was responsible to cook for Pushkar. Otherwise he was on his own. He decided to play along with the drama by making a show of drawing a cup of water for the old cripple. As soon as Pushkar got close enough to hand over the cup, the old man pulled three gold dice out of his pocket. All of sudden Pushkar was not going anywhere.

"Where does an old cripple meditating in caves get a set of gold dice?"

"Precisely right, my boy! Never meant for my hands, these dice were meant for nobility. Someone like yourself. As a gesture of my gratitude ... here, take them. Hold them for a minute."

When the Brahmin priest leaned forward, Pushkar could not understand how the bamboo cane was able to bend so sharply without snapping or collapsing. It bent to a ridiculously impossible angle. The old man saw the prince's perplexed expression and just smiled back. Without Pushkar noticing, the old man had put the dice in his hands.

"How do they feel?" asked the man dressed as a priest. "Bet you've never held gold dice before? Tell them what number you want to come up."

"What are you talking about?"

"Just talk to the dice. Tell them what numbers you'd like to see come up when you throw them. Do you like snake eyes? Just think one-one-one. And throw the dice on the ground."

Pushkar was feeling increasingly disoriented. Was the old man a complete nut? *Tell the dice what numbers I want?* But how did the Brahman get his hands on a set of gold dice? In the years since Nala had brought Damayanti home following the swayamvara, Nishada had experienced an enormous surge in wealth. Between the improved methods of farming and the trade caravans Nala led to the west, the palace coffers of Nishada had to construct new vaults to hold all the gold that kept pouring in. But he had never seen or heard of anyone using gold to make a set of dice. Was this really happening? Or had he taken a hit from the chillum without realizing it? Was the high altitude of the Himalayan region causing him to hallucinate?

"They're as real as your thoughts, boy!" snapped the cripple. "Just throw them."

Pushkar did not so much throw them. It was more of a drop. Actually the dice fell out of his hands. The prince was considering his options. If he made a run for it, there was no way the old cripple could keep up with him. Regarding Damayanti, well, she'd just have to take care of herself. This old man was giving Pushkar the creeps. He had to be someone other than who he appeared to be. Old Brahman don't just walk around on dusty mountain trails in the middle of nowhere carrying gold dice. It just doesn't happen.

"What do you see down there? My vision's a tad blurry."

Pushkar looked down. One-one-one. Just like he said.

"I hear your brother likes to gamble. So much that sometimes he can't stop. if you had this set of dice, how long do you think it would take for you to win his inheritance?"

"You know who I am?"

"Course I know who you are. And I know who you are with. But I'm not bothering with her today. I've waited a long long time to see her again. But there'll be time enough for her later."

When the old man said 'long long time', it sounded like he meant lifetimes ago. Pushkar was definitely creeped out. But for some reason he could not move. He could not lift his feet off the mountain to start running. Nor could he take his eyes off the gold dice. How long would it take?

23. Dark Witness

One winter evening Nala was sitting close enough to Damayanti and Virasen that he felt as though the three of them were sharing the same breath. Except for the candle burning on the altar the garden was pitch black. The season of shortened days was the prince's favorite time for meditation. In the mornings they gathered well before sunrise. In the evenings Damayanti did not sound the sacred Om to commence the meditation until the sun had vanished.

For Nala the darkness invited a stilling of the million-question thoughts which drove him to push his beloved and father away the rest of the day. In truth the prince did not want to continue living in isolation. Yet aside from these transcendent moments in the garden he did not know how to bridge the chasm which he himself had erected. And so during the evening practice he frequently wished the communion of sacred time could go on through the night and beyond in an endless uninterrupted repetition of the mantra.

Om Shakti Om ... Om Shiva Om

With his eyes closed the only evidence the garden was packed with disciples was the vibration of peace. In his travels the prince had been offered the hookah in the palaces and hashish dens where so many business contracts were negotiated. Despite the varied attractions imbibed along the trade route between Nishada and Persia, no inebriate approximated the depth of enveloping equanimity Nala felt in his own garden seated between Damayanti and Virasen.

The hair-trigger temper which previously got Nala and his father into fights in so many of these same establishments had softened in both of them. It was as though the demons inside the prince and king had been tamed. While no one dared speak of it, everyone breathed more freely in the kingdom as a result of their newly acquired state of surrender especially Uttani and Damayanti. Frequently in the boisterous company of these proud men, the queen and princess exchanged tacit glances of appreciation for the mantra Great Swan had bestowed on them. The knife-edge cloaked beneath the bantering veneer of bravado men projected in their day-to-day affairs had become a weapon to expose the false fortress of the minds which had isolated these men from the women they claimed to love.

When the practice was completed Damayanti asked the assembly if there were any questions. Prince Nala spoke about a shift he had noticed. During meditation he heard the mantra recited in an angry voice which surprised him. In the damp chilly darkness Nala posed a question.

"If I was the one hearing the mantra, whose voice was speaking it? And why is he so angry?"

Addressing the assembly in a clear calm voice Damayanti explained how the prince's inquiry marked a crossroad every yogi must face. The million-question mind resides at the periphery and can only see the world from the outside looking in which was always distorted. Due to the discipline of the practice Nala was seeing himself from the center looking out. His mind was calming down into a new plateau of perception where he simultaneously perceived himself as the one reciting the mantra and the one hearing the mantra. This dual phenomenon as both doer and observer represented an opportunity for the prince to heighten awareness and freely choose his reality. In essence Nala was inching closer to the center of his beingness as opposed to operating from the unconscious periphery of the habitual mind. The way to explain the source of anger in the voice would best be revealed by reciting the manta. And keep listening without judging, analyzing or blaming the voice. The princess instructed everyone to close their eyes and silently recite the mantra.

Om Shakti Om ... Om Shiva Om

Damayanti asked them to explore qualities woven into the inner sound of the mantra. Was there a dominant emotion? Damayanti allowed silence to pass between each comment. If there was, did the voice shift from one emotion to another? Or did it stay locked into the same emotion? Damayanti was herself reciting the mantra. The dominant emotion in the

24. Would Somebody Please Scream?

On the morning of the seventh swayamvara anniversary the kingdom was unusually quiet. Every square inch in the royal garden was covered with grass mats and people sitting in meditation. Damayanti was seated between Virasen and Nala in the place of honor.

The sole member of court who refused to meditate was Pushkar. In a semi-distracted fashion the young prince was firing arrows at a target. One after another he was producing mediocre results. Out of the periphery of Pushkar's vision a hunchbacked Brahman priest clutching a bamboo cane hobbled onto the field. Just like when he was climbing the mountain trail, Lord Kala walked with a tortuously slow limp. Pushkar studied the way Kala clenched his teeth which seemed to coincide with putting weight on his right leg. Was it all just an act? Or was this deity actually experiencing agonizing pain with every other step? Pushkar thought he had witnessed brief moments when Kala seemed to move his body normally. If he really was a hunchback, how did it happen to a god? I mean ... can't gods heal themselves? Or get other gods to heal them?

Pushkar decided there was something really 'off' about the god of time. In Vedic scriptures precious little had been devoted to Kala. Maybe he wasn't really a god after all. Like clockwork the Brahman repeated the pattern of a murderous step ... a pause ... then a gliding step ... then a murderous step ... a pause ... then a gliding step. Fueled by the desire to inflict pain and humiliate Kala, the young prince cocked and fired an arrow. Despite the distance the arrow struck the bamboo cane just as Kala leaned down on it. It was a remarkable shot snapping the sinuous shaft in half. Just as the hunchback was about to fall awkwardly, he stopped his body in mid-flight. Suspended in space, the lord of time grinned at Pushkar.

"Nice shot," said Kala. "Got more arrows in your quiver?"

Frozen in time Pushkar could not lift a hand to reload. He could not even move his lips to plead amends for his puerile deed. Completely helpless Pushkar watched Kala regain his balance in his hunchbacked way and walk over in staccato tick-tock fashion. When he reached the paralyzed prince, Kala tapped him on the cheek a few times.

"My stepmother Goddess Saraswati is tired of listening to your whiney prayers about protecting your brother from himself and me." Kala reached under the prince's tunic revealing a small leather chest pouch. He smiled and pulled out three gold dice. "So here are my little friends. Isn't that sweet? You've been keeping them close to your heart. Have you been practicing?" With a wave of a finger Kala released Pushkar from his frozen state.

"I won't hurt my brother or my father."

"Do you think I didn't hear you the first time? Or the second time? How many times do you have to say it before you actually believe what you are saying?"

"I won't hurt them."

"This is getting boring. Look, I'm going to be the one who hurts your father and brother. Just pick up the pieces so your kingdom doesn't fall into ruin. Got it?"

Pushkar did not scream out to sound the alarm. Nor did he run to the garden to warn his father. The prince said nothing. And he did nothing.

"That's why I gave you the gold dice," explained Kala. "Now here's what you are going to do. Are you listening? The dice are your anniversary gift. Tonight after everyone else has turned in, you are going to hand them to Nala. He'll be mourning. So he won't be able to sleep. Ask him to throw the dice once. A little brotherly wager to take his mind off what ails him. He will accept and lose. You are to keep things low-key. Hand him the gold dice again and tell him to throw them a second time. Very small stakes for the first ten wagers. Then slowly up the ante. Be ready to stay up all night. By morning you'll own the kingdom."

"Why are you telling me all this rubbish? I am not going to do it."

"You can keep saying you won't. But you and I both know you will. Because you want to be king. And you don't want your father's legacy to be stolen by an archrival. Know what I'm saying?"

"Go away!"

"You could protest a lot harder," sneered Kala. "Stick around kid. This is going to be fun. You won't want to miss it."

When the meditation was over Virasen decided to forgo his regular garden stroll with Uttani because he had promised to help Pushkar hone his archery skills. Uttani made a long face when she learned his plans. But on this special day who could stay glum for more than a second? Already scores of gardeners were watering plants throughout the garden. A raised altar was being assembled so the large crowd of spectators would be able to see the re-enactment of the swayamvara where Damayanti passed *Indra's test* before wrapping the lotus garland around Nala's neck. Even though this event had happened only seven years ago, every detail had already passed into folklore. Every year the citizens of Nishada demanded the princess walk the lines of suitors to again face the four imposter Nalas before recognizing her perfect beloved who happened to be their favorite prince.

So even though Damayanti must have heard her mother Queen Bhavani say a million times that a swayamvara represented the single pinnacle moment in the life of a princess, Damayanti felt as though she got to relive her swayamvara every year. Plus Nala and she got to celebrate this joyous ritual of love with the many Nishada women and men whom they adored. In recent years she had established a new tradition of letting people assume the positions within the suitor lines and take turns wrapping garlands around each others' necks. It easily became the most festive day in the year on the Nishada calendar. So this morning Uttani had plenty of organizing tasks to insure all the preparations were being made.

Both Nala and Damayanti were whisked upstairs into the palace to put on their ceremonial garb. Damayanti was praying she could still squeeze into the sparkling sapphire Valley of the Flowers gown. Trailing in the wake of their parents, Sumitra and Samadhi squealed with delight in anticipation of seeing their mother and father fall in love with each other all over again. The girls' only regret was that they didn't have matching dresses to go along with their mother.

Unbeknownst to them Damayanti had a surprise. While it was next to impossible to fabricate exact facsimiles of the original Tapasvini design, Damayanti had begged a favor from the famed supermodel apsara. Could she weave the girls their own specially designed dresses made from a million tiny gemstones? Accompanied by her sister posse of other apsaras, Tapasvini held a stunning ruby dress over Sumitra's shoulders which drew a chorus of ooohs and ahhhs from all present. A sequined emerald dress of unsurpassed beauty drew similar rave reviews for little Samadhi. Nala did his best not to squeal louder than the girls. His heart gateway kept fluttering open at the sight of his daughters assuming the center of attention. No force of nature in the universe could drag him away from this beauty pageant of the girls donning and modeling their new Tapasvini designed dresses. In fact Sumitra whirled in circles in front of her Daddy so he could see her every ruby sparkling on her body. Then the young princess waited for everyone to settle down before she ordered Nala to bend down to one knee. After her older sister performed the nuptial ritual, Samadhi took her turn. The women's quarter was jammed with apsaras and onlookers eager to see the princesses in their new dresses practicing their finest garland bestowing techniques on Prince Nala.

Back on the archery field Virasen brought his palms together over his heart. He bowed his head as he crossed the wide grass field in the direction of the hunchback Brahman standing next to Pushkar. The king felt badly when the aging Brahman advanced in his direction to meet his pranam. Every other step for this holy man looked like an act of torture. Virasen thought for a moment. He could not recall seeing this crippled priest in any Nishada temple. He must have journeyed here to celebrate the anniversary. Virasen could not imagine the difficulties involved in traveling great distances for a man of such deformed condition.

"Welcome to Nishada, Brahman. I hope you'll receive our hospitality for many days to come. Let me know if there is anything I can do for you."

"Actually there is. Seven years ago on a Vidabhar cow path you issued a challenge to me. Today I'm here to accept it. Prepare to die."

Before Virasen realized what was happening, Kala sprung through the air. Like a wound-up catapult releasing enormous tension in a split-second the lord of time knocked Virasen to the ground. Quicker than thought Kala locked up the Nishada nobleman in a sideway stranglehold. Helpless to defend himself Virasen could not speak or breathe. But he motioned a finger for Pushkar to fire an arrow into the back of Kala's heart. This was Virasen's only chance.

"Sorry, Pushkar is not going to help you," teased Kala. "Because he wants to be king. Don't you?"

"Shut up! My father is dying. Don't you have any respect?"

"If you knew what he did to me," snapped Kala, "you'd have less respect for him than I do."

Virasen was fighting for his life. He was mouthing the words that he could not speak. But it was impossible to understand so Kala loosened his grip. "One more day, Kala," pleaded Virasen. "Just let me have this final day!"

"As the lord of time, I'm the one who gets to decide when your time is up. And guess what?" In one swift motion Kala snapped Virasen's neck. "Your time is over." Kala dropped the body of the king to the earth.

Frozen in the same spot since Kala's arrival, Pushkar felt numb. Had he really done nothing ... said nothing ... while Kala murdered his father? He could not believe his cowardice. What would people say? He had done nothing to defend the most virtuous man Pushkar had ever known. Though he had done it as a lark just a short time earlier, why hadn't the prince fired the arrow when it actually could have made a difference?

"Go! Scream! Do something! Anything! Just let them know what I did! Now!"

Pushkar refused to budge.

"Do I have to strike you with this bamboo cane to get you unstuck?"

"I won't give him the dice."

"Fine! I don't care. Do I look like the sort of god who doesn't have a back-up plan? Now Agni, he might not have a back-up plan. Varuna? Same thing. Yama always has a back-up plan. And I definitely have a back-up plan. So if you don't take the kingdom, someone else will. Cuz your bro is going down. Think about it. But not now! This is the moment when you start sprinting toward the palace like a lunatic screaming, "The king has been murdered! The King has been murdered!"

Pushkar stayed put.

"Look, kid. Your arrow was not going to hurt me. Cuz it was never going to leave your hand."

"But I could have tried."

"Well, it's too late now. So play your part in this drama. Or you're going to written out of it." Kala reached back and lashed his bamboo cane across Pushkar's face. Blood gushed out over his dead father's body. Not content with one blow Kala pelted the prince repeatedly with remarkable ferocity considering his infirmity. The ripping of his flesh was the closest facsimile Pushkar would experience to opening his seven gateways. The sting of each wound felt liberating. Instead of running to the palace Pushkar fell on top of his father sobbing uncontrollably.

A passerby saw the assault and started screaming. "The king has been hurt! And now Pushkar is being assaulted! HELP! HELP! HELP!"

25. Uttani's Lament

The calamitous news brought an avalanche of people down to the archery field. Somehow even with a crippled body Kala had already fled. With blood pouring from his swelled up face Pushkar sported the battle scars of a warrior who had put up the good fight. Even though he hadn't. The young prince was peppered with questions. The royal physician was checking for Virasen's vital signs.

No one was prepared for the words spoken by the physician. "The king is dead." Nala cried out in disbelief extolling him to check again. There had to be a mistake. His father was the lion on the battlefield who had survived so many encounters where the odds were stacked against him. It just wasn't possible. How could this man be killed on his own palace archery field. Where was everybody?

"Who did this?" Nala grabbed his brother by his tunic and lifted him into the air.

"The crippled god of time Kala." Pushkar recounted how seven years ago before the swayamvara just outside the Vidabhar capital Virasen had challenged the lord of time to a duel with the stakes that if Virasen won, he would be granted the time to watch Nala grow up to become king. Today was the day Kala decided to accept their father's challenge.

Nala searched his memory. During the journey from Nishada the father and son had raced each other up and down the rolling Vidabhar hills. Nala recalled it as the highlight of time spent with his father because Virasen and he were approaching the horizontal relationship of equal friends ... as opposed to the vertical top-down hierarchy fathers must impose on their sons. That day he did recall his father shouting to the sky in jest how he wished he could wrestle the god of time for a chance to keep Nala forever by his side.

"Was it a fair fight?" demanded Nala. This was a warrior's sort of question. For Nala the answer would fill in the details of what had happened here. Did Virasen defend himself with honor? Was he ambushed? Had his murderer used a sleigh of hand to conceal a weapon? Nala was trying to make sense of what would never make sense.

"How fair can it be for a god to fight a human?" Pushkar asked describing the Brahman disguise worn by Kala. "Father never stood a chance."

"And what did you do?"

"I drew and aimed my arrow at the back of Kala's heart. But he froze my body in a suspended state of time. It was awful to watch. Father pleaded with Kala to give him one more day. He begged over and over. Just a final day. But Kala said he had already waited too long to settle an old score. A terrible injustice tracing back many lifetimes. And he said you were the next one on his hit list. Then Damayanti. He mentioned a transgression the three of you did together."

As he spoke Pushkar was staring at his brother. Despite the hordes of people frantically trying to do something, the field got suddenly dead quiet.

"After he snapped father's neck and tossed him aside like a twig to the earth, Kala released me. As soon as I realized I was free, I jumped on him. I pummeled Kala with everything I had. But he just laughed and beat me with his bamboo cane. The pain was nothing. I wish I could have held him here longer. I kept hoping you would show up. Perhaps if it had been the two of us fighting side by side, we could have slain him."

"Ah, Pushkar! I am so sorry," cried Nala. He scooped Pushkar into his powerful arms and hugged him with all his strength. The two brothers shared the pain and shock of their loss. Upstairs in the palace Nala had been laughing along with so many others at the pageant show of Sumitra and Samadhi showing off their new swayamvara dresses at the same time his father and Pushkar were fighting for their lives. "For so long as I draw breath," Nala murmured, "I will never forgive myself."

Damayanti was embracing Uttani who had collapsed on top of her husband. Like the other women the queen had come after the signal had been given that the threat was neutralized. Uttani could not have imagined what she would see on the archery field. All she had heard was that there had been an assault where Pushkar had been practicing archery. Her great warrior was the one who had always come home alive. Many times he had been wounded. But always alive. Now he was dead. None of it made sense. It had to be a mistake.

Uttani shook Virasen. He had to wake up. This time was supposed to be their time. The queen had been cheated out of years by the war campaigns. Like a good wife she had waited for Virasen. And waited. It could not end like this. She grabbed Damayanti and screamed for her to heal her husband. When Damayanti hugged Uttani, the queen broke free. "Not me! Him!" She threw Damayanti onto the king's body repeating her pleas. "Heal him! Now!"

The queen turned to anyone who would listen. "We can meditate together and heal him. Join me!" She extended her hands out and beckoned her subjects to come together which they did. "We have powerful minds. So I want everyone to close their eyes and picture my husband as healthy, strong and alive, strutting like a lion on the prowl. I want you to picture him breathing here with us."

"SHIVA!" she screamed, "You come here right now. I need you! My Virasen needs you! Come to heal my beloved! NOW!"

But no one came. And Virasen did not move. And he did not breathe. And it was the saddest day in the lives of every Nishada. Everyone wept inconsolably. All celebrations were forgotten. Uttani stayed by her dead husband through the long day's suffering into night. She would not let anyone else touch him. And she would not let anyone else touch her. She wanted this last twenty-four hours together with him alone.

technique harkened back to their earliest years of training. It was as though they were once again young lads wrestling more for the connection of one body touching another. At least for today neither brother exerted any effort toward one-upmanship.

"Can I show you the gift I got you?" asked Pushkar after the two of them had stopped to catch their breath.

"No, you can't," reprimanded Nala sounding more like an older brother castigating a sibling than the heir to the throne putting a subject in his place. "Are you crazy? Not today."

Like a younger brother who was accustomed to getting away with actions that he ought not to be able to get away with, Pushkar reached into his chest pouch and pulled out the set of three gold dice.

"That's a really strange gift," cried Nala shaking his head in disbelief. He gave sarcastic emphasis to the word *really*.

"I know. I've never seen anything like them either. Aren't they beautiful?"

"That's not what I mean. You know about father's edict against any form of gambling. So, Pushkar, put the dice back in your pouch. If you leave immediately and throw the dice in the river, I won't have you have locked up in chains. Now go!"

"Don't you want to hold them?" Pushkar tossed the dice at his brother who caught them in mid-air. "You got to admit," continued Pushkar, "they were made with perfect balance. Try throwing them."

"Pushkar, what are you trying to do?" Nala's voice cracked and his gut tightened up. A darkening transmutation came over the prince as though the dice contained some sinister intension. Nala stumbled a few steps backwards away from his brother. "I have to hold myself together. I can't be playing games with dice. Especially now. Take the dice and get out!"

"I'm trying to help us forget about what happened to father." Pushkar advanced forward to match his brother's retreat.

"Throwing these dice is not gonna do that." Nala placed both hands over the space between his navel and ribcage which only caused the third gateway to close up even tighter.

"Let's wager who has to serve the other dinner," offered Pushkar. The boys grew up doing precisely what Pushkar was doing right now. So there was a familiar seduction between the brothers pulling Nala into a vortex of darkness. The prince could feel his belly knotting up into a fist. He knew he should have punched Pushkar and thrown those damn dice into the river. Instead Nala hurled the gold dice in disgust onto the floor.

The young prince leaped toward them shouting the three numbers staring back at them. Then he scooped the dice into his hands and gave them a shake. "So what are we going to wager?" Pushkar purposely lifted his voice into a falsetto reminiscent of the voice of his youth. He was trying to transport the two of them back in time to their early days in the palace.

"Okay," sighed Nala. "One time. Then take the dice and throw them into the river. And I don't ever want to see those cursed dice again. Is that clear?"

When Pushkar nodded in agreement, Nala declared that whoever won got his dinner served to him by the loser. Pushkar threw the dice onto the grass mat floor and called out the three numbers. He had won.

Oddly enough, even though his belly was shriveling up into an increasing state of nervous tension, Nala felt suddenly better. The tightening sensation was familiar. So he felt comforted. Once again Pushkar came up with the next stake. Whoever wins gets to choose a tunic from the other. Without remembering what he had said only a moment earlier Nala threw the dice. Pushkar made sure to be patient. His plan was to start with silly stakes reminiscent of ones the brothers had staked when they were boys throwing dice in this same room after wrestling one another. Back then Nala had always won. Because even when he lost, he would impose his strength on the younger Pushkar to get his way. And while Nala had forgotten this part of their game playing, those memories remained fresh in the mind of the younger prince.

As adults the rules of honor clearly dictated boundaries of what constituted right and what constituted wrong. So it was unimaginable Nala would impose his strength to trump a throw of the dice in order to win as he had done in their youth. Honor made it possible for one man to challenge another. And honor made it impossible for the other man to refuse. For instance, if a guest challenged the host or a younger brother challenged the elder, the host or elder was honor-bound to accept and play for as long as it pleased the challenger.

The most illustrious example of this code of honor happened many years earlier in the nearby kingdom of Hastinapura between two sets of stepbrothers: the Kauravas and the Pandavas. Duryodhana the Kaurava brother had challenged Yudhisthira the elder Pandava to dice. In that instance, as well as today's game, the match was rigged because Duryodhana at the last instant substituted his uncle who was a master at dice. Even before he touched the dice Yudhisthira never stood a chance of winning a single throw. But because of honor Yudhisthira could not refuse.

And the elder Pandava king gambled away not only all his wealth and kingdom. He also lost each of his four brothers. He even gambled himself away. Then he staked a wager against his wife. And lost. Fortunately his wife Draupadi was shrewd enough to negotiate a technicality in the code of honor to petition for fourteen years of exile as a preferable option to becoming slaves. How's that for fun on a Friday night?

Following in the footsteps of the scheming Duryodhana, the younger Nishada prince profited from the ancient code of honor in tandem with Nala's natural weakness of thinking he could always win the next throw. In this way Pushkar kept the game going long after any reasonable men would do. Each day since returning from Damayanti's meditation retreat in the mountains Pushkar had practiced throwing the gold dice. In every single throw the dice had obeyed his commands. So naturally it was impossible for him to do anything but win again and again and again. And Nala was getting more and more agitated. But he could not stop himself. Neither could Pushkar. And unfortunately there was no parent ... no guru ... no spouse ... no one with even this slightest modicum of common sense to stop them.

Soon the brothers got embroiled in the fierce vibration of competition. Pushkar won all of Nala's steeds. Pushkar won all Nala's jewelry and clothing. Pushkar won all of Nala's money. It was surprising to Pushkar how quickly he had been able to transition from the goofy trivial wagers to the really juicy high-stake ones. That is, high-stake for Nala. Soon the younger brother could see the finish line.

It was actually anti-climactic when Pushkar won Nala's claim to the throne. Pushkar had expected to feel euphoric ... a feeling of supreme victory. What Pushkar failed to realize was that not only was Nala being injured by this psychically violent game ... so too was Pushkar ... his entire energy field was collapsing into the third gateway between his navel and ribcage. Even though he was winning at dice, Pushkar was losing his spirit. So naturally it was be impossible for him to experience any genuine euphoria from winning this sort of game.

In fact, because his third gateway was progressively collapsing with each victorious throw of the dice, Pushkar was starting to lose self-control. Pushkar entertained the preposterous possibility of staking a wager for Damayanti. You know ... like in the story between the Kaurava and Pandava stepbrothers ... he knew how much Nala loved Damayanti ... after all, they were perfectly matched beloveds ... and he also knew Nala could not refuse. All Pushkar had to do was say, "All or nothing. With one more throw, you can get it all back. What else do you have to wager, brother?"

When Nala refused to come up with anything, Pushkar would say something to the effect ... funny how Draupadi and Damayanti are so similar. Both were the most beautiful women of their era. Both names with the same first letter. Both wives who helped their husbands get out of a pickle throwing dice. Oh, forgive me, brother. And, forget I said anything. Let's get some sleep.

All Pushkar wanted was a single night alone with Damayanti. Think of the bragging rights! But he also knew that at her swayamvara Damayanti had received multiple seals of protection and blessings from the gods. Any man who defiled the princess would be dragged down to the darkest pits of hell by demons, gods and humans alike. He could never rest his head anywhere without fear. Fortunately for Pushkar, the dice throwing was just a game to him. He could pick up the dice. And he could set them down. He didn't get the same crazy glaze over his eyes that Nala got. Even when Nala had nothing else to stake, he demanded they keep throwing the dice. So Pushkar went back to the well of his father's death.

"At one point father was flailing his hand toward the palace," said Pushkar, "as though he wanted me to get you. The last word he managed to speak was your name." Pushkar pocketed the gold dice and got up off the wrestling mat. "I didn't know if he wanted to say goodbye or if he thought you could make a difference. But I couldn't move. I screamed out your name over and over again. But I guess no one heard."

Nala punched the floor and sighed. Pushkar was pleased with how easily he had broken the spell over the gambler. Now he just had to square away the rules of his brother's exile. They were pretty simple. After Virasen's funeral Nala had to leave Nishada within a day and never return. As his final duty to Nishada, Nala would dissolve the king's ashes into the holy Ganga river at The Footsteps of God. Henceforth the exile prince was banished to wander in the wilderness. The dazed elder brother agreed without a hint of protest.

Once again the dice touched Nala's hands ... before he even tossed them ... he had already imploded into the third gateway. So by now the man was a complete wreck. Pushkar had done to his brother what he had told Kala that he would never do. Tomorrow the new heir to the throne would justify his actions by saying that if he hadn't done it, someone else would. The death of Virasen was what really led to the annihilation of Nala's spirit. The game of dice was just an excuse for Nala to do to himself what he truly wanted to do. And that was to punish himself to the very core of his being.

Just before Pushkar left the room, Nala lifted his head out of his hands. "The girls were parading among the apsaras in their swayamvara dresses. They looked even more beautiful than their mother on the day she blessed me with her lotus garland." Nala grabbed his belly and fell to the floor as though he felt the pain of being gutted with an invisible spear. If Pushkar's gut had not also been collapsed, he might have felt compassion for his brother. Instead he silently sneered with disgust. Too bad I didn't angle for that final stake.

"You know ... both of them insisted," sputtered Nala, "insisted on putting ... lotus garlands around my neck ... probably at the exact moment father ... got his neck snapped by Kala."

Pushkar thought to himself... when this is over, brother, you are going to be useless to Damayanti. Instead he said, "Brother, you've really got a sense for poetry." Now it was the younger brother's turn to put sarcastic emphasis on the word 'really.' Pushkar knew it was time to get up and leave. So he did.

The next morning before dawn Pushkar ran through the palace gate toward the river. At the bank he looked to see if anyone was watching. When he was sure he was alone, he reached into his chest pouch. In a single motion he grabbed the gold dice and tossed them as far as he could across the surface of the water. Then something strange happened. Strange in that sarcastic way Nala had spoken the night before in the wrestling room. Before they hit the water, the three gold dice turned into three black crows. The birds flapped their wings and flew to a perch not far away from Pushkar.

"You humans are strange," croaked one of them. "You tell Kala there's one thing you absolutely will never do. And then you go and do it. Over and over and over again. I'll tell Kala you owe him one. But if I were you, I wouldn't expect much in return."

27. Banana Tree Farewell

"You did what?" asked Damayanti in disbelief. She inspected the left side of the lifeless man. And then the right. She interlaced her fingers and turned her wrists to reach her upturned palms toward the heavens. What on earth was going on, she wondered.

He repeated himself in the same slow hypnotic manner of speech. Damayanti insisted Nala order his four stoutest soldiers to throw Pushkar's sorry ass into the dungeon. This situation was not complicated. Pushkar had violated Virasen's edict against gambling. In particular inciting Nala to gamble.

Nala reminded Damayanti that Virasen was no longer king.

"So what? Did you change his law? If not, the law remains in effect. When you sent out messengers earlier today announcing your father's death, did you not include something about upholding all existing contracts as the law of the land? In effect affirming a continuance of Virasen's law?"

This law of the land stood out as the first responsibility established and maintained by the structure of a kingdom. The law created order around which people understood how to behave with one another. The reason subjects yielded authority to nobility was because they prized this order as a great improvement over the chaos where rogues and thieves simply took whatever they wished. Every member within any royal hierarchy was trained from birth to defend and uphold this law of noble authority. Certainly Damayanti and her two brothers had grown up asking and answering questions about this precise subject with their teachers, their father Bhima and their mother Bhavani. So she rightly assumed that Virasen had inculcated his sons in the absolute necessity of being prepared to assume this position of noble authority in the event of Virasen's death. What Pushkar had done was punishable by death or at the very least lifetime exile. So Pushkar should have been the one packing his gold dice and whatever else he could fit into his chest pouch. Pushkar should be the

"One, Pushkar knows how to exploit his older brother's weak link better than anyone. Two, these weren't actually gold dice. I'll bet Dwapara and two of his minions shapeshifted into gold dice. Long ago the clan of crows were given to Kala by his stepmother Saraswati. And Dwapara is the king of the crows. He possesses a devious mind and is completely devoted to Kala. Three, men have their codes of honor. Especially warriors. And they cannot deviate from them. Not even a tiny bit. As females, we may think these codes of honor are absurd. But men take them very seriously. Were there any witnesses to the gold dice?"

Damayanti shook her head.

"Then forget about them. You can't mention the gold dice."

"Why not?"

"By now they will have already shapeshifted back into crows. So you have no proof. Pushkar will simply claim they played with ordinary dice."

"But that's a violation of the code of honor."

"No, it isn't. Men can lie to one another and keep their honor. As long as it serves a higher purpose. Such as Pushkar's belief that he is saving Nishada from his brother's gambling ways. I told you. These codes of honor men follow will never make sense to us. First thing we've got to do is get your sweetie back in his body. Poor thing. Let's fill him with light."

"I already tried. But he won't take it in."

Chandri clapped her hands and stomped her feet. Her body started dancing as though to music audible only to her ears. She waved Damayanti to follow her lead. Together the goddess and princess linked hands weaving a kinesthetic tapestry of energy around the prince. Fine strands of moonbeams shot out from the pores of Chandri's skin. Nala was enveloped in a healing light of pastel lunar hues. The goddess brought her lips close to Nala's ears where she whispered moon mantras. Damayanti leaned in close right behind the goddess fascinated by the vibration of mantras she had never heard.

Slowly the glaze in Nala's eyes cleared. He flexed the muscles in his arms and legs. His eyes rolled into the orbs of their sockets. He opened his mouth and stuck out his tongue making odd bestial sounds.

Over the prince's belly Chandri painted symbols in rays of moonlight fired out her fingertips. After she was done, she laid Nala down on the bed and instructed him to close his eyes.

"As I suspected Dwapara penetrated Nala's third gateway with his black crow energy. I'm sure the prince didn't realize what was happening until it was too late. He abandoned his center of will to Dwapara. None of this would have happened without someone really close to him giving him the dice. Because he let his guard down. Plus he was already vulnerable from feeling guilty about Virasen's murder. Pushkar betrayed Nala's trust which contributed to his decision to give up. Once that happened he was all too easy to manipulate into wagering away the kingdom. The dice would have shown numbers in Pushkar's favor."

"That's unfair. How is that not a violation of the code?"

"If you can't prove the dice were rigged, then it's not a violation. Like I said, you are not going to understand. These codes of honor don't make sense because men want to pretend they are acting honorably, but they also want to take foolhardy risks that are not honorable. If men were serious about their code of honor, they would never gamble with real stakes. Period. End of story. If that were the case tonight, there would not have been consequences to this mischief. But then Pushkar doesn't steal the scepter from his brother which was his true aim."

"So what do I do tomorrow? At noon Pushkar is going to announce Nala's exile."

"Can't tell you that. What I will remind you is that you can't mention the gold dice. That will only make Nala look even more foolish. And no one will believe you. That's part of Dwapara's spell."

Chandri predicted Nala would still be a shell of himself tomorrow. Slowly he would start to take back his center of will. So Damayanti would need to take the lead with Pushkar. The princess assured Chandri that she would be ready to put that pathetic twerp of a brother in his place.

The goddess embraced Damayanti in lunar light. She said it was time to return to the heavens. Quicker than the speed of thought Chandri danced on a moonbeam out the window and back to the moon.

Damayanti would not risk stepping into the palace court without laying her head down on the earth one more time beneath the banana tree. Like so many times once she closed her eyes the princess immediately fell asleep and entered the dreamtime. So many friends were waiting here. Devas of the groves: mango, amla, guava and almond. Flower devas: lotus, marigold, water lily and jasmine. Herb devas: tulsi, cardamom, cumin and ginger. Jungle devas: sal, bamboo, teak and mightiest cathedral of trees the banyan. Garden devas: ashoka, orchid, rhododendron, and, of course, her beloved banana tree.

Owing to the tragedy inflected by Lord Kala at this time yesterday and the fury of planning surrounding the much anticipated swayamvara anniversary that was not to be, our heroine had been distracted from the plants to an unprecedented degree. Instantly she felt the protective canopy of love that the plants granted without asking anything in return. So pure was their nature. So giving were their hearts. Nothing had to be said. No action to be taken. For the princess had returned home to the sanctuary of the earth.

It never ceased to amaze her how easily she could accumulate layers of guarded restriction in her own energy mantle without noticing she had done so. Being with the plants in their realm afforded her the reflex of purification that came so effortlessly. Here was no pretense, no hidden agendas, no posturing, no grand plans for tomorrow, no nightmares from yesterday. Amidst the nestled fauna of so much timeless innocence Damayanti let herself fall as she had done a million times before. And for the million and first time she floated on the currents of lifeforce that nurtured the plants who in turn enlivened this planet with molecules of breath. The balance point between the realms of plant and animal lived in this majestic place whose treasure Damayanti had many times wished she could bring back with her to humanity. It was from this place where sprung the creation of the marvelous Nishada gardens, the groves, the cultivation of the prized herbs and so many other miraculous transformations.

Here the princess was humbled. Here she felt herself soften. Here was where she melted into the sisterhood of the divine feminine. Here she heard the billion voices of the plant devas calling out the message.

Enduring love is initiated by the feminine,
Open your gateways to receive light
From All That Is. Sweet princess,
We, the sisters of Shakti,
Embrace you as one of us.

At the seat of her spine she felt the burning that seized her breath. For a moment she clenched every muscle in her body. Then the gateways opened. The root center at the seat of her spine, the sex center just below her navel and the will center just below the lower crest of her ribcage. In the yielding of the third gateway she felt the warm awakening in her belly. And she knew her friend the saffron deva was not far away. His fragrance wafted through the air. Her entire body was covered with goose bumps. From the opening in her belly a wave of euphoric bliss washed over the field of plants. And the voices of the sisterhood and the plant kingdom rejoiced.

Today I am leaving all of you behind ... where together we have created so much beauty and love ... take my heartfelt gratitude with you ... if I had more to give ... you know I would ... right now my heart is heavy ... with what I know I must do ... when in truth I would rather stay here with you ... and leave human beings to their unpredictable fits of madness and violence ... but I will not abandon my inner temple ... and I will not abandon my beloved ... in this time of need ... may we meet again in the sanctuary of the sisterhood.

Here Damayanti was touching and embracing all her devas. And they were all touching and embracing her in a pure orgy of light and love that was sacred beyond words or thought. In particular she reached out to the saffron deva. She had trusted him when on the surface there was little reason. A voice in her belly had told her to take a leap of faith. In the mountain fields atop his billion tiny orange stamens he met her inside the gateway of will and showed her how to hold the inner scepter of power and listen anew to the song of her voice. And sing she did. Since those days of the mountain meditation retreat she made it a point of inviting the saffron deva into her center of will during her meditations.

In the hectic period of marathon activity characterizing the days leading up to the swayamvara anniversary she had felt his constant presence as a tender loving caress in the center of her body. Now he told her that she was ready to wield the scepter of power. Challenges would come. In the ordeals that lay ahead she would kindle the spark of innocence where others would kindle despair. One day celebrations would return.

The princess felt a twinge of guilt for inciting so much hope in the growing of saffron here in Nishada. Without her guiding hand and her team of seasoned foremen she was certain the fields of saffron that were showing such promise would fall into chaos. Other plants would invade these fields. And the saffron deva would be elbowed out of this realm.

She heard what had become the cherished sound of his laughter. The saffron deva asked Damayanti if she thought this was the first time he was being pushed out of a field by other plants. He told her that he had come as a friend and out of love. Not the need to increase his dominion. Shiva had petitioned him to be of service to the beautiful princess of enduring love. What a tandem, he had thought. It was not every day that the lord of destruction asked a favor of a simple plant deva. Never had the saffron deva spoken truer words when during their first meeting he had extolled Damayanti's cherished virtue as the single most respected human within the plant realm. This was his message to her. Trust the voice in your belly. From this place ... she felt him there ... the goddess births creations ... you and she are one ... march on, honorary sister of the plants ... march on.

28. Ritual of Fire

The cold flesh of his father's dead body brought Nala back to life. He had a duty to perform that was part of a grand cycle of life. It was his duty. And he must do it. Through the night Uttani had remained by the side of the corpse. This first touch instantly told Nala that his father had departed. Virasen was no longer residing here. Yama had come. And Yama had gone with his noose tied around the soul of Virasen.

What was left required tidying up. The body was washed with sacred water carried a great distance from the holy river Ganga. Nala and Pushkar lifted the body. Uttani and Damayanti laid down the white vestment. When the sons of Virasen lowered the body, the wife and daughter of Virasen sewed together the seam enclosing the body in the white fabric.

From the archery field the sons of Virasen carried the body to the riverbank. These steps were part of the initiation of passing the authority in the family from father to son. Nala welcomed shouldering the weight. He had been well prepared by Virasen. A few times Pushkar spoke to Nala. But Nala heard nothing. It was just the wind blowing by his ear. He felt the earth support his steps. And he felt free where before he might have felt a burden. He wanted to take these steps. He wanted to take his part in the grand cycle of life.

At the riverbank the sons of Virasen placed the body atop the pyre. Nala had overseen the selection of only the choicest seasoned wood which had been soaked in wax. A team of Brahman priests recited a litany of mantras. Among them was an invocation to Agni the god of fire. When Nala spotted the arrival of the fiery red-robed deity he lit the flame and ignited the pyre. Then Nala sat beside his mother and watched the body burn. Even after the soul left the body, any subtle traces of remaining impurities could pull the soul back like tiny invisible threads.

The ancient ritual of fire served the two-fold purpose of incinerating these impurities to make easier the next journey for the soul and it gave an undeniably visceral experience of finality to Virasen's life and death. The sun took its time ascending to its zenith while the flesh burned. When the flesh was gone, the Brahman priests used rakes to push the bones back into where the embers burned brightest. Bones take a long time to burn. The sun continued into its descent.

All this time Nala thought of his father and the impermanence of life. He knew he had made a grave error. In trusting his brother he had not listened to the inner voice. In catching the gold dice he had gone against his truth. The prince knew he possessed a weakness in his belly. He was not possessed by a rakshasa demon. No, he was just human. He had weaknesses and flaws that made him susceptible to fall. All day he heard the voice tell him to invite his most loyal captains from their dharma platoon to join him in the wrestling room that night. But the message sounded silly. Why would he need loyal captains to watch his brother and he wrestle?

Now the prince would pay a price. As he watched the priest collect the ashes into a white urn, he knew that he would take back what he had so thoughtlessly given away. It might take some time. He might lose years of his life. He might lose a great deal more. But he would get back what he gave away.

On his other side sat Damayanti who had been repeating the mantra since her arrival. Now she said a silent prayer for the soul of her father. In her heart there was sadness. And in her belly there was passion. Without stirring from her seated position she petitioned Lord Shiva and Goddess Shakti to bestow truth and power in her every thought so that her words would leave her lips with a precision like darts dipped in the pure white yoga light that came from the lineage of Shiva-Shakti.

Immediately after this ritual Pushkar was convening his first royal court. Damayanti touched her forehead to the earth. She asked for the grace of her guru. Then she brought her hands together over her heart. Never could she have imagined that her journey from Great Swan would have led her into the place she now found herself.

When the Brahman handed the urn to Uttani, the ritual was complete. Damayanti rose to her feet armed with the certainty of knowing who she was. And who Nala was. And her faith in the steps that lay ahead. Together the prince and princess ... women and men who sat at the riverbank ... made their way to the palace.

29. East Gate

In the full royal assembly Damayanti did not wait for permission to speak the truth which needed to be heard. Without the slightest nicety of royal protocol she jumped to her feet and cursed Pushkar. From this day forward he would carry the burden for every Nishada subject devastated by this mysterious coincidence between Virasen's murder and Pushkar's theft. No one had ever seen the princess seethe with such wrathful fury. Our dear sweet Damayanti possessed the warrior visage of Goddess Kali. If she had been wearing a belt of skulls, everyone would have expected the princess to plunge a hatchet into Pushkar's belly and lick his blood.

Damayanti predicted the scepter of Nishada would burn in Pushkar's hands and he was destined to die a lonely dishonorable death. In short the princess acted as Nishada's judge and jury in pronouncing the verdict of public opinion. From the outset the reign of Pushkar was doomed.

The response of the newly coroneted king gave people a glimmer of hope at the end of this dark tunnel of madness. The young lord dropped to one knee and held out the royal crown.

"Damayanti, even with your sharp tongue, I am magnanimous enough to put your honor above mine. As your brother-in-law and king, it is my responsibility to love and protect you. Please take this crown. And be our queen."

A hush fell over the room. Pushkar vowed to step down as king. Damayanti would rule the kingdom. Not Pushkar. And not Nala. As queen, Damayanti would have complete control of Nishada. Further if she accepted, Pushkar would agree to reduce Nala's exile to a period of fourteen years after which he could return. However Nala could never become the king.

Now that Pushkar had everyone's attention he turned to his elder brother and asked if he had ever revealed to Damayanti how he had lost all Nishada's gold on the horserace prior to the swayamvara. Without waiting for a reply, Pushkar surmised that if not for all the wedding gifts and acumen Damayanti brought from Vidabhar, the kingdom of Nishada would have been plunged into ruin. As long as their father was alive, Virasen protected Nala from himself. But with Virasen's death, Nala's weakness had now been exposed. The bottom line was Nala would always make a flawed king.

"Before anyone rushes to cast me as the villain," continued Pushkar, "please remember, no one coerced Nala to throw the dice. Fortunately by wagering with me, the kingdom of Nishada did not lose a single gold coin or grain of rice. As king, my first deed is to offer the crown to Damayanti. Help me to get through this nightmare. Hurting my brother is the last thing I want to do. But I could not let him fritter away the kingdom our forefathers and all of you have worked so hard to create."

Throughout his spontaneously crafted soliloquy Pushkar extended the crown toward the princess. He sincerely wished she would take it. Pushkar knew he was out of his depth. Already Uttani had decreed that she could not stay in Nishada with her younger son as king. The young man was confident he could travel west along the trade caravan to the wealth of Persia. He could negotiate contracts with neighboring kingdoms. What he could not do was grow saffron, amla and the myriad crops that filled the royal coffers and fed the people. What he could not do was feed the spirit of the people with the vibration of mantra. What he could not do was liberate the minds of the people by speaking the wisdom of the soul.

The kingdom needed Damayanti. And so did he. Despite his petulance Pushkar was not so arrogant as to overestimate his capacities. While he had never once walked down to the palace garden, Pushkar had long regarded his sister as the conscience of the people. After all Virasen had yielded to her within the first year of her arrival as his guru. She was the one who possessed the wisdom to lead a kingdom. If Damayanti left Nishada, Pushkar knew that her predictions of doom would inevitably come true.

This moment was the one and only chance in Pushkar's life to achieve greatness. If Damayanti accepted the crown, dharma would return to Nishada. Order and equanimity would be restored. In a scenario where no choice offered the right way, Pushkar was convinced he had somehow stumbled onto a path to regain virtue for himself and his people.

"Pushkar, you expend all your energy working to portray yourself in the best light ... when in reality ... even on his worst day Nala is one hundred times the man you are."

"My brother is possessed by a dark side you don't know about because he fights day and night to hide it from you. But it's there. Anyone who knew him from before the swayamvara knows exactly what I'm talking about. And they're just too weak to speak of it."

"Fool! Everyone possesses a dark side. Look at beautiful Chandri. Even she does not stay in full brightness all the time."

"Nala and I share the same blood. So I can see weaknesses where you are blind. That dark side is going to destroy him and everyone close to him."

"For shame, Pushkar. You should have been supporting your brother yesterday. Instead you hid behind the code of honor and attacked him when he was most vulnerable."

The verbal joust between Damayanti and Pushkar grew in intensity with each word fired back and forth. Even so the princess kept her mind and heart open to the universal body within and around her. The princess did not shrivel her body as Nala had done yesterday when he held the gold dice in his hands.

"If I could win this crown away from Nala with such ease," shouted Pushkar, "how long do you think it would have been before someone else would have done the same thing? Nala said himself that enemies of Nishada have sent spies to exploit any signs of weakness."

"And he never expected you, his brother, to be one of them! If Virasen were still here, he'd thrash you to the marrow to teach you a lesson about loyalty and real honor. Don't offer me that crown. Hand it back to your brother. And drop to your hands and knees to beg his forgiveness."

"Strong words from someone who has never seen Nala gamble."

"He took the biggest gamble when he gave his heart to love. So if he is a gambling man, at least, he is *my* gambling man!"

Damayanti could not stop herself from running to Nala and washing her hands up and down his body. She could see that his third gateway refused to crack open to even a sliver of light. And she wished it was in her capacity to heal her beloved so he would show everyone assembled here the goodness in his soul. "And if there are a hundred people in this court today, ninety-nine of them feel the same way I do." Damayanti whirled her body in a full circle. Her hands extended out to familiar faces Nala and she so dearly adored. Then the princess flexed a terrible glare at the man world of men and honor she was parting ways with everyone. The queen handed her son the urn holding the ash remains of Virasen.

Simultaneously both Damayanti and Uttani dropped down to touch each other's feet meeting near the earth. The two women hugged and laughed. Then they wept. More than anything left in this earthly dimension Uttani desperately wanted to join Nala and Damayanti on the pilgrimage ahead to the Footsteps of God along the banks of Ganga. Nala would need his mother to stand beside him when performing his final duties as a son. She needed to be there to bid farewell to her beloved as his ashes were immersed in the sacred river.

However, as exiles, Damayanti and Nala were banished to travel alone. What's more the Footsteps of God were a great distance away. And Nala and Damayanti's two girls needed Uttani too. Instead the queen promised to deliver the girls safely to Bhima's palace in Vidabhar. Damayanti promised to look after Uttani's son. Then the mother and daughter brought their hearts together in a final embrace. As the guru of her departed beloved, Damayanti vowed that any impurities in the soul of Virasen would be washed in the holy Ganga waters. His soul would be set free at the Footsteps of God.

Now was not the time to hesitate. As much as the women wished to remain together, they knew better. Recalling her time with the clan of the winged sisterhood Damayanti whispered in Uttani's ear.

We, sisters of Shakti,
Embrace you as one of us.
In celebration we sing in your voice
In crisis we hold energy in your heart
In meditation we dwell inside the rainbow shaft
Awakening through you in every sister
Our initiation is for life.
This is how we as sisters live the life of enduring love.

Om Shakti Om ... Om Shiva Om
Om Shakti Om ... Om Shiva Om
Om Shakti Om ... Om Shiva Om

Inside the east gateway of the capital Damayanti and Nala turned back. In the hush of the jam-packed stone square Damayanti examined the familiar lines on so many faces. Together the prince and princess had crammed so much love and work into seven years of living with these Nishada kinsmen. For a moment she reconsidered taking control of the kingdom. If they marched back to Pushkar, what would he do? These people were poised to rally to their side. All this absurdity of throwing dice and men's honor could be forgotten. If she just took a step back toward the palace. Any reasonable woman would have snatched the scepter from Pushkar and reset the kingdom back on a righteous course.

Instead she took Nala's hand. Together they turned to face east. Strange as it seemed, even to her, the princess felt liberated by the actions of the past day. Something in her belly welcomed the annihilation of everything she had created. At the seat of her spine the rainbow shaft of light shot up through her belly. When her third gateway flew open she felt a scepter of light inside her more powerful than anything back inside the palace. Together Nala and Damayanti walked out the east gate taking the first step of their pilgrimage to The Footsteps of God.

30. Who's Gonna Fix this Mess?

The murder of a beloved king triggered certain inevitable outcomes. Ambitious men wasted no time fabricating intrigues. Rumors got circulated by paper-pushers seeking to jockey ahead of one another. In every quarter of the kingdom pilfering ran rampant. Ordinary people withdrew into the sanctuaries of sacred groves, Shiva temples and homes praying for the return of lost memories.

Virasen always taught his sons the first duty of a king was to exemplify dharma for his people. Dharma being the ever-turning wheel of cosmic law. To observe ourselves on this grand wheel of life is to see the place of every sentient being ... large and small ... wise and foolish. It is to embrace the totality of one's destiny as a human embodiment of God. The second duty of a king revolved around safeguarding stores of food, gold and soldiers. The third duty necessitated installing a trustworthy circle of advisors to guide the citizens of the kingdom. But when the king gets murdered and his heir duped into gambling away his throne, how can anyone trust noble authority or bother with cosmic law? In Nishada, survival became the order of the day.

From the palace Pushkar made a show of marching out into the capital streets. With a retinue of soldiers in tow the new sovereign lord tried to convince his populace that life could return to normal. Of course it could not. And it would not. In hurried fashion musicians fanned ahead blaring conch shells to announce his presence. But no one ventured out.

Pushkar strode through the narrow cobble stone labyrinth. On the door of a gemstone merchant he pounded a fist loudly as though he was bearing great news. When no one answered, the young man shouted out that it was

Pushkar son of Virasen announcing himself to his people. Not some barbarian invader demanding tribute of gold and virgins. When the merchant's wife meekly opened the door, he pushed his way in whereupon he tapped the shoulder of her son.

Lord Kala had advised young Pushkar the only way to carve a distinct legacy for himself was to promote a young generation of Nishada leaders. The gemstone merchant's son was one of many untested young men to join his rank of ministers. Messengers fanned out in the four directions announcing the serial of tragedies: Virasen's death at the hands of Kala, the dice game between Nishada's princely heirs, the exile of Nala and Damayanti and the coronation of Pushkar.

To win back the love of the people Pushkar gave away rice and silk robes. He hired bards to re-enact his heroic attempt to save Virasen from Kala during preparations for the swayamvara anniversary followed by two brothers grief-stricken game of dice which led to his serendipitous ascension to the throne. Pushkar was anxious to spin his offering of the crown to Damayanti as a portrayal of the first magnanimous deed of a man destined to take his place in the lineage of distinguished Nishada kings. He had retained enough of his father's education to recognize the hazards of being labeled a despot.

With the departure of his father, brother, sister and mother it quickly dawned on Pushkar that he had no one with whom to celebrate his newfound power. Oddly he never considered this price when he was implementing Kala's nefarious plan. Now as though he had contracted his brother's condition, like some contagion, Pushkar began obsessing over the bittersweet taste of victory. Day and night the young king could not control his thirst for more wagers. Pushkar routinely challenged other noblemen to games of chance. But once the gold dice turned back into crows, the son of Virasen quickly learned that life was not like tossing Kala's gold dice. Most subjects begged refusal to join in Pushkar's theatrics. Gambling so soon after the recent calamities screamed out like a crass abomination. Sadly these refusals fueled an already helpless sense of outrage in the youthful lord. The prosperous kingdom of Nishada disintegrated into a hopeless morass from which it was unlikely to recover for many years.

31. Samadhi & the Palanquin

Shimmying off the cushions inside the curtain-enclosed palanquin the girl stepped down from the vehicle. When her bare feet touched earth she sprinted away from the heavily traveled trail into the forest. In her mind Samadhi had plotted an escape in order to find her way back to her mother and father. She knew she could not return to Nishada. And the way could not be on the road ahead.

The young princess knew her grandmother had been entrusted with bringing the girls to Vidabhar where they would be safe. But Samadhi was not looking for safety. She was looking for her mother and father.

Her short legs darted furiously through the dense underbrush. Here her size worked to her advantage because she was able to slither between vegetation where adults were repelled. There was a slight delay between her jailbreak and anyone noticing. So she felt elated that her plan had worked when she dropped exhausted on a patch of dirt surrounded by a thick tangle of rhododendrons twisting high toward the forest canopy.

Samadhi rubbed her hands together to ready herself for the task of formulating the next step in her plan. The girl poked a finger in the dirt and drew a picture of herself. Her parents had set off to The Footsteps of God where Nala would perform his final duty to Virasen by depositing his ashes into the holy waters of Ganga. But where was the Footsteps of God? She closed her eyes and spoke the mantra aloud.

Om Shakti Om ... Om Shiva Om

Then she opened her eyes and rubbed her hands together. In the dirt with her finger she drew a downward pointing triangle and a line connected to a circle. Next she added arms, legs and eyes. Drawn to the left of herself, this figure was her mother. On the earth she wrote the words Om Shakti Om. And why did they leave me behind? I could have helped. Then she closed her eyes and said the mantra again.

Om Shakti Om ... Om Shiva Om

Again she opened her eyes and rubbed her hands together. To the right of her self-portrait Samadhi drew an upward pointing triangle. Then she drew a circle and lines to the associated body parts. Below the image of her father she wrote the words. Om Shiva Om. The girl believed that if she invoked the mantra all by herself that it would possess a supernatural power.

Many times Samadhi had sat in the garden listening to her mother tell the entire kingdom that by repeating the mantra one could perform miracles. What the girl wanted was simple. Just an ordinary miracle. Nothing special. Just like bringing a baby into the world or growing a garden where there had been rocks and weeds. All she wanted was to be transported to where her mother and father were located at this moment.

Since the uproar over her grandfather's murder and her uncle taking her father's inheritance, Samadhi had not had a moment to herself. Queen Uttani and the palace handmaids had been smothering her with so many confusing messages that even when she invoked the mantra, the young princess had been unable to feel its power. If she could just get away from everybody else, she was convinced the mantra would not let her down. Samadhi closed her eyes and spoke the mantra.

Om Shakti Om ... Om Shiva Om

Why wasn't it working? It had been more than an entire day since Samadhi had seen her mother and father. And while she was used to long absences of her father from his annual caravans west, she had rarely gone so long without the caress of her mother. The girl had no doubt that she could transport herself to them. If she just repeated the mantra enough times. So she kept invoking the magical words.

In her mind her mommy was Goddess Shakti and her daddy was Lord Shiva. Neither of them could do wrong. Nothing was beyond their powers. Samadhi dwelled in a place of pure innocence.

Every time she opened her eyes Samadhi expected to see her real mother and father. Not just a picture in the dirt. When it didn't work, she began working the mantra to summon them to her. All the while she had been hearing Uttani and the others calling out her name with increasing urgency. It was only when the tiny princess started crying that Sumitra crawled down on her hands and knees and snuck under the thick rhododendron leaves where she discovered the hiding place.

Sumitra saw the pictures drawn by her younger sister in the dirt. And she understood. Sumitra inched cautiously closer to Samadhi. She looked into Samadhi's eyes to see if it was okay. When Samadhi bit her lip and nodded slowly, Sumitra drew herself into the picture. Then she took her sister into her arms. And together they cried out the primal appeal of two girls desperate to get their lives back to normal.

The sisters crawled out and dusted themselves off. Samadhi refused to go back into the palanquin. She insisted on walking beside the men and their families. She knew this was how her mother and father were traveling. On their own two feet. As the youngest member of the royal household Samadhi had recently caught onto the fact that there were certain truths that adults kept from her. But even she knew there were no comforts for exiles.

Like clockwork Sumitra chimed in that she would not climb into the palatial conveyance either. On the second day the queen decided to forgo the luxury of being carried to Vidabhar. From then on, all of them were exiles. When it rained or they were exhausted from the tedious monotony of walking all day, even then, the girls and queen refused the comfort of the palanquins. Traveling in this fashion slowed their progress considerably which had the effect of heightening the tormented feeling of loss.

32. If I were a Man

Just as she had done every night dating back to her days as a girl, the queen sang evening prayers after dinner. In short order the girls curled up on either side of their grandmother before crying themselves to sleep. In the midnight silence of the forest Sumitra was haunted by a dream in which the lord of time was still squeezing the life out of her grandfather. Virasen flailed his arms at the child as though begging for her intercession. When he was dead, Kala tossed the king aside like a ragdoll. Then the hunchback god turned toward Sumitra. The young princess pirouetted in a whirl showing off her ruby swayamvara anniversary dress as she had done for her father. On her lips she was poised to ask if Kala could see her sparkle. Just then the apsara Urvasi screamed for her to run. The hunchback god and Sumitra smiled at each other. Then he chased her down a long endless corridor filled with bright lights, many doors and the echoing of his demented laughter. When the girl screamed out to her daddy for help, Uttani instantly woke up. The queen caressed Sumitra's cheek awakening her from the nightmare.

"It's okay, Sumitra," whispered the queen. "I'll keep you safe through the night."

Eventually Sumitra slumped back into the exhaustion of slumber. Here was the first time Uttani allowed her own tears to fall. There was something so heart wrenching in the suffering of an innocent girl which eroded Uttani's instinct to hold herself together. The tears released a potent venom which Uttani hastened to wipe to avoid searing the skin of her granddaughter.

At sunrise the queen was relieved to observe the girls applying themselves to the task of preparing to walk south. The journey took them through ancient forests and pristine rolling hills. As long as the queen sought to uplift the spirit of the girls, she could avoid a widow's burden of mourning the loss of her man. In the last seven years Virasen had become her new best friend and steady companion. After decades of war campaigns the king had finally learned how to slow down and appreciate life. Their mutual discipleship afforded the king and queen an undiscovered inroad to intimacy. When they meditated together morning and night Uttani felt their love deepen in ways as spacious as the unimpeded sky. Her most closely guarded aspiration of walking alongside Virasen on the path to human liberation was being realized. Their love had endured every challenge in life with their twilight years as the fruit of their labor. But now Virasen was gone. Against all sense of righteousness the life of the king had been stolen from her by the god of time.

The first whispers of each morning had become a flutter of disorientation for Uttani. Where there should have been her beloved, there were little Sumitra and Samadhi. Around the camp where there should have been her sons and guru daughter, there were no leaders. Only followers waiting for their queen to signal the rhythm of a new day. There was no kingdom anymore. No palace garden. No meditation to start the day. No sons to light up the palace. No Damayanti to calm her fears of being stripped of love.

On the fourth day of the journey Samadhi insisted her mother and father would start the day with meditation. So the little princess instructed the queen to gather everyone. Then the girl ordered several foremen to follow her into the forest to pick flowers while other men scurried to fabricate a makeshift altar. In a clearing the young princess was thrilled to spot a buttercup whose bright yellow petals reminded the child of her mother. One of the men returned to the camp holding a hydrangea loaded with a hundred petals of varied shades of royal blue. Without so much as a word of debate everyone agreed the flower reminded them of Nala. Anxious to please the fiery young princess, another foreman was not paying attention when he stumbled face first into a lotus pond. Inches from his prone figure he picked the one and only lotus flower from the shallow waters.

When he stepped into the camp soaking wet, the foreman wore an expression of vindication for every man and woman who had made the original journey from Vidabhar seven years ago. He used both hands to lower the prized flower as the altar centerpiece. As Damayanti's favorite flower, the lotus kindled memories of the beautiful princess, her guru Great

Swan and the garland used to declare a perfect love for Prince Nala to all the world.

The last man returned with the tender green buds of a bamboo shoot. The simple offering touched her heart so quickly Uttani didn't have time to censor her tears. As the balance of strength and flexibility the bamboo was a reflection of the man Virasen had become in his later years. A king bold enough to shift the direction of the entire kingdom to adopt Damayanti's new agrarian methods shepherding a new level of prosperity for every Nishada. Yet a king humble enough to take his daughter as his guru. Everyone sat quietly as the last offering was added to the altar. Since Damayanti always set fresh flowers and lit a candle in front of the clay statue of Great Swan, Samadhi was determined to hold onto the umbilical connection to her mother.

The foremen and their wives welcomed back the familiar ritual of meditation with the same gusto as their queen. When Uttani chanted a single Om, everyone closed their eyes and resumed the practice in front of the altar. For a moment it was as they had done so many times before in Nishada with the single Om of Damayanti. Throughout the meditation tears streamed down the face of the queen. It took all her focus not to blubber aloud. To her surprise, the torrent of emotions gushed through the gateways at the seat of her spine and in her belly.

Where was the musk scent the queen had inhaled along with the mantra so many times? It had been Uttani's greatest joy that the king had become Damayanti's first disciple because it meant Virasen would always be there beside her when she opened her eyes after meditation. A man and a woman expressing their love side by side every morning and every night. As the rainbow shaft rose up to pierce the gateway of her heart, Uttani realized a woman's dream coming true.

Here now was the unimagined sadness of knowing when she sounded the Om and opened her eyes, Virasen would not take her hand. And he would not ask her to walk around the garden. Not today or any other day. Seated at the altar she was beginning to feel Virasen's loss. Not just think about it. But really feel the loss. And it tore through her with a force she could no longer control. Uttani wished the stabbing pain would just rip her in half so she could be done with this life.

Instead lo and behold the fourth gateway of her heart cracked opened. The rainbow shaft flooded the center of her body with dazzling light. All her life Uttani had been preparing for this moment. But where was her guru to celebrate the removing of the obstacle of the heart? And what good was it to open even a single gateway with no beloved to share the awakening? To say the victory felt hollow was the cruelest understatement. Uttani would gladly forgo ever opening this gateway again if it could get her one more walk through the palace garden with Virasen.

Uttani performed the awkward task of chanting the closing Om. With the vibration of Om resonating on her lips Uttani decided her only hope was to let her heart shatter into pieces. The queen took Samadhi and Sumitra into her bosom and just held them there. No one else moved as Uttani made the most hideous gut-wrenching sounds.

In the evening Uttani assumed the center position once again leading the practice of repeating the mantra. The mood was palpably different than it had been during previous evenings. Now instead of bracing themselves against the night, it seemed like the darkness was an old friend returning home.

For once the girls weren't fidgeting. Everyone sat close together. Like a family. For Uttani the mantra provided much needed solace to the disturbing violation of thoughts intruding on her day. If she were a man, Uttani would have set out to avenge the murder of Virasen. No matter what it took, she would stalk and kill Lord Kala. Then she would have returned to Nishada to smite her wicked son Pushkar. Next she would coronate Nala and Damayanti so they could sit again on the throne. Only this time Damayanti would hold the scepter for the kingdom. Not Nala. For he clearly needed to be tethered to the will of a wise woman.

But Uttani was not a man. And indeed, the queen had two young granddaughters to look after. Someone had to prevent the violence from destroying everything and everyone. And this someone was almost always a woman. Someone like Uttani.

Like a seamstress spinning the wheel round and round she worked the mantra to weave the fabric of her soul. And despite the almost intolerable pain she felt alive again. Just to utter a complete round of the mantra required the grace of god, guru and two little girls. These morning and evening meditations saved Uttani from a life with a heavy heart. She had no way of knowing if she would ever see Nala and Damayanti again. But the gateway of her heart was open which it never had been when she meditated beside Virasen. Who could figure the inscrutable ways of unlocking the secret of enduring love? Certainly not me, thought the queen, as she chanted the eternal Om signaling the end of the meditation.

Uttani had never ventured to Vidabhar. Nor had she had met King Bhima or Queen Bhavani. So she had no way of knowing whether Bhima would welcome or cast them out for fear of offending the newly coroneted King Pushkar. Someone had to guide the girls to Vidabhar. Then Uttani would see what happened next. If Bhima embraced the girls, perhaps she would stay.

Even if opening the heart gateway felt like life's most excruciating pain, Uttani cherished having Samadhi and Sumitra rest their heads on her chest. She could see so much of Damayanti in Samadhi. And Sumitra looked just like Nala when he was six. Or she might set out on a pilgrimage to the fabled abode of Shiva situated on snowy Mount Kailash in the faraway Himalayas. So arduous was the pilgrimage that few devotees ever returned. The prospect of a one-way trip was part of the attraction. For Uttani it would be embarking on a pilgrimage to be reunited with Shiva and Virasen.

If King Bhima refused the children, Uttani did not know where she would go. She would certainly never go back to Nishada. Whenever the queen was not repeating the mantra, these were the sorts of thoughts spiraling through her mind. Not once but over and over again.

In the stark wilderness the full moon provided quite a sight. Sitting beside the fire Uttani tracked its progress rising slowly through the canopy of trees toward the sky's zenith. When the moon came into full unobstructed view, the queen spoke a prayer.

"Sweet Chandri, guide us through this darkest hour of our hearts."

A tiny crystal of water popped inside a log scattering ash into the nearby night. Sumitra took her younger sister's hand. And the two of them looked from the fire up to the moon. Then the princesses repeated the same prayer their grandmother had spoken.

"Sweet Chandri, guide us through this darkest hour of our hearts."

Like the fire something in Uttani's heart popped as she listened to the simple purity in the voices of the girls. She realized these children were here on the journey to guide her, and not the other way around. If not for Samadhi, she would not have resumed the meditation practice which was essential to resuming not just her life ... but the lives of everyone Uttani was entrusted to lead. If not for Sumitra, she would not have shed her own tears. Even so, the despair was palpable in the evening air.

"Do you think you are the first ones to feel uncertainty in the darkness?"

The moon goddess posed the query as she danced atop a moonbeam stretching across the night. Wearing a sequined dress of lunar crystals Chandri showed off the full glory of her figure reflected in this time of the month. As the body of the moon waxed, so too, Chandri's body changed shape. But tonight she appeared to the queen and girls in her most voluptuous beauty.

"Who was the first?" asked Samadhi.

"Listen closely, girls!" replied the moon goddess. "And I will tell you how this entire universe was created out of total darkness."

The queen and the princesses sat upright while the goddess waved first her arms and then her hips. It was the way of the moon. Whenever she told a story, she needed to move her body. Around the fire the goddess danced wildly with moonbeams spraying from her fingertips and toes. She howled. And she cried. The goddess made no attempt to censor emotion. She was emotion flowing in the body movement and the raging sound of her voice. With carefree madness she laughed. And then she launched into the story. Her words had a hypnotic effect on the exiles from Nishada.

33. Birth of the Universe

In the beginning God dwelled in a realm where nothing existed. Everything was just dark chaos flowing in a formless stochastic state. During this pre-creation phase, the dimensions of space and time had no reference points. For a very long long time God was all alone.

Then out of nothingness the moment arrived to kickstart things. The Supreme One manifested a triune of gods: Brahma, Vishnu and Shiva and a triune of goddesses: Saraswati, Lakshmi and Shakti. Comprised of male and female, each couple had their own *dharma* or duty to perform in order to create the universe.

Brahma and Saraswati arrived to birth the flickering consciousness of life. Vishnu and Lakshmi existed to sustain the flame making life possible for every fragile sentient creature within the infinite cosmos. Shiva and Shakti stoked the flame with so much energy as to destroy the illusion that life was anything more than a dream. In this fashion of God's perfection every sentient being was born to evolve into the conscious awareness of itself in its divine origins.

Brahma and Saraswati became known as the creators of the universe. Vishnu and Lakshmi were called the sustainers of the universe. Shiva and Shakti acquired the moniker as the destroyers of the universe. All three tasks relied upon one another in an intertwined symbiosis of evolution.

It was no coincidence these supreme beings, whose arrival predated the universe itself, were split into the polarity of gender. For while God is One, any being who manifests a physical form must operate in the world of polarity. Light and shadow ... high and low ... near and far ... space and time. The divine male and female triunes were not perfect in their every thought, word and deed. Just like everyone else who came along after them, these gods and goddesses arrived here to evolve. They just happened to start much further along the evolutionary scale than the countless beings who followed in their footsteps.

How do I bring order to chaos? This question was the first thought Brahma pondered as he sat atop a lotus pad growing out of Vishnu's navel amidst the backdrop of nothingness. Back then Brahma did not see himself as the lord of anything. He was just the first guy to sit in supreme contemplation of what eventually became the universe. At this juncture he was feeling lost. Surrounded in all directions by vast emptiness Brahma did not know where to start. So he closed his eyes and meditated on the riddle which refused to leave his mind. *How do I bring order to chaos?*

After a couple million years Brahma took in a long slow inhale. Then he made a vow. He would not exhale until he got a clear answer to the conundrum. So he held his breath for one hundred thousand years. At the outset before universes are created, it always starts this way with seemingly endless stretches of inactivity. The first thoughts of cosmic contemplation take awhile before they make any sense.

One day Brahma heard a presence speak from the depths of the cosmos. The mystery was clarifying his confusion through a feminine voice.

"Order is distilled from chaos with consciousness."

The voice belonging to Goddess Saraswati stunned Brahma by tackling his question so succinctly. He inhaled with such force that the chaos was shaken into a state of readiness. Suddenly life was going to start happening any second now. Then as many dreamers often do Brahma sat smitten in awe for another million years. He would have meditated on Saraswati's seven words in intoxicated bliss forever. And that's a pretty long stretch of time, even by cosmic standards. However Saraswati was not going to sit idly and watch her husband daydream his existence away. Saraswati offered to give the lord of creation some pointers. Brahma had to figure out how to create something out of nothing. This sort of thing required a basic knowledge of the way the universe works. So he petitioned Saraswati to illuminate his mind. Over the course of many million years under her tutelage, Brahma acquired the ability to sense, think, comprehend and communicate.

Patiently Saraswati showed Brahma how to observe the chaos of his own mind. She instructed him on the subtlest nuances necessary to pierce the veils of illusion. The goddess showed Brahma how to meditate deeper into the cosmic mind where he discovered infinite possibilities of creation.

From this place of unparalleled awakening Saraswati spoke of four sacred texts called the Vedas. One page at a time the goddess expounded upon the mysteries of the universe. In this way the lord of creation became absorbed in the balance point between the nature of time and timelessness ... between the nature of space and emptiness. Slowly he began to recognize how acquiring inner consciousness made it possible to shape the potential chaos around him. This realization coalesced into tremendous reserves of power in the mind of the creator of the universe.

Just then a new source of anguish plagued Brahma. With so much power accumulating inside him, the lord discovered he had no idea how to exercise it. Once again he petitioned his beloved to illuminate his mind. Brahma was sure Saraswati had been keeping one of her Vedas from him. You know the one explaining how to create universes. In silence he prayed the goddess would give him the final missing piece. So he could get on with his *dharma* and get out of the dark.

While he was sitting in cosmic meditation Brahma felt a soundwave of energy spike up the seat of his spine. The sound possessed energy. A low resonant rumble ... lammmmmmm ... that went on and on. In addition the wave possessed the qualities of intense light and heat. Lord Brahma was fascinated by this phenomenon which arrived out of the chaos. Then it stopped. The lord of creation was perplexed. What was the source of the sound? In complete silence he had been sitting for so long contemplating Saraswati's words. Then Brahma began to mimic the sound. In so doing he began spontaneously reciting the first mantra of creation.

Out of nowhere particles of gas and dust separated by vast unimaginable distances coagulated into the swirling forms of galaxies. Across the cosmos Brahma sang out in an attempt to merge with the twanging wave of sound. Why had the mysterious sound stopped? From his lotus pad Brahma repeated the first mantra of creation again and again. All the while millions of galaxies congregated in enormous clusters around Lord Brahma to form the beginnings of the universe. Summoned by the mantra the newly emerging reality possessed an intelligent consciousness. Something like the emotion of gratitude was being expressed by the creation. Brahma felt it as he heard the voice of countless trillions of stars speak the words. *I am here. I am now.*

Without fanfare Saraswati plucked two strings. Another energy wave higher in tone reverberated in Brahma's sexual organs igniting an intense arousal ... vahmmmmmmm ... The lord exalted in the delightful pulsating sensations. The wave of energy had returned. But this time it carried a different quality of awakening. Lord Brahma felt an intense desire to leap off the lotus pad in search of the sound. But in which direction would he fly?

He cast his gaze up and down ... left and right ... then forward and backward ... outward and inward. The lord of creation was considering his options when the sound stopped. Just like before. Brahma doubled his focus reciting the second mantra of creation. The galaxies ignited in a single glorious web of brilliant lights of innumerable hues. Determined to impregnate the source of the sound Brahma kept reciting the mantra which fueled the web of light to solidify into the planets that revolved around the stars.

Saraswati smiled as she gazed upon the emerging creation. It was a marvelous sight to behold. While a woman must wait nine months to hold her offspring, Saraswati had waited eons. Now her only child was being born. With the pride of a new mother she smiled hearing the voice of an entire universe speak the words, *I am the creator of life.*

The goddess cast her gaze downward to the stringed gourd in her hands. The instrument was called Veena. And it was the original source for all the sounds of the universe. Veena was an extension of the goddess. And the goddess represented the embodiment of purity. So the soundwaves carried the purest vibration as Saraswati plucked the first, second and third strings in succession. The goddess was pleased to observe the balance between feminine and masculine energies working perfectly.

This time the soundwave struck Brahma square in the gut ... rammmmmmm ... he felt the air around his belly pushed aside as though the sound possessed its own conscious intention. Each wave was definitely seeking out a specific place to burrow into his body. The burning sensations were increasing with each note. For the first time he noticed that the previous two notes were contained within the resonance of this third wave.

Brahma recited the third mantra of creation with thundering fury. Billions of planets hummed with the vibration of the mantra. In an instant Brahma created atmospheres, oceans and lands across the entire creation. In response to the mantra, the reality pushed back in the direction of Brahma by announcing itself with the words, *I manifest power in the cosmos.*

When silence returned Brahma thought to himself: I have a universe to create here. I cannot indulge myself in idle pleasantries. I must get to the bottom of this mystery. Brahma was losing patience with his inability to discover the source of the sound.

Just then a huge wave pierced his heart ... yammmmmmmm ... and the lord felt a flutter of emotion unlike anything in his previous experience.

Was it love? Yes, he thought to himself. This is love. Not of a beloved. This is the love of an entire creation. Over and over from every direction he heard the words. *I am love. I am love. I am love.*

Inside his divine body Brahma noticed four gateways had opened. Arising from the seat of his spine, the sound flooded the lord with so much burning light that he felt liberated from any urge to take external action. And, just like that, Brahma was content to remain in his awakened state of samadhi. His impatience was quelled. Even when the wave subsided, the lord was not disturbed or perplexed. The wave had penetrated four gateways. His heart was cracked open. Brahma gushed love everywhere reciting the fourth mantra of creation. Instantly sentient beings of every size and shape populated the lands, oceans and skies from bacteria to insects, fish, reptiles, birds and animals. Brahma was in love with his creation. With the extra juices of energies gushing from his heart the lord recited the fourth mantra again and again. From Brahma's love emerged the most remarkable of all the forms he had yet created. Human beings took their first steps into creation. Back then humans were so pure and radiant that they looked just like the gods.

Saraswati looked inside herself to summon all her strength. As the first mother of creation the goddess yearned more than anything to go down to earth. Her single wish was to cradle everyone of her newborn children. In the way only a mother can fathom these nascent humans were so glorious in their first clumsy steps. Here was the moment of great challenge for the goddess. Would she stay true to her dharma by completing the cycle of birthing the universe? Or would she succumb to her maternal instinct to succor her newborn children embracing and singing for them the lullabies of creation?

One after another the rhythmic twang of strings marked the fifth wave. Lord Brahma broke into spontaneous sound ... hammmmmmmm ... as though Saraswati's fingers were plucking the strings inside the god of creation ... Brahma was powerless to control these mysterious waves. Not that it mattered. The lord took in a deep breath and savored the moment. The birth of the universe was no longer just a thought in his mind. It was actually happening. And Brahma was sitting right in the center of everything. The lord belted out the sound of the fifth mantra of creation.

Just as gateways inside Brahma were opening so too were the voices of his children. Across the cosmos creatures of every species began to speak with unreserved joy, *I express the truth*. The fifth mantra added the dimension of communication which fueled a flowering contagion of creative collaborations arising from the newborn races of the universe.

The goddess played the first six strings of her Veena. Instantly the door to the sixth gateway melted inside the lord's skull where the pineal and pituitary glands yielded a most intoxicating auditory elixir. The soundwave reverberated across time and space ... SoHmmmmmmmmm ... in a simmering inferno of pure energy. The universe was cooking in anticipation of the heightening state of samadhi enveloping Brahma. Now he spoke for all the universe to hear. In the mantra were contained the words: *I am that I am.*

Nothing concerned the lord of creation anymore. Over and over he recited the sixth mantra. From the third eye of Lord Brahma located in the center of his forehead stepped forth a procession of gods and goddesses whose dharma it was to govern the creation.

First out of the gate strutted Indra into the universe with the supreme swagger of a lord confident in his abilities to rule the heavens. Next were redheaded Agni and blue-misted Varuna the gods of fire and water walking side by side. Close by with his noose draped in hand walked Yama followed by a celestial band of apsaras and gandharvas singing and dancing in celebration of the extraordinary birth of the universe.

Next to emerge from Brahma's third eye were pairs of divine couples: Surya the sun god and Chandri the moon goddess ... Vayu god of the wind and Bhumi the earth goddess ... Budha the god of Mercury and Shukri the goddess of Venus ... Brihaspati guru of the gods and Gayatri goddess of the Vedas ... Soma god of medicine and Ushas goddess of dawn ... Ganga & Yamuna the river goddesses ... the Ashwin twins protectors of universal polarity.

Marked by song and dance a period of festivity ensued where the gods and goddesses embraced one another. An enormous cloud of sparkling lights wafted over the divine assembly. These sparks were the spirit devas whose dharma was to oversee the animal and plant kingdoms. Next to join the cosmic party were the mythic Kinnaras whose bodies were part human and part horse. Their job was to act as the bridge between the animal and human realms. Then came the eight Vasus, eleven Rudras and twelve Adityas followed by Kubera the god of treasures flanked by his mighty Yaksha warriors who were the preservers of heavenly wealth.

All pressed palms together over their hearts and bowed heads in pranam. Overhead Lord Vishnu and Goddess Lakshmi made their appearance riding atop Garuda the golden eagle soaring high through the heavens. As the sustainers of the flame of life, Vishnu and Lakshmi were universally adored by all sentient beings. The birth of the creation was nearing its completion.

All that remained was for Shiva and Shakti to announce themselves. Rather than strut, walk or fly into the universe, as the other immortals had done, the destroyers of the universe were seated in meditation. Instead of embracing their devic peers, the two cosmic beloveds gazed into one another's eyes. In meditation Shiva had been resting the back of his left hand on the top of his right palm. Now he spread open his arms. The ascetic slid his slender tongue along the sensuous contour of his upper lip. Then he smiled with a hint of mischievous certainty. In an instant Shakti giggled and leapt high into the air. She did three backward somersaults before landing in his arms. The two yogis wrapped their limbs around each other with a level of such supreme passion that every member of the celestial assembly felt included in the embrace. Yes, the cosmic beloveds had indeed joined the party marking the birth of the universe.

The opening of the seventh gateway was beyond description. Lord Brahma knew he must birth a final creation for the universe. So his countless children to come would have a wayshower .. a clue ... to join him in arriving into this transcendent state of consciousness. So he mustered all his mental power. The soundwave was the primordial all powerful sound ... Ommmmmmmmmmm ... he felt his crown spread open like the thousand petals of the most beautiful lotus blossom grown from the muck and mire of his mind.

The seven soundwaves flushed open the seven gateways. Brahma's entire being was purged of even the tiniest speck of impurity. He felt like a groom prepared to step onto the altar to embrace his bride. The soundwaves were booming so strongly that from the nothingness ... time and space were fluttering back and forth. Brahma kept his seated asana. With closed eyes he could see galaxies ripening to take shape. Amidst so much madness Brahma continued internally reciting the creation mantras. All was quiet in the eruption of sound. All was still in the endless waves of energy. All was Brahma. Brahma was all. The repeating words of the mantra were simply: I am God.

Arising from the crown of Brahma was a white clad goddess seated atop a white swan. As the goddess of wisdom, arts and purity, Saraswati stole the breath of every god and goddess. Brahma could not fathom how anyone so stunningly beautiful had emerged from him. In the presence of the entire celestial ensemble Brahma pronounced his love for Saraswati.

cosmos which is a big no-no because it roused Shakti from her meditation. Trust me, you don't want to piss off Shakti or Shiva. Getting both of them angry is always a bad idea. With a pained facial expression Shakti whispered that she had to go to assist her sister. Instantly the supreme ascetics materialized in Brahma's heaven.

Sobbing on the floor in supplication Brahma knew he was in serious trouble. Whenever the meditation between Shakti and Shiva is interrupted, it is no trifling matter. The fabrics of creation are ever seeking to come apart at the cosmic seams of time and space. If that happens, the universe dissolves back into chaos. For this reason the divine triune couples: Saraswati and Brahma, Vishnu and Lakshmi, Shakti and Shiva had to perform their dharma to maintain the cosmic balance. Dalliances of lust were not part of the divine plan. Not for the triune couples.

So it was with trepidation Brahma welcomed Shakti and Shiva into their home. Brahma tried to assuage the situation with small talk about new species Saraswati and he had created down on earth. But Shiva would hear none of it. The lord of yoga ordered Brahma to be silent. Saraswati was pleased Shakti and Shiva had come to her defense. After a thousand years of meditation, the silence was broken by the arrival of Vishnu and Lakshmi. Suddenly here were gathered the emissaries sent by God to create, sustain and destroy the universe. All in one place and time.

In his capricious escapade Lord Brahma had unwittingly sown seeds of unhappiness in the minds of all creatures. From now on the impulse of lust had been infused into the male polarity with the power of one third of the triune. To decide what should be done the three goddesses huddled up in meditation apart from their mates.

When the goddesses returned, Shakti and Shiva embraced. Side by side Lakshmi and Vishnu stared long and hard at Brahma. As punishment Saraswati pronounced there would be no temples of worship dedicated to Brahma. On earth no one would ever pray to Lord Brahma. Henceforth Brahma was banished in residence within his palace in the highest sphere of heaven. Only from here could Brahma add new life to his creation. His penance was to remain in meditation on the self for so long as this universe existed.

Shiva never uttered a word. When the lord of yoga opened his arms, Shakti leapt high into the air. The goddess giggled in delight as she flipped backward into three and a half somersaults. Then she landed diving headfirst into Brahma. As the creator of the universe Brahma was the universe. And the universe was Brahma.

When the goddesses had their private pow-wow, they realized that Brahma's actions had created a cataclysmic imbalance of the male polarity. During their meditation the three goddesses could see down on earth and other planets. The contagion had already spread far and wide. The male members of every species were seeking the conquest of love inside their feminine counterparts instead of embracing the love inside themselves. And the females were scheming ways to stand out as the most beautiful one in order to attract the most powerful male. The imbalance set in motion by Brahma was growing stronger. So the triune of goddesses distilled the essence of love into a powerful elixir.

When Shakti dove into Brahma, the goddess dispersed herself through him into every particle of matter throughout the universe. Shakti deposited a drop from the elixir behind seven inner gateways located inside every sentient being. Shakti volunteered to donate her body to the universe. Instantly Shakti sent tsunami waves of energy everywhere. And her physical body no longer existed. In an instant it had dissolved never to return. Not during this cycle of the universe. After Shakti and Shiva destroyed the universe and after the seemingly endless period of chaotic emptiness and after the subsequent emergence of a new universe only then would Shakti regain a physical form.

All seven gateways inside Brahma flew open and his consciousness was elevated to levels rendering the god drunk with madness. Brahma prostrated himself on the floor calling out to Shiva by the name Mahadeva which meant the greatest of gods. Like a beast he howled for Shiva to be his guru. With extraordinary difficulty he managed to scream out, "Teach me how to keep Shakti from destroying me."

The remaining members of the triune smiled. Without speaking aloud Saraswati and Shiva made a pact to transmit the secret of enduring love to ardent seekers. Together they started with Brahma as their first disciple. The white swan who bore witness to this pact was none other than Great Swan. So what started with Lord Brahma's indiscretion grew into the journey of the goddesses and Shiva working together with Great Swan coming down to earth to guide Princess Damayanti.

Chandri announced it was time to complete her journey across the sky.

"Don't stop, Chandri!" shouted Sumitra. "Teach us the secret!"

Through the dense forest of trees Chandri pointed to a sliver of the moon. It was disappearing into the horizon. "Girls, it's time for sleep."

"No!" demanded Samadhi. "You must tell me about my mommy."

"And Great Swan!" exclaimed Sumitra.

The goddess stepped on the last moonbeam and danced her way back into the moon. As she glided and twisted her body away, Chandri instructed the girls to dream about what she had told them. "When you want me to tell you another story," she said. "Look up at the moon. Call out to me. And I will come. Especially while you are waiting for Mommy."

"When is she coming?" cried Samadhi. "And where?"

"What about Daddy?" asked Sumitra. "Isn't he coming too?"

34. Ceremony of Ashes

The beating of the drum was the signal to gather at The Footsteps of God. Played by the captain of the gandharvas Chitraratha, one might expect such a famed warrior to pound a fierce bellicose rhythm. Actually his strokes were the most tender carresses on the skins producing a sound of poignance and love that was somehow heard far and wide. The gandharva had been playing at Ganga's riverbank for days joined not by other warriors but by a host of apsaras. From their lips they sang love songs carried up into the highest heavens and drifting down into the nether underworld cities of the nagas at the bottom of the deepest seas.

Throughout the day humans and celestials had been arriving in ones and twos and in groups as large as ten. All the while Chitraratha played his tender beat. Now as the light of day signaled the first sign of fading into darkness, the singing apsaras fell silent. Atop distant Himalayan peaks silhouettes of twinkling light marked the bonfires of yogis and saints whose prayers had been cleansing the molecules of air, water and earth. Chritraratha held his hand still. The ceremony was about to begin.

Urvasi rose to her feet and sang a solo.

Day into night and night into day the wheel of dharma turns.
Not even the most powerful gods may block its justice
Long long ago this very same Virasen
in the highest celestial realm of Lord Brahma's palace
commited a crime against a god
Now as one of us he returns.
And we are touched with the joy of reunion.
For we see how humanity has opened
the gateways of love anew for our dearest brother.
Come home, brother. We love you.

The crowd of humans and gods parted. Nala knew this was his time. The exile prince made his way to the riverbank where Damayanti followed quietly in his wake. She wished Uttani were here to see the turnout for her fallen husband and to say goodbye one last time. Urvasi's song sent Nala's mind to seek out memories that might make sense of her words. As he hoisted the white urn high above his head for all to see, Nala was reminded of the way Damayanti had hoisted the garland of lotus blossoms when she walked the swayamvara lines of suitors. With so many eyes set upon him, Nala wondered if his beloved princess had felt any of the ambivalence that he was feeling now. He wanted to defy the wheel of dharma. He wanted to bring his father back to life. Nala wanted to start the story all over again from the beginning. But he didn't know when it had started. Urvasi had sparked questions in his mind.

What had Virasen done to merit being murdered in his own home on the morning of his son and daughter's swayamvara anniversary? Where was Kala's honor? Hiding in the guise of a cane-toting crippled Brahman? Where was the justice? How would this wheel of dharma turn for the prince now that his father was gone? Was he next?

Nala could not stop wondering if his enemy was here tonight among the other celestial ones. Would he dare attend the ceremony of ashes for the king he had slain? The mind being the mind, it cannot stop itself. Once started, only the buddhi ... the witness ... can stop the ravings of a disturbed mind. And Nala did not wish to stop.

When he got to the bank, Nala turned in a circle three times. Keeping the urn held high, he spoke with the loudest voice he could muster. "Come out, Kala! As all of you are my witnesses, I challenge the god of time to tell me where his honor is. Is it hiding in the robes of a crippled Brahman?"

"No, Nala! Not here!" whispered Damayanti. Up and down both sides of the riverbank murmuring voices echoed disapproval over the watery surface. Suddenly even Ganga herself started gurgling to drown out the voice of Virasen's son. "This time is for your father," protested the river goddess. "Do what is right! Set his soul free!"

Ganga was right. Nala had a duty to perform. From the depths of his soul he knew these words had to be spoken. "I love my father. And I cannot let him go. If I thirsted to slay a man in the twilight years of his life, I would never ambush him after he meditated. As a warrior I would challenge him to meet on the field of battle at his convenience. I wouldn't deprive him of his dignity by slaying him unarmed."

Nala stopped. Even with so many beings crammed into the close quarters along the banks of the holy river, there was only silence. Nala turned to Chitraratha who had gathered all of us to The Footsteps of God.

"Explain it to me, Chitraratha. What crime could my father commit against a god?"

The proudest of gandharvas Chitraratha looked down at the water. Nala thought that surely Urvasi would set things straight. After all it was her song that disturbed his mind.

"Urvasi, you, who professes love for my father, tell me what he did? You sang of a gandharva committing a crime. Well, what crime?"

The apsara with the most beautiful voice remained silent. Nala was becoming even more agitated. He felt the gods had been engaging in a conspiracy against his father. Why hadn't they warned him? And why were they continuing the conspiracy even here at the ceremony of ashes for this man? Nala was certain Indra would explain. When everyone else in heaven and earth was silent, Indra was never at a loss for words. Ever since their encounter on the Vidabhar cow path. the exile prince thought of Indra as his second father.

"Indra, once you asked a favor of me. Now I ask you to return it. As the one who never shirks the cosmic spotlight, tell us. What crime did my father commit? Against an angry god, what chance did he have? And why didn't you warn him?"

"Nala, you must not stop the wheel of dharma. Perform your duty as Virasen's son. Put his ashes into the river." Indra could have issued an edict in his typical bombastic manner of speech. But he didn't. His delivery was slow. And his words were filled with compassion. All those gathered at The Footsteps of God were sending light around Nala. Such was the power of the human heart that it could take even a single ray of this compassion and perform miracles. And that very same heart could shut out all the brilliance of so many gods and luminaries as though they were adversaries rather than allies.

"Once Damayanti had her moment to walk the lines of men and gods and hoist her lotus garland," replied Nala. "Well, this is my moment. And I'm going to hoist this urn high until I get my answer."

"Nala, only the heart can reveal the answer. Trust me. The mind will never get it. And it's not what you think it is. Your father is waiting for you to set him free. You must let him go."

The words were not spoken by Lord Indra or another of the many immortals in attendance. On her hands and knees Damayanti had crawled toward her beloved. She grabbed one of his feet and set her forehead on the other. Our heroine was not begging. At The Footsteps of God the energies were so intoxicating that it was easy to get lost in the clouds of the mind. A spell of dizzy confusion had overtaken Nala. By touching his feet the princess grounded his body back onto the earth. It was while she held him that Damayanti spoke to calm his turbulent mind.

Nala had done it. He had committed the most dreaded breech of protocol that a son could do. The gambling prince had made the ceremony about himself rather than his father. He had brought the perpetrator of his father's murder here to The Footsteps of God. What could Nala do now for an encore?

From the urn Nala removed the lid. He handed it to Damayanti. "My beloved," he whispered with tender affection, "what would I do without you?"

"It's perfect, Sweetie," replied the princess. "As long as you and I are together, everything will always be perfect."

"I can let him go now."

Nala had not known where to turn. To Indra? To Urvasi? To Chitraratha? To Shiva who was not here? Where was the one famed for commingling in places of the dead? Everywhere had felt like the wrong place to look. Finally he turned to Damayanti. A single tear ran down his face.

The thought came to him that if he had never fallen in love with Damayanti, Virasen would never have challenged the god of time that afternoon and he'd still be alive. Such was the nature of the human mind. By some miracle ... call it, love ... the gateway of Nala's heart opened. And he saw the absurdity of believing the steady stream of rubbish put forth as credible thought by his own mind.

If Nala had refused Indra's favor and walked away from the swayamvara line, who could say how the lord of time would or would not have responded? What Nala could declare with certainty was that without Damayanti by his side, he would never have known how to open his innermost being to life. She had been the constant light in his darkest hours of despair. Together they had celebrated the simplest pleasures and created miracles.

What she had said was so true. As long as she was by his side, everything would always be perfect. If only he could keep his heart open long enough to see the perfection. And the gift of Damayanti was that she lived with this open heart. That she saw this perfection. And somehow she possessed the patience to let Nala trail after her along their pathway of enduring love.

Mercifully Nala tipped the urn spilling its contents. As the gritty white ash made contact with the holy water, the lord of death Yama and Virasen appeared on the river. Yama was dressed entirely in black except for a pair of gold earrings and the noose he tied around the wrist of the departed king. On the surface of the water Yama led Virasen out into the middle of the river. Assembled here were scores of gandharvas and apsaras.

Yama removed the noose from Virasen and stood to one side. One by one the gandharva warriors and apsara nymphs hugged and kissed Virasen. They were welcoming home their brother. Damayanti wished she could be out among them to give Virasen one final embrace. Now Nala felt relieved. There were no signs of death or suffering upon his father now. He could see Virasen was thrilled to be moving onto the next adventure in the journey of his soul. Nala too wished he could run out onto the river and hug and kiss his father. But he had already drawn enough attention to himself. He knelt down and lifted Damayanti into his arms. Tonight she would be his apsara. And he would be her gandharva.

Here at The Footsteps of God where the earthbound veils of illusion between the realms of matter and spirit were at their thinnest ... where the river goddess Ganga flowed down as the mighty confluence of innumerable snowy Himalayan streams... and where ascetic yogis set up ashrams sequestered in the dense jungle forest in all directions ... here Virasen re-acquainted himself with his celestial kin ... and here he cut the final thread holding him to what had been his blood kin.

The last gandharva to kiss and hug Virasen was Chitraratha. Like long separated brothers they made no attempt to censor their laughter or their tears. The final apsara to embrace Virasen was Urvasi. Nala and Damayanti were not the only humans to blush at the site of this reunion. Yes, she loved him like a brother. But maybe there was something more between the two of them. And he definitely loved her. With each kiss and hug the form of Virasen shapeshifted more fully into the immortal body of a gandharva. Sweeping Urvasi into his arms he looked every bit as radiant as any member of the celestial constellation. Next Indra took Virasen's head into his hands and inhaled the aroma of the returned comrade as though he were his own son. Finally Virasen was back where he belonged.

The vibration of energy had been building inside Damayanti's body. With each kiss and embrace Virasen received, she felt the opening of gateways up her spine. The first three opened with swirls of red, orange and yellow light. When Virasen and Urvasi touched hearts, the green light of the heart gateway opened up for Damayanti. She said a prayer to Goddess Shakti that everyone assembled here could feel the warmth of the green light.

Damayanti closed her eyes and melted into Nala. The rainbow shaft of light was rising vertically up into the gateway of the heart where it poured horizontally from her heart to Nala's heart. Then she felt the energy surge from his root gateway into hers making a loop of light that fused these four gateways together. Damayanti had never felt the energies of male and female so perfectly attuned. Among the gandharvas and apsaras the same fusing surge of male and female energies was happening. This ceremony of ashes had turned into a celebration of light and love.

Indra announced that the earthbound portion of the ceremony of ashes had been successfully completed. Virasen turned to his son and smiled. Lord Indra explained that the moment of death offered an opportunity to clear impurities resulting from past actions. Long ago this ceremony had been scripted to occur at The Footsteps of God to assist in the liberation of Virasen's soul and awaken the realization of the true nature of death and life for all in attendance.

Everyone watched as Indra, Virasen, Yama, Agni, Varuna and the others piled into Pushpaka. Damayanti wished she could leap into the celestial chariot along with the other apsaras and gandharvas to witness the next part of the divine ceremony. What Indra could not divulge was that Goddess Saraswati and Kala were waiting for Virasen. The karmic debt between them would finally be settled.

Damayanti and Nala sat on the riverbank of Holy Ganga. They listened to the sound of her water flowing downstream. Here was a sanctuary where Damayanti and Nala could make a home. Nearby were forest ashrams where ascetic yogis were living on roots and nuts. Upstream were the mountain spirits who sustained the cave dwelling saints so they could meditate uninterrupted for eons of time. No one cared about exiles here.

The princess took the hand of her beloved. In earnest she whispered for Nala to remember what it felt like to open the gateway of the heart. He whispered the mantra. Both closed their eyes.

Om Shakti Om ... Om Shiva Om

05 Exile – Truth Gateway

Blah – blah – blah ... blah – blah-blah
So many words ... so little truth

Isn't it time you told your love story?
Why do you think Shiva sits in silence?
He's waiting for you
There's room for all of us in the temple
So sing, sisters! Sing!

in his consciousness as the inevitable confluence of these two seemingly different paths.

With its enormous difficulties Kailash offered a tangible high-risk high-reward goal. And it offered the great promise as the big Sugar Daddy of all sacred spiritual destinations. So the princess and exile prince rested by the river for three days to gather strength and provisions.

With the approach of dusk on the twelfth day of the pilgrimage Nala felt a stabbing pain in his heart as he gazed at his beloved. Once regaled as the world's most beautiful woman Damayanti was wasting away with each step toward Kailash. Berries, nuts and roots were becoming more scarce the higher they climbed into the matrix of mountains. The Himalayan terrain went up and down. Up and down. On and on this way. Sometimes Damayanti and Nala were below the tree line where it was easier to find shelter and food. But the trajectory ahead involved spending more time above it.

Now as gusts of frigid northern air blew through her single robe there was little to keep the chill from seeping into the marrow of her bones. Despite the inclement conditions the princess never complained. While her spirit remained strong, Damayanti's pace had begun to lag.

The exile prince felt like a fool for failing to insist on Damayanti joining one of the royal parties heading south after the funeral. At The Footsteps of God numerous offers had been extended to both of them. But Nala simply could not sit in Bhima's palace waiting for Kala's next move. He had to take a course of action to strengthen his chances of defeating the god of time. Or at least do anything and everything to prevent Kala from abducting the love of his life. And he knew Damayanti would refuse to leave his side. Surely if there was anyone who could help them, it was Shiva.

Around a bend in the trail the exile prince spied a fat crow dining on the tawny corpse of a mouse. Behind a boulder Nala stealthily crept up so close that he could have snatched the crow by the scruff of the neck. Instead he stripped off his robe. Quickly he glanced back at Damayanti bringing a finger to his lips as a signal for silence. Then Nala smiled because he knew how much a warm meal would mean to them right now.

With splendid grace he leapt forward casting the robe as a net to catch the bird. Once he had the crow pinned to the ground he would strike it with a rock. It was an excellent plan executed with perfect precision. At the same moment however the crow leapt into flight. Both Nala and the fat crow were in the air simultaneously. The princess observed the encounter with trepid fascination. What would happen next?

If Nala had paused to consider the breed of bird, he might have exercised caution. During the early creative phase in the life cycle of this universe Lord Brahma had assigned the crows and vultures to act as timekeepers for his crippled son Kala. It was their dharma to support the lord of time in recording the exact moment of birth and death for every sentient being in the book of time. That fat crow had been waiting on the trail for this moment.

The crow eluded capture but flew close enough to snag the robe in his beak. With a strength belied by his size the bird pulled the robe away from the outstretched prince. Then he nonchalantly settled down on a nearby branch. In order to speak the crow nimbly transferred grip of the robe from beak to claw. He introduced himself as Dwapara Chief Timekeeper for Kala and the time consortium.

"Lord Kala sends his regrets for the ill tidings befalling both of you. For Princess Damayanti he has a message."

The crow flexed his shoulders and snapped his beak open and shut. Turning one eye to drink in the princess, now it was Dwapara's turn to smile. It wasn't every day a crow beheld such breathtaking beauty. Even in her emaciated condition the princess was still a ravishing sight to drink in. Dwapara reveled in this close proximity to the famed princess by making ecstatic clucking sounds. Then he composed himself. He had his dharma to perform. The crow took in a deep breath and spoke in a perfect facsimile of Kala's voice.

"To end the conflict, Damayanti, all you have to do is think of me and speak the words, 'Kala, please accept my heart as a token of our enduring love.' And I vow to take you into the corridors of time where I will show you the threads of cause and effect making up the tapestry of your past lifetimes. We can move through time going forward and back so you can see who you are by knowing who you have been. After which I will cater to your every need. In the celestial realm you will live as a goddess by my side. You can sing devotional love songs in Indra's palace alongside the apsaras as often as you like. That's a big step up from a hut by The Footsteps of God or your father's

parts. Wouldn't you say that makes us intimate friends?" Dwapara tilted an eye in the direction of the princess. "Pardon me, Princess Damayanti, if my words offend your ears. I speak without censor because of the debt your husband owes my master. Until it is paid in full, Nala will continue to suffer hardships even more dear."

Tiwari did a spot-on impersonation of Nala's private conversation with Pushkar back in the wrestling room talking with obvious anguish about his two girls clamoring to be the first one to put a lotus garland around his neck at the exact instant the lord of time was snapping Virasen's neck. The crow even paused in order to inflect the same awkward guttural sound Nala made owing to the difficulty of getting the words out.

Damayanti was struck by the guilt her beloved felt for doing something so beautiful with their daughters. It was as though Nala felt he had snapped his own father's neck because he had been experiencing love at the same moment Virasen faced death.

Smerfta impersonated Pushkar's reply about Nala having a real sense for poetry. Dwapara claimed that after winning everything from his elder brother Pushkar deliberated long and hard about giving Nala one last chance to win everything back. He was willing to risk it all to spend one night alone with Damayanti. Pushkar was struck by the coincidence of how Draupadi and Damayanti were both universally regarded as the most beautiful women of their time, and both suffered the indignity of exile because their noble husbands momentarily lost their sanity gambling away their kingdoms to games of dice with their brothers.

Dwapara asked Nala if he could picture how that outcome would have turned out. Back in the wrestling room Pushkar withdrew the wager before Nala had time to reply. Smerfta lent voice to express the inner thoughts of the soon-to-be monarch. Pushkar wanted to execute Kala's plan for his coronation to have as little contact with Damayanti as possible. More than any Nishada general, minister or even Nala, the younger brother feared the wrath of his elder sister.

The crows were hooting and clucking after each bit of commentary. Bantering back and forth between themselves, they were having the time of their lives. All the while Nala wished he could hide under anyone of these Himalayan mountains. In his naked state he stood exposed to the sting of every barb. Rapidly his energies started collapsing into what he felt was a black hole of shame.

Damayanti took the chin of her beloved into her hands. She forced him to look into her eyes. And she assured him that she did not care about anything these crows might say. The princess told Nala to think of Virasen as he hugged and kissed his gandharva brothers and apsara sisters. She told him to picture the two of them sitting side by side on the riverbank of Ganga gazing at the water. Neither of them needed to rule a kingdom to find a meaning in life. The meaning was right here in their love.

Damayanti recited the mantra aloud. After the first round Nala joined along.

Om Shakti Om ... Om Shiva Om
Om Shakti Om ... Om Shiva Om
Om Shakti Om ... Om Shiva Om

While it was evident Dwapara reveled in flexing his mastery of invective sarcasm, neither he nor his mates dared utter anything flippant about the lord of destruction or his beloved Shakti. Nor were they going to recite the mantra along with the humans. Since they got what they had flown north for, the trio flapped their black wings in unison. To the rhythmic whoosh sound of pushing air, the crows took flight. They had delivered their lord's message. In his claw Dwapara clutched the prized object of conquest: Nala's robe.

After 108 repetitions of the mantra Damayanti and Nala were silent. They gazed into each other's eyes. Their breath was calm and deep.

The princess untied her robe. On the pointed edge of a jagged rock she tore off a section large enough to act as a loin cloth. Then she wrapped her scantily clad body in what was remained of her robe. Nala was unable to utter a single word of gratitude. Instead he bit his lip to keep from weeping. And he quickly concealed his shame in the cloth. Together they would celebrate each victory. Together they would share the burden of each challenge.

intimacy the exile prince had always experienced a delay. Just as on the day Damayanti laid her lotus garland around his neck, Damayanti was the one for whom all the gateways opened. She had always been the initiator into the mystery of love. Many times since that day she had asked. And many times he felt the moment of clumsy awkwardness. As a yogi Nala simply would never measure up to his beloved. But both of them had learned to make space for the awkwardness and stay close to one another.

With the ripe scent of pine boughs flaring through her nostrils the princess yielded willingly to her exile warrior prince. Their bodies quickly filled the hut with steamy warmth. Together they made slow passionate love. In particular Nala touched his beloved with a poignant tenderness as though he might never touch her again. At her toes he started with teasing strokes before working his way up her feet, calves and thighs. He took his time. Nala felt a primal need to instill every part of her body inside himself.

It is a universally known fact that the glands of yogis who have opened their inner gateways operate on an accelerated level. In particular, when the barriers to the heart gateway have been removed, the thymus gland secretes the most intoxicating substance called ojas which circulates throughout the body rejuvenating tissues, muscles and organs and stimulating higher levels of consciousness. Getting past the fourth gateway is like passing through a yogi's tipping point. Each time Damayanti opened the heart gateway her body produced more ojas than it had the previous time. In minutes all the bruises and soreness in her body from the weeks of trekking were suddenly flooded with oxygenated blood and this amazing elixir.

The ojas healed Damayanti in every way. Even though she had barely eaten for days, the princess felt no hunger. In all Damayanti's places of womanly beauty ... such as her perfectly round breasts and the breathtaking curves of her hips and thighs, the moist glow of her lips, cheeks and eyes ... in short, Damayanti's fullness of beauty returned to her previous pristine luster. A byproduct of the ojas was that it released the most deliciously irresistible aphrodisiac.

Nala inhaled her fragrant scent heightening his already aroused state. From previous occasions the exile prince had learned to restrain himself. He took in a long deep inhale to imbibe the ojas spilling out from his beloved. Then he held his breath. The ojas circulated throughout Nala's body. By the fifth cycle of breathing in the ojas he too felt young and strong again. All his hunger vanished except for the overwhelming desire to devour Damayanti. With passionate fury Nala tasted her flesh.

Into the night the princess sang out her love song in sanguine tides of ecstasy. Damayanti melted to the touch of her beloved as he penetrated her every defense. With rhythms varied between gentle and strong Nala moved his hips. All the while he continued to imbibe the ojas wafting from the princess. He ran his hands through her long black locks. Occasionally he grabbed a fistful of hair and tugged exposing her neck to his assault. She felt stabs of pain followed by orgasmic spasms shooting through the orifices of her body. Instantly she felt the boundaries of her beingness expand dramatically as though she could easily fit the entire Himalayan matrix into the palm of her hand. Damayanti felt as though she and Goddess Shakti had merged into one being.

"For all time I promise to love you. Through all space I promise to love you. In all thought I promise to love you. In all action I promise to love you. Damayanti, I promise my love will overcome every challenge."

Nala spoke the words without any real sense for exactly who was speaking. Of course it was him. But he had not planned the declaration. The words emerged from some hidden depth inside himself. And they provoked powerful waves of emotion in both Damayanti and Nala. Each clasped the other more tightly. With unrehearsed intensity they wept freely. It was as though both of them had been granted permission to grieve the loss of love for a thousand deaths and a thousand lifetimes.

No matter what happened tomorrow or in the days ahead, neither of them would forget this moment. More than ever Damayanti and Nala were bound in their love for one another. The love was being impregnated into the subatomic structure of their cellular DNA. One to the other. Damayanti to Nala. And Nala to Damayanti. This must be the love of which Chandri spoke on the swayamvara eve. A love to endure into generations of yogis yet to be born.

With each ripple of lovemaking Damayanti felt the pressure building inside the fifth gateway of truth. Breaking this seal would require Damayanti to speak and live her truth with greater integrity.

Here she felt so close to Nala that she trusted the truth unfolding before them. She even trusted the awkwardness of her invitation to Lord Kala. Inside her throat, where the pressure was building, Damayanti felt that she had spoken truth earlier when she intimated that Nala and she had committed a sin against the lord of time. Even if she didn't know how or what they had done. But she was frightened of what Kala might do.

The lord of time had slain the mighty warrior Virasen as though he were an insignificant insect. He had decimated the phalanx of protection bestowed by Indra, Yama, Agni and Varuna as Nala and Damayanti's wedding gift. The four gods had promised no foe would penetrate the seal. Yet Lord Kala had managed to turn Pushkar against his father and brother. It had taken seven years. But the lord of time had plotted and executed his crime to perfection. If no one could stop Kala inside the Nishada palace gates, who could protect Damayanti and Nala out here in the wilderness?

As slow and steady as the lovemaking had built up to its glorious climax, the careening stream of fearful thoughts flooding through Damayanti's mind dissolved it in seconds. Suddenly Damayanti was back to being Damayanti. Shakti was back to being an elusive goddess permeating all matter in some mysterious unfathomable code. Damayanti gasped from a stabbing spasm of heartache. For she also felt keenly aware of being separated from her beloved.

In the darkness Nala groped awkwardly to find her lips. He too was disoriented. In his fashion Nala recovered by teasing the princess with the subtlest movements of his tongue. Then, just as quickly as Damayanti had ridden the ecstatic highs and asphyxiating lows of her emotional roller coaster ride, the exile prince experienced a sadness whose source he could not identify. With a silent tear running down his cheek Nala re-pledged his enduring love for Damayanti. The princess licked the salt tear with her tongue and pulled Nala's already close body even closer. It was as though Damayanti was trying to freeze this moment in time. But the domain of time belonged to someone else.

The princess closed her eyes. Instantly she slumped into a state of deep intoxicated sleep. Next to his beloved, the exile prince remained remarkably alert. In the afterglow of love this was a common occurrence between them. Damayanti was the one who immediately dropped into the kind of exhausted slumber where nothing could arouse her. Her body was integrating the energetic openings in an inward feminine fashion. Meanwhile Nala's body was integrating the energetic openings with an outward vigor of feeling ready to bound across mountaintops.

This aspect of yoga ... the yoga of sexuality ... was the realm where Nala had practiced so diligently as to excel beyond all Damayanti's expectations. The exile prince had become adept at retaining his seed and drawing his sexual energies up ... rather than exhausting himself by shooting them out ... and he had mastered the adroit skill of guiding his beloved in the interplay of rhythms between the masculine and feminine waves of sexual ecstasy ... the yogi lovers had discovered that they would arrive at the same place of opened gateways if they were patient ... if they trusted one another ... and trusted love ... but, alas, it was only in this compartmentalized act of lovemaking where the exile prince opened the first two gateways ... all the while the other five remained sealed like locked vaults whose codes had been lost.

Nala had the impulsive thought that he must get to Shiva immediately for the great yogi was the master code breaker. If anyone could open the sealed gateways, it was the god of destruction. If the exile prince was going to defeat Kala, he had to possess all his faculties. Opening the seven gateways would exponentially increase his personal power. Obviously he needed the help. Otherwise Nala was going to continue to suffer further indignities. He had abandoned his father in his moment of greatest need. He had gambled away all his possessions to his brother. He had offended the gods along the banks of Ganga during his father's ash ceremony. He had even lost his only robe to a lousy crow. Nala pondered what else could the lord of time take from him.

Nala waited until he was certain Damayanti had drifted deeply into the realm of dreams. Carefully he disentangled himself from his beloved. This last encounter was what he wanted her to remember of him. Tonight was finally his time to face the crossroad. The moment to define the pilgrimage of a hero's life.

With the aftereffects of the ojas coursing through his body, the exile prince had the inspired thought that he could find the way to Kailash quickest if he went by himself. Even at her fittest Damayanti was no warrior. On the steep vertical ascents and descents Nala was constantly racing ahead of his beloved and then waiting. His natural pace was to lope twice as fast as the princess. Right now the exile prince felt certain Kala would not be content with stripping him of his robe. The god of time was coming after his final possessions. So Nala had to arrive at Kailash before Kala stole his body and mind. The exile prince was pitted against his adversary in a race against time.

Surely no one in the wilderness would dare harm someone so fair, pure and kind as Damayanti. Her fame would also protect her. Now that she had gotten her mojo back, Damayanti would try for a day or two to catch him. Even then she would still possess an abundance of strength to return to Bhima's palace in Vidabhar. These were some of the bewildering thoughts racing through Nala's mind.

If Nala abandoned Damayanti here on this solitary dark mountain pass, she would finally be free from the misery of his million-question mind. From their first meeting back at the hunter's pond Damayanti had always eclipsed his light. At the swayamvara Nala had squandered the gold of Nishada on a horserace wager only to be bailed out by the princess. When Nala failed miserably in his management of the royal farms, it was Damayanti who spoke to the plant devas locating the perfect spots for the crops to flourish and lead Nishada to prosperity. When Nala shunned his father after the wedding, it was the princess who ignited a deeper meaning to life which Virasen shared with Uttani. Again and again Damayanti had taken actions to correct the disorientation which happened as a result of Nala's missteps. For years the shame had been growing inside that it was always Damayanti who acted as the caravan leader finding their way home. But not even Damayanti could undo Nala's foolhardy decision to throw those three gold dice. Nala took a step up the mountain. It was time he moved on to find his own way all by himself.

But if he stayed, the two of them would face the challenges ahead together. Wasn't this commitment to face challenges together one of the secret ingredients to enduring love? Nala took a step back down the mountain. He could never abandon Damayanti.

If Nala did abandon Damayanti here on this solitary dark mountain pass, the princess would be spared the unnecessary suffering of a pilgrimage which was never hers in the first place. While he had moments of blind selfishness, Nala was not completely oblivious. He saw how dearly Damayanti wanted to settle down and make a home at The Footsteps of God. One does not embark on a pilgrimage to Kailash just because your husband needs to go. That's doesn't count as legitimate motivation. Not for this bad-boy of holiest pilgrimages. Very likely she would backtrack to The Footsteps of God and find her way back to the girls at Bhima's Palace in Vidabhar. Nala took two steps up the mountain.

But if he fled, the Nishada exile would be violating the oath he made before pouring Virasen's ashes into Ganga. *As long as you and I are together, everything will always be perfect.* That moment of enduring love at The Footsteps of God with Damayanti would stay with Nala for as long as his soul held light. Nala took two steps down the mountain.

If Nala seized the initiative here on this solitary mountain pass, he would be heeding the warrior voice inside his gut. There were campaigns a hero must wage without his sweetie pie. This Kailash pilgrimage was one of them. Nala ran three steps up the mountain.

But if he stayed with her, the pilgrimage would be so much easier. How would Nala have handled those three crows without Damayanti? She had brought him back to his center. And, boy! Did that feel great! Nala ran three steps down the mountain.

The indecision was driving Nala crazy. Up the mountain. Down the mountain. Up. Down. Up. Down. Would death be better? Or to abandon my beloved? For the sake of love she had endured his woe. Nala wanted to shake his beloved Damayanti and ask her opinion. What should I do? Damayanti had always had the answers. And this was precisely why he had to perform the most cowardly act of abandoning his beloved on a solitary pass under a moonless Himalayan night. And why? Because she always had the answers. And he had to finally discover the answer for himself.

Nala made a dash up the mountain. After this moment the exile stood no more at the crossroad. Nala had shattered his paralysis by choosing his dharma. And he wasn't going to screw it up. He would find Shiva and perform any penance necessary to become his disciple. Once and for all he would learn the secret of enduring love for himself. Not through Damayanti. And he would bring the secret back and share it with his beloved. Then his radiance would match hers. And together they would face Kala or any foe with enduring love as their only shield.

Along the rocks and patches of dirt Nala groped with his hands to find the way. Performing this feat on a pitch black night in the uneven Himalayan terrain would have been suicide for any ordinary man. But Nala got his underbelly close to the earth and slithered like a snake over the treacherous pass cloaked in nocturnal darkness. Once he got out of hearing distance he whispered the mantra over and over.

Om Shakti Om ... Om Shiva Om

It was true. Nala the exile prince was doing the very thing no husband ought ever to do under any circumstance. He was abandoning his beloved wife in the wilderness on a pitch black night high in the Himalayan mountains without food or water. [Take note: Fellows-Don't follow Nala's example!] Just as Nala had done the very thing no son ought to do under any circumstances at The Footsteps of God. Just as Nala had done the very thing no king ought to do under any circumstances with the gold dice in his hands. Just as Nala had done the very thing no suitor ought to do under any circumstances in the horserace before the swayamvara. Nala had a

crossed over the Himalayan pass. With each step the princess was sniffing the air. Yes, she told herself. Nala passed this way.

Many times Damayanti stubbed her toe or ran into a tree. Each obstacle only fueled the princess onward in her passionate quest to reconnect with her cherished beloved. The more desperate the pilgrimage got, the more she rallied to keep moving forward. Damayanti was practicing something Great Swan had taught her many years earlier. *The mind can overcome any obstacle when it aligns with the heart and soul. This is when the seven gateways open. And Shakti reveals herself as the essence of cosmic love.* It was these words Damayanti repeated to herself over and over. Not Kala's words spoken through Dwapara.

I will find Nala. She told herself. I will find Nala because I have already found myself. I am Damayanti. And I am Shakti. I am the essence of cosmic love. Damayanti was still riding the ripples of elation from hearing Nala promise to love her through all time, space, thought and action. He had promised his love would overcome every challenge. For a woman there existed no stronger intoxicant. With each mountain peak she crested, Damayanti kept sniffing the familiar scent of Nala. The princess was just getting warmed up. She was poised to charge after her beloved across every mountain and valley and ford every stream and ocean. Against all odds Damayanti was closing the gap between herself and the exile prince.

Meanwhile Kala landed his chariot in this very space. The god of time had dropped what he was doing the instant he saw Nala go off on his own. This was his chance. So he waited on the trail for Damayanti to rush into his arms.

In the darkness Damayanti heard a strange sound ahead. Was it Nala? She called out his name.

"Why have you abandoned me? My love! This charade of hide and seek must end now. Wait for me! I need to be held in your arms!" Damayanti sniffed the air. She was confused. She could still smell Nala's scent but something didn't feel right. "*As long as you and I are together, everything will always be perfect.* Don't you recall saying these exact words at The Footsteps of God?"

These words played like a cruel song in her head. She called out his name again and again. Each time she raised the volume of her voice. She hoped that wherever he was, he could hear her.

Damayanti possessed an enchantingly beautiful voice that the wind carried far enough away for someone else to hear. Someone looking for the princess. Someone who instantly recognized his chance. It wasn't his intent to frighten her. But it was a pitch black night. And he wasn't Nala.

"Witnessed by all the worlds, I passed *Indra's test* for you." Damayanti's voice had turned to pleading. Part of the secret of enduring love was observing how quickly one's consciousness could swing from fear to love or from love to fear. "I bestowed my lotus garland upon you." With a sinking feeling in her gut the princess was tilting toward fear. "Please, Nala, come out of the dark night! And hold me!"

When the lord of time dragged his foot on the earth, Damayanti saw nothing. But she heard the peculiar cadence of his tortured step. Before he could say anything, she ratcheted up the decibel level of her voice and really started screaming. "Nala, help!"

The princess cried out to her friend Chandri. But the moon goddess was nowhere to be seen. Damayanti pleaded for Shiva to come to her aid. But his meditation was too important to disturb. The noble damsel called out to Indra, Yama, Agni and Varuna. These were the Gods whose nuptial blessings included a promise to protect her union with Nala against any foe. Yet oddly enough her pleas were greeted only with silence. It was as though the entire universe had abandoned the princess to this solitary fate. She thought quickly. Who else could she turn to? She searched her memory for anyone who had thought kindly of her. And then it came to her.

"Vibhishana!" she screamed with all her might. "Fulfill your promise now!"

Hadn't the rakshasa king promised to protect her in the dark of night? As his name echoed out into the night, she wondered if she had erred. The princess had never felt more vulnerable. The last time she had put herself in a place of such pitch black darkness had been the night of her initiation in the lake of dreams. But tonight was different. There would be no guru to catch her if she fell in the remote wilderness. Was it wise to call out in distress to a demon? Would he remember the single black rose he set at her feet at the swayamvara? And the promise he made in front of a hundred thousand spectators?

Damayanti did not personally know any rakshasas. But it was universal knowledge that they drank human blood and ate human flesh. Would her body make a tasty morsel for one so fierce as the king of rakshasa demons?

Again she heard the sound of the dragging foot on the earth. And she heard a voice call out her name. She was surprised. Where she had expected the voice to envelope her with the hunger of lust, it sounded injured. Who was this intruder? Was it the god of time?

Before she could call out to the intruder, the air surrounding Damayanti whipped debris of loose branches and pebbles into a swirling vortex. The princess heard a whooping sound in her ears. Seeing nothing she feared for the worst. Then the wind built up to a crescendo as her body was snatched into the air as effortlessly as an eagle would snap up a mouse.

Vibhishana flapped his enormous black wings and lifted her high above the trees. She yielded completely to his mercy. The demon king told the princess that his services were at her disposal. With infrared eyes that saw much more acutely at night than day he had no difficulty finding her once she called out his name. When Damayanti asked if she had in fact been at risk, Vibhishana confirmed that the lord of time was closing in less than ten body lengths away. The demon king could not explain why a god was behaving like a stalker. It was odd to say the least. "Obviously he covets your beauty as all of us do," said the demon. "Fortunately the rest of us possess some code of honor. Later on I might go back and thrash that rascal."

The princess recounted how she had awoken only to find Nala missing. She told Vibhishana to take her to him at once. She hastily explained that the two of them were on a pilgrimage to Kailash and that he could never make it there without her help. The demon demurred. "Nala is safe. He is not injured. But I'm sorry, princess. The fact is he does not want to be found."

"I don't care. Take me to my beloved immediately. Kala's already killed Virasen. Who do you think he's going after if he can't find me?"

In her normal affairs it was rarely necessary for the princess to reprimand others. But tonight was not normal. When the demon failed to deviate his flight path, she grew testy.

"Vibhishana, you said your services were at my disposal. So take me to Nala at once. Or drop me from this height. And I will locate him myself."

"Princess, I am so sorry. But I am taking you back to Vidabhar. I know if you stay out in the wilderness, you will keep trekking north in search of Nala. But you will not find him.

Dear Damayanti, I have lived on your planet for thousands of years. And, believe it or not, I have studied the ways of men in greater detail than yourself. Your beloved must find his own way. He cannot do it with you constantly by his side. Because your brilliance eclipses his. Over and over again you save him from himself.

While you may hate me for it, I must take you to your father and mother ... to Uttani and your beautiful girls. Every night Sumitra and Samadhi cry themselves to sleep calling out your name. Every child needs her mother. And you have two girls that even a demon can see need you."

The princess swung her fists at the demon. She kicked him. She bit him. But Vibhishana possessed more strength than an entire army. No blow caused him to release his grip on the princess. She cried out in protest. Nala needed her now. She was certain of it.

The demon wished to speak kind words. But he had none to say. So he sang an ancient hymn to Shiva and Shakti. After a time the princess was too tired to fight against such a formidable foe.

38. Kala's Curse

"For you, I'll make an adjustment. Brahma will never notice. The guy is way too busy making big wheel deals to bother with details. You give me what I want. And I'll give what you want. Just tell me."

"Five hundred years," demanded the naga Karkotaka.

"Done!" shouted the lord of time. "You know what I want?"

"I should have asked for a thousand. You must really want this guy's life to be a living hell."

"Get the job done today & you'll get your thousand. Five hundred after today."

In the early afternoon the exile prince picked up the pace. Dancing to the heart pulse of the mountain was bringing a simple joy he had not felt in years. He was re-learning how to listen to the rhythms of nature which opened a whole new way to move through the Himalayas. This freedom was something he rarely gave himself with Damayanti because she was simply unable to cover ground at the pace of his ubermench focus. Like a panther stalking along steep mountain trails he sniffed the air. His prey was Shakti. If he could not have Damayanti by his side, he would find the goddess at every turn as he climbed further and further into the remote region. At least this is what he told himself. He was getting his second wind.

In his body he felt strong and agile. Each step was revealing the pilgrimage Nala was meant to take.

At the ford of a tributary mountain stream Nala bent over cupping his hands. In a good spot to quench his thirst he reached between boulders to catch the falling water. Hidden in the shadows was a tiny snake that bit his hand.

The exile prince screamed more from shock than pain. His instinct drove him to suck out the venom. But it was too late. The released toxins were taking effect. Amused by his success the tiny snake hissed out from the shadows where he revealed his true form. The snake was actually a much larger naga from the underworld.

"Accept my apology, exile prince," said Karkotaka. "This curse sent from the lord of time is not permanent."

Karkotaka introduced himself by way of mentioning he had been in attendance at the Vidabhar swayamvara. Up in the nosebleed section of the amphitheater he had applauded wildly when the princess of enduring love hoisted her lotus garland high into the air. He described being delirious with joy when she draped it around the former Nishada prince's neck. Karkotaka said it was one of the most thrilling moments of his considerably long lifetime.

"Did you know that once upon a time you were a proud handsome gandharva in Indra's celestial legion?" asked Karkotaka. "I am not sure if I'm supposed to tell you. But since I feel we have a connection through Damayanti's swayamvara, well, here it is. You took something away from Kala. So he is cursing you to live his fate until you pay the debt. For your sake, may it be sooner than later."

The naga bowed low in front of the prince. He asked Nala to pass along his regards to Princess Damayanti if he ever saw her again.

"Oh, one more thing. The lord of time has asked me to inform you that he has taken an idea from your heavenly benefactor Indra. Like the four gods who once stood in the suitor line, Kala has shapeshifted into your body and is making his way to the Vidabhar palace. That's where Vibhishana took Damayanti after you so rudely abandoned her in the wilderness. While Kala wants you to know that his intensions are pure, this time he will not be denied Damayanti's love."

The naga lingered to consider whether he had done everything. Karkotaka wanted to be thorough. Since he was getting an extra thousand years added to the book of time out of this afternoon's work. When he was satisfied he had accomplished every task on his mental checklist, the naga

39. Kala's Test

When the news reached her ears, Damayanti could not believe what she was hearing. On the same lightweight chariot Virasen and he had used in their first journey to Vidabhar, Nala had been seen riding through the north gate. A white dove brought the message to the princess.

Immediately she ran down to her father's court where he was seated on his throne. Damayanti jumped into her father's lap and shared her joy. Make the palace ready. Burn incense. Gather lotus blossoms to show him the way to my bedchamber. Oh, she forgot. He already knows the way. The princess squealed with delight. Her perfect beloved was returning into her arms.

The next time the princess saw the rakshasa demon king she would let him know that he did not know as much about men as he claimed. Bhima did his best to match his daughter's enthusiasm. But that was impossible.

She bounded up to her room calling out to her handmaids. Together they sang love songs while the handmaids removed Damayanti's clothes and scented her body with sandalwood oil. The princess tried on every stitch of clothing she owned before settling on a pink and purple sari decorated with pairs of kissing golden swans. One of her handmaids brushed the knots out of her long black locks. While outside two handmaids sprinted out to the palace lake to gather lotus blossoms to put in her hair and spread around the bed.

Like a mantra song she kept singing the same words. *My perfect beloved is returning into my arms.* When she was finally ready, she paced by the palace window. On the lake Hansaram and Great Swan were basking in the glory of the sun. All appeared to be in its perfect place. Then she thought of the girls who had gone with Uttani to shop at the bizarre. Should she send one of the handmaids to retrieve them? No, she thought to herself, there would be time enough for Sumitra, Samadhi and Uttani later. Now she wanted Nala all to herself in this very room where their first spark of romance ignited on her swayamvara eve.

An uproar carried from the north gate of the capital all the way to the palace as the people extended a heartfelt welcome to the exile prince. If he had been expelled and become *persona non grata* in Nishada, there would always be a sanctuary for Nala here. Nishada's loss would be Vidabhar's gain. Across the subcontinent his reputation of generosity had spread as one half of the love tandem of Damayanti and Nala. Their unparalleled turnaround of the fortunes in Nishada were the envy of every kingdom.

More than harvests and gifts the ordinary citizens were overjoyed to have their beautiful princess back home in the kingdom of Bhima and Bhavani. They recognized Nala as the karmic agent for the miracle of her return.

Inside the palace court Damayanti's enthusiasm did indeed spill into the heart of her father. Bhima sprung off the seat of his throne and ran to embrace Nala. No one had seen the Vidabhar king so energetic in years.

"Nala, I am so sorry for your loss. Your father was a great warrior and king. I am so glad I got to meet him." Bhima pulled away to look into the eyes of his son-in-law. Had Nala gotten over the tragic ordeal that had kept every gossip mill from Lanka to Tibet churning for weeks? The king saw lines of grief and sadness in his son's face which were perfectly understandable. Bhima hoped that coming to Vidabhar would be the remedy for all of them.

"Thank you for bringing my daughter home. I cannot convey how dearly I missed her. Truly she is much more to me than my only daughter. Damayanti is my best friend. My wayshower. The light of my heart. And you have brought her back home."

Again Bhima clutched Nala to his heart. The king told our imposter that his daughter was waiting for him in her bedchamber. Bhima was so beside himself that he indulged in a gesture of unusual intimacy commenting to his son-in-law that tonight might be the auspicious time to conceive an heir. He patted Nala on the back and pointed the way.

Just what was Kala's plan? He asked himself this question as he climbed the stairs and entered the women's quarters. Did he intend to stay in Vidabhar? Certainly there might be poetic justice in raising a son with Damayanti. Along with Sumitra and Samadhi the lord of time could raise the family he never had. That would only work if he permanently removed the real Nala from the equation. But he didn't want to kill Nala. He wanted the real Nala to live with his curse.

Sumitra and Samadhi made killing Nala impossible. The lord of time refused to do to those girls what Nala had done to him. In his heart Kala knew his intensions must be pure. When he murdered Virasen in the archery field, the old gandharva had paid his debt. The two of them were good with each other again. Kala wanted to come away from this story entirely free from any threads of cause and effect. He wanted freedom not just for himself. But he desperately wanted it for Damayanti and her two girls. And he even wanted it for Nala.

Here in Vidabhar he simply wanted love. Just what that would look like remained unclear. Should he behave like Nala so as not to shock her? Keeping the ruse going until the time was right? Or should he lay his cards on the table as soon as he walked through the door? Just because he was a god didn't mean Kala possessed the divine consciousness of someone such as his stepmother Saraswati. Here and now she would know exactly what to do. But he had better think quick because he was standing outside her door.

"Perfect beloved, I feel your heart close to mine. Come through the door and sweep me into your arms. It's okay. The nightmare is finally over. We are safe inside my father's palace."

Nala ... I mean Kala ... opened the door. This was the first time he had seen her in the flesh since the days long ago when she sang apsara songs in his father's palace in the highest celestial realm. His knees buckled. She was more than the most beautiful princess on the planet. For the lord of time she was the most beautiful creature in all the universe. And she was running full bore toward him. After so long how would it feel to be taken into the arms that he had dreamed about so many many times?

He spread his arms open to receive her embrace. And, just as Dwapara had laid a trap for the exile prince, Damayanti had her trap in place. She had not known for certain. Would this be her beloved? Or was this her enemy playing games with her heart? If it was the latter, no god could help Kala from her wrath.

She reached behind her neck for the swan feather given by her guru to be used in a time of dire need. The princess stroked the soft white feather across the cheek of this man or god or whoever he was standing in front of her. Instantly Kala shapeshifted back into his normal hunchback crippled body.

It took him a few moments to realize what had happened. He could not know the feather possessed the magic of the swan clan to shatter illusion. Even though his identity had been exposed, he decided to take the risk of reaching out. If they could just share a single embrace, Kala would finally spill the beans and tell Damayanti why he was obsessed with winning her love.

"I hate you, Kala! And I am going to kill you unless you tell me what you've done with my beloved!" screamed Damayanti with a rage heard by every man, woman and child in the kingdom. The princess was beside herself. It wasn't that she was concerned about her own safety. She knew she could put this pint-sized hunchback in his place. Damayanti wasted no time. She positioned herself between Kala and the door. He wasn't getting out without explaining what he had done with Nala.

Meanwhile just as the Vidabhar king had moments ago embraced the infectious joy of his daughter, now Bhima was like a heat-seeking missile charging up the stairs locked into a single target. He would not lose his daughter a second time. This vile deformity of a god would not escape his hands. Each day Bhima sat on the throne receiving news of the latest tragedies, he had been wringing a towel with his bruising hands that he imagined was the neck of Kala. Now he wanted to test his strength. When he charged through the door, Bhima inadvertently knocked his daughter into the arms of Kala.

Brief though it was, the embrace sent Kala into a state of euphoria. For the first time in his memory ... now that's a long time ... cuz the lord of time has an exceedingly long memory ... Kala cried for joy ... he didn't care that Bhima was strangling him ... or that Damayanti was still screaming bloody murder.

The warriors of the Vidabhar guard charged into the bedchamber after their lord. To their amazement Bhima was seen on the floor strangling a towel. And Damayanti was crying by the window. "Great Swan, I wish I had never grabbed you into my arms. I hate you!"

40. Mister Indestructo Meets the Lord of Death

On his daughter's say-so Bhima charged north with his deadliest assassins astride chariots flying at lightening speed. His only condition in agreeing to seek and bring home the exile prince was that she remained locked and sealed inside the walls of the Vidabhar palace. The lord of time would not be returning for an encore performance. Bhima posted the rest of his entire army around the palace. A team of sentries was responsible for following every move of the princess.

From the north Nala was making progress in his march toward Vidabhar. His unorthodox method of jumping off ledges and cliffs had its advantages in the high mountain regions. Lately though he had literally fallen into an improved variation. Along a particularly steep ledge the exile prince was limping along when his attention was diverted by the thundering sound of a precipitous waterfall. It gave him an idea. Water flows down. And down means south. So he positioned himself out where the water flowed with the fiercest current.

He closed his eyes and pictured holding Damayanti in his arms. He recited the mantra.

Om Shakti Om ... Om Shiva Om

Then he jumped. With the mantra on his lips, his body was pulverized against enormous round boulders. Like a super yogi pinball wizard he bounced at breakneck speed downstream. More than once Nala got impaled on a branch or sharp rock. Each time he took a deep breath. He opened the gateways of his body. He recited the mantra. And he kept traveling south.

Om Shakti Om ... Om Shiva Om

Pretty soon the locks of Shiva ... that is, the myriad Himalayan tributary streams and waterfalls flowing from a thousand strands of the yogi's matted hair ... merged to feed the river Ganga. At this place Nala stopped. Here was a confluence where two streams met ... one whose waters were pure white light ... and the other whose waters were pitch black ... coming together to form the source of holy Ganga.

On the bank Nala bowed low and petitioned the goddess to hasten his journey south. Golden haired Ganga was pleased that the exile prince asked for her blessing. Instantly she increased the flow of her waters flooding her banks and wiping out any structures in her path. The added water made it much easier for Nala to travel downstream. He pledged his eternal gratitude to the holy river goddess.

At The Footsteps of God he stopped to pay his respects to the memory of Virasen. But Ganga coaxed him, saying, "Keep on ... keeping on." From higher ground ascetics peered with curiosity at Nala as he was carried along the flood current. Who was this buoyant god floating in the middle of a flood? No human could survive for long against the power of mother Ganga.

They recited prayers for his safe journey and begged the river to calm herself so they could return to their ashram huts built on stilts for just such occasions. Sharing the higher ground were elephants, deer and tigers gazing with silent wonder at the floating hunchback.

At this rate Nala thought he would make it to Vidabhar by nightfall. He wondered when he would get the chance to resume the pilgrimage that represented the crossroad of his life. In his heart he knew he needed to climb to the abode of Shiva. In his gut he felt Shiva would not turn him away. In his root he saw himself as radiant with gateways open to the wisdom of his guru.

Even though his pilgrimage had been far from complete, Nala had already received tremendous boons from his decision to embark upon it. Now he trusted himself. When the spasms of fear arose, he didn't panic. Or at least he didn't panic for long. He was observing the state of panic and disengaging from his identification with it.

At the next turn in the river he expected to find signs of civilization. His memory had not failed him. Indeed there was a sizable population residing here. Ahead were archers lining both sides of the banks pulling back their bowstrings. He also saw massive warriors practicing the motion of throwing

You can guess who was fuming with commands to arms. Nala thought to himself that he would not want to face Bhima on the battlefield. The king was fearless about launching all his weapons at the lord of death. But we're not talking about the lord of time or the lord of the sun or the goddess of the moon. This was *freaking* Yama the god in black. None of the arrows, spears, vats of boiling oil, shards of broken glass or anything else got anywhere near Yama or our fallen hero.

"Does this mean I'm dead?" asked Nala. "Where are the kisses and hugs from the flirty apsaras?"

"No, you are not dead. Remember? You are in an immortal body. Don't tell anyone. But back there I lied. You owe me a solid. Are we clear?"

Nala had a flashing awareness of actually inhabiting a body. He closed his eyes. He drew in a slow long breath. And, yup, his gateways from the ground up started to crack open with flashes of light. He had never noticed specific color with specific gateways. For some reason he saw a distinct red light at the root. Orange at the second gateway. Yellow at his solar plexus. Green light shining out of his heart. His gateways started opening up like a rainbow shaft of sparkling light. He pictured himself holding Damayanti in his arms. As he recited the mantra, Nala saw a beautiful blue light coming out of his throat.

Om Shakti Om ... Om Shiva Om

Yama named his terms. I let you out of suspended animation ... cuz right now the cosmic movie is on pause ... at least your part in the movie ... if you agree to stop going to Vidabhar. Anywhere you go where there are people, you are going to get killed again. And again. And again. Cuz you look like Kala. And everyone ... I mean ... every man and woman on the planet hates Kala. Right now he's the poster boy on the #1 Most-Wanted-God List. And that's Wanted-Like-Mashed-Up-Into-Peach-Chutney List.

Nala asked for a Vidabhar update. Had Kala gotten past the palace defenses? Is that why Bhima had gone all-Rambo-on-steroids up here? Because Kala embarrassed the king on his home turf? Was Damayanti okay? Was she still in Vidabhar?

Yama broke down the high points of Kala's visit to Vidabhar including his disappearing act in the clutches of Bhima. Yama omitted any mention of Bhima knocking Damayanti into Kala's arms. He didn't see that as a necessary detail for the exile prince.

"Right now you are feeling like Mister Indestructo. You've been leaping off mountains in a single bound. Only to fall on your face. And get up! Way to go, Super Hero! You've been opening inner gateways that have been shutdown your entire life. Great work! You made the right call abandoning Damayanti in the wilderness at midnight! Brilliant! Following your intuition! Thumbs up! Remember what started all this? The pilgrimage to Kailash. Are you seeing the connection here?"

"No, my #1 priority has to be making sure my beloved is safe. Kala is obsessed with getting his mitts on her. And I can't let that happen."

"Pride divides the mind." Yama figured if common sense wouldn't work, he'd try quoting some ancient wisdom. "When the mind is divided, so too is reality. The threads of cause and effect get obscured. Buddy, right now, you've got some obscured threads!"

"Huh?"

"Don't let pride blind you. Close your eyes. Go into your heart. Let go of needing to be THE MAN. Ask yourself. Is Damayanti safe? And just listen. Don't answer with your pride-filled head."

Nala followed Yama's directions. He took in a deep breath and looked in his heart. Yup. She's safe.

"So why are you pushing the envelope with this Mr. Indestructo routine? You've had your fun. Now get back to work."

"But I can't use gravity to get back up the Himalayas. So this immortal body doesn't help me get to Kailash."

"Cry me a river, buddy. Look, I got you out of a lifetime of perpetual comatose torture. And you are complaining about climbing up a few rocks."

41. Can't Keep a Princess Down!

"Get out of my way, Jar-head! I have a rendezvous with Shiva in the temple."

"Your father laid down the law. 'If you wanna keep your head,' he said, 'the princess doesn't leave the palace.' And princess, I wanna keep my head. Am I being unreasonable here?"

"I don't care what my father said. I'm pulling rank on all you blowhard chest thumping defenders of illusion. As an emissary of Shakti, I'm telling you to get your hairy butt out of my way. I must speak to Shiva now!"

The team of sentries refused to budge. Damayanti said, "Fine, okay. We'll see who's boss around here." She sat down and closed her eyes. And she started chanting the mantra.

Om Shakti Om ... Om Shiva Om

And chanting the mantra.

Om Shakti Om ... Om Shiva Om

And chanting the mantra.

Om Shakti Om ... Om Shiva Om

The handmaids joined her in chanting the mantra.

Om Shakti Om ... Om Shiva Om

Sumitra, Samadhi and Uttani joined her in chanting the mantra.

Om Shakti Om ... Om Shiva Om

Mothers, sisters, wives and daughters of the sentries heard Damayanti. From all over the capital women walked past the guards who were their husbands, fathers, brothers and sons. None of them dared step in front of the sisterhood posse. Pretty soon the entire women's quarter was packed with the potent sound of women chanting the mantra.

Om Shakti Om ... Om Shiva Om

Only one woman wanted nothing to do with the mantra. In fact her body was breaking out in hives. Apparently she was having an allergic reaction. She needed to get the sound of Damayanti as far away as possible. And this woman was none other than the queen. No wilting lily herself, Bhavani charged up to the commanding general. The queen ordered him to immediately move the women en mass to the Shiva temple.

The general was explaining the order given by King Bhima for the umpteenth time when an even greater horde of women were jamming their way into the palace. All the recruits were chanting at top volume.

Om Shakti Om ... Om Shiva Om

Queen Bhavani was at her wit's end. The general was at his wit's end. All at once, the mothers and wives pointed to their own husbands and sons and called them on the carpet. In a way only a Vedic mother or wife could do, these women reprimanded the men in their lives with the sternest ferocity.

If there is anything in creation more intimidating than an army of angry mothers and wives, these soldiers had never seen it on the battlefield. They had no training to deal with this intensity of devotion. Everywhere the men looked they saw an army of fierce goddesses. In seconds all the men were on their hands and knees begging for forgiveness.

Damayanti, the handmaids, Uttani, Sumitra, Samadhi and all the other women and girls filed out of the palace and walked to the Shiva temple. With each step they were chanting the mantra.

Om Shakti Om ... Om Shiva Om

The princess was finally fed up with gods like Kala thinking it was okay to toy with human men and women simply because they possessed divine capacities like immortality and materializing or shapeshifting at will. In her universe, divine intervention had tilted way out of control. Through the chirpy-chirpy bird grapevine Great Swan had learned about the curse Kala had imposed on the exile prince. When Damayanti got the news, this was the final straw!

Turning her handsome rugged hunk-of-a-beloved-warrior into a hunchback crippled lame excuse for a sentient being! No, it was one thing for Kala to turn himself into the prince. But this curse business was simply going too far.

So the princess decided that she was going straight to the head of the trinity. Lord Shiva & Goddess Shakti were going to have to answer to her. Damayanti entered the temple and dropped to her knees. With great reverence she touched her forehead on the cool marble floor. Then she sat up and brought her hands together over her heart.

While the other mothers, wives, sisters and daughters continued to chant the mantra, the princess of enduring love opened her inner gateways from the bottom up to her heart. The shame of humanity was stuck in her throat. Always taking whatever morsels of light the gods knocked off the altar. Well, the princess wasn't going to wait for morsels anymore. She was going to claim her spiritual scepter at the head of the altar. She spoke the prayer. *I am not leaving this temple. I am not going to cease chanting the mantra. I will not turn my heart away until humanity is on an equal playing field with the gods. One for all. And all for one.*

The gods and goddesses say it ... you and I are One ... whatever we can do, you can do and more ... we come from the goddess and to the goddess we shall return ... Well, today was the day Princess Damayanti staked her claim. She gave no thought to failure. All her focus was on Shakti and Shiva.

She closed her eyes. She took in a slow long breath. And she chanted the mantra.

Om Shakti Om ... Om Shiva Om

This was the time to hold nothing back. The princess felt layers of pretense and illusion peeling away. Some heretofore dormant part of her was using the voice as a conduit for being more real. Being more honest. Not posing so much. The princess was no longer keeping things pretty. She was willing to let her devotion get ugly. Or whatever it needed in order to be real.

She was getting out of the nicey-nice box of being a good woman. She was done with being a good woman. What good was it doing her? Or her beloved? Suddenly Damayanti was the ravenously hungry goddess on the prowl for egos that were out of control. The bigger the ego, the better. More stagnant egos for the hungry goddess to consume. While she was raging, she felt the gateway of the throat breaking into pieces like shards of metal and glass. She wasn't sure if this was okay. She might be destroying the fifth gateway, instead of opening it. But it no longer mattered. She was out for liberation. No longer did this body belong to a princess. Because there was no princess. She took in a long slow breath. And she kept chanting the mantra.

Om Shakti Om ... Om Shiva Om

Emotions poured through the broken shards of the gateway. Rage, sadness, fear, joy, shame, bliss, anguish, love, hatred, passion. Emotions came out in the chanting of the mantra. She took in a long slow breath. Her throat was burning blue like an audio inferno. And she kept chanting the mantra.

Om Shakti Om ... Om Shiva Om

The boundaries of who was Damayanti and who else was in the room blurred. Was she the handmaid next to the body of the princess? Or was she the young girl dancing with wild abandon on top of the altar without a thought for whether her movements were sacred or profane? Whose emotions were singing through this voice? And whose voice was it? These questions opened inner gateways in the surrendering of them to the voice

consideration of reward. Again he felt shame for turning away from such a noble man. This was where Nala had been getting stuck. It was the shame. The shame of selfishly pulling away from the man who gave him life. The shame of posing as a prince worthy of acclaim and respect.

In the aftermath of his high profile wedding coup Nala had become the world famous emissary of love … the glamorous beloved of Damayanti … the male counterpart to the Dynamic Duo Miracle Workers transforming Nishada into one of the Hot Spots on the subcontinent … Nala knew he was a fraud … the miracle was the doing of Damayanti and Virasen … they had the vision … they did the work … they kept the faith … while Nala erected walls around his heart.

The goddess smiled at the exile prince. She wanted all of it. And Nala was finally ready. So he started at the beginning. And he told his life story sitting on the riverbank. And Ganga listened.

When he was finished, he got up. He left The Footsteps of God. And he would not return until it was his day to kiss and hug his celestial brothers and sisters and climb aboard the super cosmic party-craft Pushpaka with Indra. And ascend to heaven.

Nala found going up was much harder than going down. The hunchback crippled body just refused to fly. He tried. He hopped up. He was hoping to suspend his body in the air. He had seen the gods do it plenty of times. Most recently Yama back at the river near Bhima's camp. So he figured he had a god's body. It should be able to fly.

It was simply a question of mind over matter. Nala was learning how to get out of the mental box of limited thought. Not that it got his body to hover off the ground. Much less lift him into the drafts of wind coming up the side of the mountain. He watched with envy as an eagle floated effortlessly up one of the drafts.

"Will you teach me?" shouted the exile prince.

"Teach you what, crippled wanderer?"

"Teach me how to fly."

The eagle croaked with glee. "You want me … an eagle … to teach you … a hunchback human … how to fly?"

Nala limped to the nearest ledge. He felt the exhilaration of a boy about to move into unchartered territory.

"Well, I'm not exactly human," countered Nala. He wanted to leap from the ledge to show the eagle. But then he would have to climb all the way up the trail again. And that would be a real drag.

"Oh, are you the Mister Indestructo all the birds are chirping about?"

"Yeah, yeah. That's me." This incident was something new. For the first time in his life Nala was enjoying the game of notoriety. Until now he had always used one hand to fan the flame and the other to extinguish it. Now he did neither. Instead he flapped both his arms like wings.

The exile prince looked really silly. At least from the high altitude perspective of the eagle. Curious about this unusual wanderer, the bird landed not far away.

"Okay! I've never done this before," said the eagle.

"Neither have I," replied Nala. He felt his gateways opening. "So that puts us on equal footing."

"Got any suggestions?" asked the eagle. "I learned how to fly from my mother. But that was a long time ago. And I'm not my mother. I know how to fly. But I've never taught anyone. There are some things only a mother can teach."

"I can teach you a mantra," offered the exile prince.

"That sounds great," replied the eagle. His words were dripping with blasé sarcasm. "How is that going to get your hunchback body into the air?"

"Let's chant the mantra together. And find out."

"Who are you?"

Nala introduced himself. The eagle flapped his wings lifting his powerful body into a draft. After being carried up the mountain, it took the eagle a few attempts to lower himself and land close enough to resume their conversation. The eagle demanded to hear the story of the exile prince including the swayamvara and the events leading up to it. He wanted to hear all of it.

For a second Nala caught his mind complaining ... *A second time in the same day? This was going to take too long. He needed to get going on his pilgrimage. Not yak-yak stories to goddesses and birds.* But he spotted a glint of wonder in the eye of the eagle. That was enough to remind him of the wonder of life.

Why was he rushing? He had all the time in the world to meet a brother on a remote mountain. With each word he felt himself opening to the pilgrimage. The abode of Shiva was not so far away. He watched the reaction of the eagle to each twist and turn in the story. Together they laughed. And they cried. And they became brothers.

Now the eagle felt that nothing was impossible. Eagerly he closed his eyes and took in a long slow breath. Together the two brothers began to chant the mantra.

Om Shakti Om ... Om Shiva Om

The wind around the exile prince and the eagle picked up. The sun flashed in and out of focus. Underneath them the mountain shook. The two brothers took in slow long breaths. And they kept chanting the mantra.

Om Shakti Om ... Om Shiva Om

Then it happened. A pair of magnificent talons latched onto the hunchback body of the exile prince. The sound of the wings was deafening. The eagle stood by in awe. What was happening? Nala took in a slow long breath. And he chanted the mantra.

Om Shakti Om ... Om Shiva Om

The exile prince took flight. Garuda the king of eagles ... the vehicle for Lord Vishnu ... had eavesdropped on the chanting of the mantra by a member of his eagle clan. And he was irresistibly drawn to the source of devotion.

Once Nala's brother got over his initial shock, the eagle lifted into the air and flew alongside Garuda. Together the two brothers and the most glorious of all birds flew north to the snowy peaks. It did not take long for them to see the single mountain standing out from all the others spiring like a magnificent golden cathedral opening the gates of heaven. Once again Nala was on his pilgrimage. In fact he had never left it. Kailash was within sight.

"I admire your courage, Nala," said Garuda. "Many times you have done foolhardy deeds. But you have never given up. You keep coming back to your soul. I honor and believe in you."

06 Kala & Kailash – Mind Gateway

When the third eye of my Shiva opens
Fools shout, 'Hit the deck! The universe is about to explode!'
Shakti says, 'Let Shiva hit you right in the kisser!
For his light shall incinerate ignorance
The destination is so very close
Why heed the counsel of fools and turn back now?'

43. Back Where it Started

In the palace garden Damayanti sat on the bench and gazed out at the lake. Hansaram was frolicking with his beloved Great Swan. The pair glided with beauty and ease on the water. All was as it should be in the world of swans.

"Among humans," said Damayanti hastily after Great Swan swam to shore and was waddling in her direction, "Enduring love seems more elusive than it ever did when I was a girl clutching a swan in my arms. And my heart cannot accept anything less. Tell me, Great Swan. Who among my kind is truly living the life of enduring love?"

In the glory of the morning sun Great Swan basked flapping her wings without taking flight. Shedding remnant drops of water from her feathers the bird selected a patch of soft grass on which to park her tush. Between words the bird preened herself poking her beak to remove specks of dirt from her down.

"In the south lives a saint," said Great Swan, "named Amma. Her ashram serves the forgotten denizens in a remote jungle. With the four cornerstones: energy, love, God and service, Amma is modeling how to reclaim a life of balance between heaven and earth. This saint has never abandoned even one of her gateways."

Damayanti stretched her limbs toward the sky. When her guru was finished, the disciple asked the question in a different way. "Will I ever see Nala again?"

"For all we know Nala perished in his search for Shiva. I hear nothing from passing birds." Great Swan let the silence convey what could not be spoken in words. The two of them, guru and disciple, gazed at each other for awhile. When Damayanti grew impatient she swiveled her hands in rapid circles beckoning further guidance.

"Enduring love is a mystery. As I have told you many times, it takes away everything that gets in the way. At The Footsteps of God you shed tears to crack through the gateway of the heart. In the temple you raged at the gods and shouted truth to shatter the gateway of the throat. Now I cannot tell you how to dissolve the gateway of the mind."

It seemed her guru was wandering away from Damayanti's question. What did opening gateways have to do with seeing her beloved?

"Princess, you must realize how far you have come. Human love is the rarest jewel in all of creation."

As an adolescent Damayanti imagined opening the seven gateways would happen in tandem alongside her perfect beloved. Not a thousand miles away with the curse of a crippled god between them. Yes, she had experienced precious awakenings. But at what cost? She felt the naiveté of youth had blinded her to the harsh reality of love as a solitary journey. In the end, love was better directed to God and the larger creation of life than to a beloved. Even if he was *her perfect beloved.* This truth was a bitter pill to swallow because she could feel the pain of the words *perfect beloved* more acutely now than at any time in her life. And she wondered if she was actually getting anywhere with repeating the mantra and acting as an emissary of love in spreading the teachings of her guru.

"Trust the yearning that inspired you to launch this adventure. Passing through the gateway of the mind leads to inner peace. Don't stop now, princess. Not when you have almost arrived at your destination."

Great Swan waddled back to the shoreline. With her webbed feet she paddled out to rejoin her mate. Over her shoulder the white swan called out, "I love you, Damayanti. And, for what it's worth, I believe in you."

hearing. Now he understood why Shiva was called the lord of destruction. "And you must give me the foolish dream where you tell yourself that you ever loved her."

The exile prince collapsed forward. Something inside Nala's chest was shattering. He gasped for air. Had he come all this way just to die at the feet of a hermit god at the end of the world on a lonely Himalayan mountain?

Shiva reached down and nonchalantly flicked the tip of his finger into the skin just above the brow of the exile prince. A flash of lights like a bursting supernova jolted through Nala's mind and body. Suddenly he could see how his life was an attempt to possess the beauty of Damayanti. And how in every lifetime he had been trying to snatch beauty from his beloved and stash it like a precious gemstone in his own personal treasure vault. Keep it as *his* prize. *His* love. *His* possession.

Nala gagged on the vomiting ocean of tears surging from within him. Was it possible he had been deceiving himself through an eternity? Had his existence made a mockery of love? Out of sheer desperation Nala discovered that he could not hold onto this dream anymore. Not in the presence of Lord Shiva.

If it were within his power to do so, the exile prince would have destroyed Shiva. And he would have made sure Damayanti never heard a single word of the yogi's diatribe. He wanted to obliterate every trace of this moment. While he was blubbering out nonsensical words of fury and hatred for Lord Shiva and Goddess Shakti, Nala heard a quiet voice inside ask a question. "Is what Shiva saying the truth?"

Emotions continued to rip through Nala with an unremitting momentum. The exile prince was certain that when this tide was complete, there would be nothing left of him. He would be extinguished. Unlike the death of Virasen, there would be no ceremony at The Footsteps of God. No celestial ensemble to welcome him home. For what was really happening here was that Nala was the one being obliterated. Not Shiva. And he could do nothing but let go of the struggle. He saw the futility of his life. The exile prince felt he was done with this human drama. Inside he heard the question again. "Is what Shiva saying the truth?"

"Yes! Damn it, yes!" shouted Nala. "Shiva always speaks the truth. Every word. And I hate you for it." Nala rose onto his knees. He clenched his hands into fists and started pounding on the chest of the lord of transformation. From every cell in his body Nala wailed out with a primal scream of anguish. "I hate you, Shiva. I hate you. I hate your truth. I hate your love. But most of all I hate you." He channeled every ounce of his strength into blows that landed again and again square on the heart of the lord.

Shiva made no attempt to defend himself. Instead he smiled at the exile prince as a benevolent father would at a two year old having a temper tantrum. Then as though Nala's assault was less of a distraction than a moth flying to light, Shiva closed his eyes and resumed his meditation. With each pummeling strike Nala became infused with a radiant energy.

"Is that all you've got?" teased Shiva.

"For now. I'm exhausted."

"You are not tired. Give me more."

"Later."

"Did you say you came here for liberation? Or to get a good night's sleep?"

"I have nothing left to give."

"Have you ever wondered how Kala got past the seals of Indra, Yama, Agni and Varuna?"

Shiva waited for the question to sink in. Of course he had obsessed over it. Along with Vibhishana's vow of protection it seemed unimaginable that the god of time could possess the power necessary to penetrate the sanctity of so much goodwill.

"I am the one who broke the seals. Overruling all the other gods I gave Kala permission to accept Virasen's challenge. And I allowed him to curse you. And I'm the one who will make it possible for Kala to chase Damayanti into his endless corridors of time on this very night while you sleep at my feet. And I can't tell you why until you figure it out for yourself."

Nala tapped a new reserve of vitriol that he unleashed on Shiva. Again and again he wailed on the chest of the lord. He felt the hatred of mankind pouring through his heart into his fists and every cell of his body. He shouted obscenities he had never heard before. He clenched his entire body and crashed it into the lord. And he gave all of it to Shiva. Every last molecule of malice. Until eventually he collapsed.

Shiva wrapped a tiger skin over Nala's body. Before closing his eyes to resume meditation the lord of yoga caressed the cheek of the exile prince. "Today you made your first installment."

45. Kala's Trap

Ever since Damayanti's return to Vidabhar a battle of wills had been waging between mother and daughter. On more than one occasion Bhavani had told everyone in hearing distance she could not fathom how she had given birth to such a stubborn child. The queen took it as a personal affront when Damayanti engaged in her chanting vigil inside the palace and the Shiva temple. Why couldn't the princess mourn the exile of her husband in some quiet corner like a good wife? All this ruckus was not helping Nala or anyone else. Bhavani was convinced her daughter was doing all this chanting just to annoy her. From her point of view it was working all too well. The round-the-clock vigils were robbing the queen of precious sleep and giving her nightly headaches. So Bhavani had no qualms about ordering the royal physician to add a new ingredient to the already potent herbal concoction steeped into the hot water of Damayanti's evening tea.

On this night the princess fell into an unusually deep sleep where she almost immediately found herself walking down a long narrow brightly lit corridor. To her left and right were many doors all of which were closed. To get her bearings in this unfamiliar dream space Damayanti walked a good distance before she stopped. Here the princess randomly selected a door. When she pushed it open, Damayanti was pleasantly surprised to see Vishwakarman's amphitheater filled to capacity. All the guests from her previous swayamvara were here. It was as though she had walked back in time to the most pleasant day in her life.

How lovely, she exclaimed, as she stepped across the threshold. The princess thought to herself. This is a dream. And I am the dreamer watching the dream. And I am going to enjoy every second of it. Perhaps if I can dream bestowing the lotus garland to my beloved a second time, it will help me to find him in the waking world.

She entered the precise pocket of time when the tournaments ended and Lord Indra was announcing the exciting moment everybody had been waiting for. Damayanti found herself walking down the invisible crystal staircase wearing the twinkling sapphire Valley of the Flowers dress designed by the apsara Tapasvini. Just like the previous swayamvara she felt the million sets of eyes fastened upon her every move. And this time she was more relaxed because she knew the result awaiting her in the suitor lines. She drank in all the adoration that went with this marvelous spectacle of love.

Just like before she touched the feet of her mother first. With her father she lingered because she knew it was her friendship and love that Bhima would most miss when she left Vidabhar. Next she dropped her body in full pranam to her guru in her wedding dress. She could have remained all day drinking in the energy she received from Great Swan. Eventually she stood up and walked onto the lush green field where stood three long lines of anxious men waiting for her to face her destiny. Unlike the first time Damayanti gave no thought to the burden of disappointing so many powerful kings and gods. She knew everything was perfect. There were no doubts in her mind about making a different choice this time around. No regrets.

As she had done before Damayanti opened her palms to the suitors in the line. But this time she started with the first man. In the original swayamvara she had not gotten the idea until she had walked to the second line. With foresight on her side she wanted to perform this gesture in front of every man. So she stopped in front of this first suitor. Only a year or two younger than her father, this man wore the garb of an Asian king. She turned to him and extended the garland opening her palms to the man's heart while she silently recited the mantra. Both of them smiled with innocence. Just like before Bhima rose from his throne to join his daughter. And the entire amphitheater of spectators stood up and opened their palms.

Damayanti walked down the line three steps where she turned to face the next man. Again and again with each suitor she repeated the ritual. And the crowd repeated it with her. Even though it was just a dream Damayanti opened her heart to each suitor as though he was worthy of her undivided love. This time around she received the love from these men in a way she had not given herself the freedom to feel on the highly anticipated day. So repeating this gesture again and again did not get tedious. In fact she was almost disappointed when she recognized that she was nearing Nala.

What seemed odd to her as she took the three steps to move closer was that she could see the gods Agni, Varuna, Yama and Indra standing between herself and Nala. That's peculiar, she thought. I don't remember seeing them there before. What she recalled was the four gods posing as identical versions of Nala where she had to pass *Indra's test* to receive his blessing. When she had succeeded in identifying and draping the garland around the real Nala's neck, the second gateway opened for the princess. Immediately the wedding party celebration cranked up to seismic levels of happiness across the continent. Why was it different this time? Was it because she had already passed the test?

What Damayanti could not know was that this second swayamvara was a trap. Where she had landed in her dream was a multi-dimensional vortex called *the corridors of time* where Lord Kala stored the memories of all things. In this realm he reigned as the master of time. It was through his mind that she stopped at the precise door opening into her swayamvara. The details were precisely as they had been except for a few changes. This time Kala was posing as the Nishada prince. To insure she put the garland around his neck, he had relegated the other gods to embody their normal form. This time he wanted to be the one to whom Damayanti declared her love for all the world to see. Well, not really all the world, because this was a dream inside *the corridors of time*. Be that as it may, Kala was set on being the one to wear the lotus garland of the Vidabhar princess. He had put a tremendous amount of energy into creating this perfect scenario. Kala had been studying her every movement since she set foot inside his realm.

Damayanti decided to follow the protocol she had performed the first time. In front of the fiery red robed Agni the princess stopped and turned. Extending the garland she opened her palms in the direction of Agni's heart. Closing her eyes she silently recited the mantra. In front of the blue misted Varuna she opened her heart and recited the mantra. The princess did the same with Lords Yama and Indra.

Om Shakti Om ... Om Shiva Om

Now the stage was set. King Bhima, Queen Bhavani, Great Swan, all the gods and goddesses and millions of romantic devotees across the subcontinent and planet were holding their breaths. This was the magical moment when Damayanti, not only extended the garland to Nala and repeated the mantra, here is where the princess hoisted the garland high. Nala went down on one knee. She repeated the mantra. Everything was ready except that she could not feel the rainbow shaft of light rising up her spine. Something was wrong. When she opened her eyes and examined her surroundings, the bodies of the men on all three lines were shapeshifting until all the hundreds of kings and gods looked like exact replicas of Nala.

The princess cast the lotus garland onto the ground and broke down in tears. Still maintaining his imposter disguise Kala stepped forward to take the garland and put it around his neck. Within full view of everyone Damayanti screamed that she already had a husband and would never accept another. Like a hungry tigress she sprung to her feet ready for Kala's trap. Pouncing on top of him the princess stared straight into the god of time's soul and declared, "This time, Kala, you will not get away. On your knees now!" Damayanti ordered the god of time to explain his obsession with stealing her love and destroying her beloved.

The scenery of the amphitheater surrounding Damayanti changed to a previous lifetime long long ago when every clod of earth and drop of water radiated a primal purity. The elements of air, fire, earth, water and ether charged the atmosphere. Every sentient being knew every other sentient being. The scale of imagery expanded to include the celestial realms. Here Indra led a traveling entourage of apsaras and gandharvas singing divine love songs. Damayanti was one of these apsaras. One day inside Brahma's palace, the Lord Creator became smitten with Damayanti while she sang a beautiful love song to God. In just a momentary glance the two of them made love. It happened so quickly. Needless to say, Lord Brahma was one very potent dude. They exchanged a passionate glance. Instantly Kala was born. This was how it was when celestial beings gave birth.

As an apsara devoted to Lord Indra, Damayanti made little effort to conceal her contempt at the prospect of becoming a mother. Other apsaras took turns hugging and kissing the infant and simultaneously cooing and cajoling Damayanti to reconsider her decision. This baby boy was so pure and beautiful. The apsaras insisted they could share the responsibility. So even if Damayanti felt no maternal affection for the boy, he would still be lavished with so many adoring aunties that he could not help growing up happy and a blessing to everyone in Indra's court. Damayanti was gratified to hear these words of support from her celestial sisters. She saw that indeed Kala was a beautiful happy boy.

the royal physician had added to her daughter's evening tea. That I promise you. And she did not include the royal physician among the team of experts trying to rouse Damayanti.

To their credit both Sumitra and Samadhi did their best to remain calm. As far as anyone knew, their father was lost somewhere in the remote Himalayas last seen searching for Shiva. And their mother was stuck in a state of suspended sleep. Each of them clung to one side of Damayanti. The girls refused to be separated from their mother. Without telling anyone else they used their fingers to draw the symbols of their mother and father on Damayanti's body over and over. It was the girls' secret medicine that they hoped would bring them back home.

After twenty-four hours of failed attempts a soothsayer suspected Kala had something to do with the odd phenomenon. Once this idea got out into the palace rumor mill, Great Swan held a vigil at Damayanti's bedside repeating the mantra aloud.

Om Shakti Om ... Om Shiva Om

All members of Vidabhar society, high and low, joined along dedicating their meditations to Damayanti. Within days this practice spread to neighboring kingdoms. Pujas and fire ceremonies were performed with extraordinary fervor by Brahman priests and saints. Girls and boys put aside their games of jest to recite the mantra. Soon the entire continent was invoking Shakti and Shiva to assist their sleeping princess of enduring love.

Om Shakti Om ... Om Shiva Om
Om Shakti Om ... Om Shiva Om
Om Shakti Om ... Om Shiva Om

At the far edge of Creation inside Lord Brahma's palace the mantra reverberated through the thick adamite walls, as though they were flimsy bamboo, interrupting Brahma's meditation. This was risky business. For if Brahma lost the thread of his meditation longer than an instant, the entire creation could dissolve until he remembered who he was. And then the next cycle of universal creation would begin again from scratch. Fortunately for all of us Saraswati squeezed her husband's hand. She assured him that she would handle the matter. Smiling back at Saraswati, Brahma wondered aloud what good karma he had performed to deserve such a wonderful wife. Then he closed his eyes and resumed his one-pointed meditation upon his creation of all that is.

In the next instant the mantra invoked by humanity dissolved *the corridors of time* and returned the princess to Vidabhar. When Damayanti awoke from her long slumber, Kala was still clinging to her feet hanging off the end of the bed. And, yes, Kala was still sobbing uncontrollably. As soon as Bhima got over this shocking sight, the Vidabhar king jumped onto Kala and began strangling the god of time. Deceived by Kala in his first attempt to seduce Damayanti, Bhima possessed the fury of a father determined to keep his daughter safe. So much so that he was choking the life out of Kala.

46. Shiva Payment Plan

Two weeks had passed. Each day Nala sat at the feet of Shiva. While in meditation a question arose in his mind. What did Shiva mean when he said, 'You don't even know who Damayanti is. So how can you love her?' Damayanti is my wife. Of course I know her. And of course I love her with all my heart.

Without disturbing his one-pointed concentration Shiva responded from his mind with a tone of infinite patience. 'Do you know who you are? Do you love yourself? Don't answer right away. Look into your soul. Discover the truth without rushing words or thoughts. Be silent. See yourself as if you had never seen yourself before.'

Nala could not see the point of looking into his soul if he was incapable of loving his perfect beloved. "Of what meaning is there to life without love?"

Shiva adjusted his posture and opened his eyes to look down at Nala. 'Why do you think I sit here by myself?'

From the swayamvara eve Nala recalled gazing into the eyes of the lord and seeing the union of Shakti and Shiva. The reputation of Shiva consisted of being a renunciate ascetic who had given up everything for God. Perhaps when he gave everything up, he did it for love. Love for Shakti. Love for the creation. "Can you help me to see what you see?"

Shiva instructed the exile prince to sit closer. Nala inched up so that their knees were bumping. For a fleeting instant he entertained the thought of leaping into the lap of Shiva. "Enduring love takes away everything that gets in the way," said Shiva. "Close your eyes and see who I am. So you can see who you are. I am a mirror. Shakti is a mirror. The mantra points the way."

Nala did as he was told. He closed his eyes. But all he saw was emptiness. Nala wanted more instruction. "How do I see you? How do I find the mirror?"

Shiva interrupted the track of Nala's million-question mind. "Enough talk. Meditate."

47. Nothing in the Universe Like Mother's Love

When Damayanti realized what was happening, she broke free from Kala's grip and leapt up. In a heartbeat she was standing on the bed pointing her arm like a scepter at her father. The princess ordered him to release Kala. Her voice commanded obedience. The room became perfectly still except for Kala's shuttering sobs. Bhima was awestruck. Never had he seen his daughter take charge with such fierce unequivocal authority. He wondered what in heaven and earth was going on here. In the only chance she might ever have to rid herself of this miserable creature who had cursed her husband, murdered her father-in-law and stalked her ceaselessly, Damayanti stepped forward to protect this wretched immortal. Standing before him was not the same princess who had been chanting day and night in the Shiva temple. What magic spell had the lord of time perpetrated on their princess?

"I am the one who hurt him," confessed Damayanti. "Not the other way around." She ordered everyone to leave the room immediately including Sumitra and Samadhi. In seconds the room was empty. But I'll bet there was a crowd on the other side of that door. Instantly the princess swooped down to the floor and took the pathetic god into her arms. Oddly enough, as she gazed into her son's misshapen face, the shaft of rainbow light ignited at the seat of her spine climbing through her first gateway. In his eyes she was again transported back to Brahma's glittering palace at the farthest edge of creation where she abandoned her newborn son. Damayanti clearly saw how the romantic dream of being with Nala traced back like a lost thread to the time when she abandoned Kala. How for thousands of years she had made the love of her perfect beloved more important than her love for the rest of universe. How she had cloaked herself in a cocoon of romantic dreams. She also saw how this romance had crushed anyone who interfered with her dream.

Cradling Kala into her arms, the princess felt the shaft of rainbow light climb up through the second and third gateways gathering new spinning energy like a controlled tornado. Just as the rainbow shaft passed through the fourth gateway of her heart, the god of time stopped sobbing. Resting his immortal cheek right on her chest, Damayanti expanded her energy body into Kala's energy body. Finally the princess relinquished her ancient resistance to embodying the mother.

As the rainbow shaft shot up applying pressure to her throat gateway Damayanti expressed love in a lullaby dissolving the final illusion of the romantic dream so her body merged with Kala. Her ancient apsara voice washed every pore of Kala's skin like a mother's tenderest balm. With the innocence of a child Kala wrapped his arms around Damayanti just as her sixth gateway burst open. Damayanti connected the threads of cause and effect back to the decision to abandon her son. With tears streaming down her face, she begged Kala to forgive her and promised to never again abandon him. Inside her heart she opened a sanctuary where Kala had been waiting for eons to be held. The god of time had not quit his job with its myriad duties to perform. The records of time would still call out to Kala for his particular attention to detail. He would maintain the cosmic cycle of souls first moving into matter and then returning to the universal body of God. But here and now the lost love between mother and child had finally been reconnected.

Damayanti touched the angry lines of twisted muscles in his throat that had been screaming across time. For so long these muscles had been waiting for a mother's caress. With her touch they melted like butter in the heat of the sun. Damayanti pictured her two girls and wondered if she had been caressing them enough and expressing to them how much she loved them. Next she smoothed out the lines of sadness clenching Kala's face. Her fingers seemed to know where to stop and probe with the softest tiniest strokes.

The humpback shoulders of the time lord straightened out with remarkable ease when Damayanti ran her open palm in a downward slope dissolving his lines of shame. Next she turned Kala on his belly and washed his spine of the fear that had knotted up his nervous system. What amazed her was how gracefully his body was resetting back to its original pristine state in which he was born. One by one she laid out the appendages of his arms and legs. In his gnarled forearms and fists she felt the frustration of waiting so long suddenly drain away. With each touch Kala sighed. He didn't resist any of it. Nor did he move toward her. In innocence Kala was content to yield everything to his mother. Whatever she gave would be perfect. He was done with making demands. He had been doing that for long enough.

This was the nature of the troubled mind that even an immortal being could twist himself up into such perversely contorted deformities that no god could fix. Not even his father Brahma. Or his stepmother Saraswati. But in the Vidabhar bedchamber, where a young princess had spent her days gazing out at a pair of white swans frolicking on the palace lake, Kala allowed his mother to heal what the heavens could only tolerate. Saraswati had constructed the bridge across which Kala had walked. It was unusually long but today he had reached the other side.

Now Kala was no longer the victim of a chance rendezvous of celestial passion. And Damayanti was no longer an apsara addicted to the bliss of cosmic romance. Both mother and son possessed a new capacity for compassion. In themselves and in each other they recognized a depth of being that superseded any role they could play in the world as mother-son, lover-beloved, deity-mortal, creator-creation, perpetrator-victim, conqueror-conquest. In a mother's touch they discovered a level of existence that was pure energy defying words or containment of any kind, which if Damayanti were allowed to describe it, she would have called it 'enduring love.'

The play of life was not an illusion designed to torment or limit our consciousness. It was a gateway designed to embrace and express this enduring love. Damayanti no longer cared if she opened her inner gateways. She no longer needed to be the perfect mate for her perfect beloved. In this same room where Nala and she had first merged their hearts, Damayanti experienced herself as the perfect beloved. And her mate was all of creation.

She understood what Shiva had meant, when on her swayamvara eve, he spoke about the paradox of his constant embrace with Shakti. To embrace Shakti or Shiva meant to embrace all of creation. In this union there could be no distinctions. Now the mantra had a voice of its own. As though the creation was speaking to the creator. And she didn't bother to discern which she was. Creation or creator. The gateway of her mind was flooded with pure consciousness where all was one. And one was all. Together Kala and Damayanti held one another in this state of pure being.

A restriction that felt like the metal band of a royal crown was lifted from Damayanti's head. As her third eye opened, a flood of streaking light started pouring out of her body through the opening. It looked like a vast tunnel sucking out stagnant thoughts, emotions and toxins. The colors shifted from blue to green to violet to yellow to gold to white. It was a pageant of light cleansing her mind.

The princess saw with crystal clarity. For the first time she understood what Great Swan meant when she said that for love to endure, it has to include all beings. Not just the one perfect beloved ... Not just the ones who meditate ... And not just the ones who honor Goddess Shakti and her sisterhood. The great wheel of dharmic law was bringing all beings together in a dance of liberation that included the seemingly cruel actions of Kala and the tormented sufferings of her beloved husband Nala alongside the innocent play of Sumitra and Samadhi. All of it was perfect. She didn't need to fix Nala or save him. With his own place in this grand cosmic drama, the exile prince would find his own way. With her gateway open Damayanti saw what actions she had to take. Her one prayer was that this gateway would remain open long enough to take the steps that lay ahead.

repeating the same mistakes in the future. Don't you get it? Virasen had to leave in order for you to get through the third gateway."

"No, I don't get it. And I don't want to get it. Virasen was more than my father. He was my best friend ... my guru ... my wayshower to truth."

"He took you as far as he could. Back at the hunter's pond Virasen told you now was your time ... Goddess Shakti was calling you ... and he was right ... but you weren't listening. Virasen had a debt that he paid with his life. Right now you have a debt to pay the lord of time. When you have taken care of it, you will be free. And hopefully more evolved in your consciousness."

"What must I do?"

"Observe the mind. Each time you judge yourself or another as right or wrong, observe the pattern. And stop! Suspend the million-question mind. Replace belief with mantra. Replace thought with breath. This action which is an inaction is yoga where the center expands into the periphery. And all points merge into one."

"You're kidding, right? You might as well say, 'Hey, Nala, let's go for a walk on the moon.'" Nala reckoned there must be rare super-advanced souls who could put into practice what Shiva was teaching. But he wasn't one of them.

"If you want to know the truth, that's why I ran away from Damayanti."

Without any shadow of doubt Nala could see his beloved possessed the gift. She could observe the patterns of her million-question mind without judging herself and others. She could replace beliefs with the mantra. She could replace thoughts with the breath. And Nala saw clearly he would never be up to the task. In this regard the exile prince was absolutely convinced he would always come up short.

"I know this about myself," declared Nala. "I see the opening in the gateway of the mind. I can watch others go through it. As I have watched Damayanti. But I can't pass through the gateway. In this regard, Shiva, I am damaged goods. I have always been damaged goods. And I hate it. I truly do because this shortcoming is costing me everything."

Shiva remained motionless. In perfect equanimity the original yogi seemed to be observing his own mind. Or he was observing some great hidden mystery. Whatever was going on, Shiva waited a long time before disturbing his reverie.

"Everything you just said is the perfect explanation for why I yield to Shakti. The male mind analyzes, conquers and creates inanimate things. The female mind intuits, nurtures and creates life. When disturbances arise, you default to the male mind. And you are hurting yourself there."

Nala wanted Shiva to keep talking. What he was saying was making sense. If he could just figure out how to shift over to the feminine mind, Nala felt a glimmer of hope that he could find his way back to loving himself.

Rather than speak further Shiva beckoned for Nala to come closer. When he complied, the lord seized the crestfallen exile prince into his powerful arms. Clasping Nala tenderly the great ascetic yogi held the exile prince as a nurturing mother holds a bewildered child. Shiva whispered in his ear. "I love you, Nala. And I believe in you."

excited was Kailash that he forgot the part about his pilgrimage coming to an end. He only heard the part about getting to ask the lord of yoga for answers to the million questions that lived in his mind. So he closed his eyes and took in a long slow breath. He repeated the mantra.

Om Shakti Om ... Om Shiva Om

"What is the source of the mantra's power?" asked the disciple.

"Two ingredients must come together to bestow a mantra with power.

First is God existing without form, time or any sort of limitation. This is the infinite emptiness ... and the infinite fullness ... the great mystery ... what dwells beyond the beyond ... and resides inside the gateways of the soul. You don't have to search for this ingredient ... because God is everywhere ... every time ... every thought, every word and every action. There is nowhere you can go that God is not.

Second is the one who recites the mantra. It can be an ascetic yogi sitting quietly in the forest or inside a mountain cave who hears the voice of God whispering in his ear. If the sound calms the mind, the yogi is likely to repeat it. If the sound continues to calm the mind, the yogi is likely to keep on repeating it. If after this period of continued repetition the seven gateways open for the yogi, a rainbow shaft of light will issue forth from the yogi out into the universe.

Others may see this light and be drawn to its source. Or what appears to be its source. For the ascetic yogi knows the true source has nothing to do with anything he or she is doing. But the ones who are drawn to the light see the yogi. And they think the yogi is the source of the light. When they ask the yogi to teach them how to access this light, the yogi creates a ritual to facsimilate the conditions under which he or she discovered the voice. And the yogi calls it a mantra.

If the seekers of the light are properly initiated ... and if the original source of the sound and light continues to infuse the universe with its presence ... and if the ascetic yogi continues to repeat the mantra with frequency ... and if the seekers of the light begin to repeat the mantra following the steps given by the ascetic yogi ... then the power of the mantra is revealed to the seekers of the light."

Kailash ingested the words of his guru like seeds of light to sprinkle upon the soil of his mind again and again over the course of his life. Kailash asked another question. "What is the secret of enduring love?"

"In the palace garden you asked this question. Don't you remember? While I cannot improve on Damayanti's answer, I can repeat her words.

"The secret is simple. All we have to do is realize the love already dwells within us. All the love anyone of us can ever give to the perfect beloved. All the love we can ever receive from the perfect beloved. This love already exists in me. And in you. And in everyone. Pretty simple, huh?"

Just as he had done that morning in Nishada with Sumitra in his lap, Kailash asked a follow-up question. "So why it is a secret?"

"Because no one believes it. Everyone keeps looking for love outside themselves. So what starts out as a simple axiom becomes an impenetrable secret. And we develop seemingly powerful minds that get us further and further away from enduring love. Then we have to unlock seven gateways ... that used to be open all the time ... before we can discover this simple secret."

The words spoken by Shiva had the effect of opening all Kailash's gateways save one. So sensitive was the body of the exile prince to the enormous flood of light that even the slightest movement caused ripples of turbulence not unlike the effect he had felt of leaping into the most powerful current in the waterfall. With each energetic activation came a responsibility. And Kailash was realizing how fortunate he was in his first meeting with the princess to receive her rainbow shaft of light arcing over the hunter's pond into his chest. That was his first activation. And he was feeling pretty certain this current one would not be his last. In the awakening of the gateway of the mind, Kailash was certain his guru would always be inside him.

"What separates gods from humans?"

Before responding Shiva flicked his finger against the middle brow of Kailash's forehead. Instantly Kailash experienced the melting of six gateways. The rainbow shaft ignited up the spine pushing him to sit bolt upright. From this asana Kailash drank in each spoken word as the sacred transmission of wisdom from guru to disciple.

"Gods too are instruments of the divine. Just like all sentient creatures. Sometimes humans forget and think the gods and goddesses live in a perfect state of love without a care for the feeble suffering of humanity. But nothing could be further from the truth. We are the gatekeepers of the love vibration for humanity and all of creation. That's what qualifies us as gods. When we cease to beckon all sentient beings to enter the temple of seven gateways, we get reminded real quick to straighten up and fly right. Or we lose our divinity.

I wish I had been at The Footsteps of God to see my warrior shed an old skin to emerge into a familiar new one. I heard about Urvasi and their loving embrace. I still wish I could have borne witness to his transmigration. I loved Virasen not to claim ownership of his soul. I loved Virasen to claim freedom for my own soul.

My soul is eternal. Even as a young girl I always knew this truth. But no one bothered to see anything special about me. Because no one thought this young girl could realize such things about herself. And no one told me that I was not my soul either. So it was really my affair to choose.

Neither Virasen nor Nala were the easiest men to be around when they were young because they had an itch to conquer that took them away from their own souls. And anyone who abandons their own soul cannot get close to another soul. It is impossible. And, probably for the same reasons that no one asked when I was a girl, Virasen never asked me to show him the way to his soul. So I waited while I stayed true to my own soul.

Then a beautiful woman came into our lives. Like a river so quiet and composed whose waters invite peaceful reflection, Damayanti tamed the tormented lion inside my Virasen. After he petitioned her for initiation Virasen came into the bosom of his own soul. I quietly watched his eager steps before I asked to be initiated.

Instantly I felt at home with the mantra. And my warrior and I were meditating side by side where our souls mingled. Virasen was no longer running away to vanquish some foe. Then someone else asked to be initiated. And someone else. And someone else.

For seven years our souls were linked as one. Not just Virasen and mine ... but a kingdom of souls sat each morning and evening in a paradise garden ... and she was the light we followed to get out of the endless night of the ever-conquering mind that never conquered anything. As a soul family she showed us how to make love more important than fear.

When I die, I will not look back. My soul is already free. And I am ready anytime to make my own journey to The Footsteps of God. And I am thrilled to walk with Prem Ma today. Even though she claims no family, she is still my daughter. And always will remain inside my soul.

And the girls ... well, they are the reason I did not join Virasen on the funeral pyre ... and thank God for Sumitra and Samadhi ... their love sustained me when I lost my way. Here is what I learned from them on our journey out of Nishada.

Life events which liberate the mind rarely start out as happy ones. By remaining steady in the presence of the soul, even when the mind gets super turbulent, I discovered a crossroad where a moment earlier there had only been one way. The girls showed me how to see the crossroad. And while I don't know for a fact, I believe that the only thing I'll take with me when my ashes are dropped into the holy river is what I learned at the crossroad. Bless Samadhi and Sumitra for being acorns that did not fall far from the tree.

There must be something special about girls and their capacity to recognize the eternal nature of the soul. This story started out with a girl doing something no one told her to do. To scoop a swan into her arms and demand that Great Swan teach her the secret of enduring love.

It ends with a grown-up girl giving everything away including her family. And what happened next? We all followed after her anyway. She gave us away. But we came right back with a greater sense of who we are.

I think that's the secret. You give it away with so much love that it comes right back with even more love than before you gave it away. At least that's my story. Probably no one will ever ask me to tell it. But I'm sticking to it.

Uttani took in a long slow breath. And she recited the mantra.

Om Shakti Om ... Om Shiva Om

Next to Uttani walked Bhima. The two of them looked much more alike than either of their spouses had to them. With each step on the pilgrimage there emerged a remarkable ease between them. Anyone who did not know would have assumed they were married.

Without saying a word about the lord of time, Uttani helped Bhima to accept Kala as a gift from heaven. So much healing had happened in such a short time.

Nothing pleased Kala more than walking alongside his mother while she laughed with the two girls. After his healing back in Vidabhar, nothing surprised him more than the princess announcing her plan. As the lord of time part of his job required anticipating all sorts of contingencies. But he never saw this one coming. It was one of those rare epiphanies which made hanging out with humans so splendidly human.

Kala had a theory that the tidal wave was Varuna's way of getting back into the story. At the swayamvara Kala was pretty sure Varuna felt jilted when Damayanti lowered her lotus garland around the prince's neck. Do you remember how he didn't want to leave? Chandri and Yama found ways of sneaking back onto the stage. Indra always found a way to snag great lines. Agni had made an appearance in his fiery red robes at the ritual of ashes. And Varuna was feeling left out. At least this was Kala's line of reasoning.

When the aqua god showed up in Vidabhar the mist in his eyes was bluer than normal. If Kala hadn't known better, he would have guessed Varuna shed a tear or two on his way down to earth. Varuna and Kala had never been on the best of terms. Frankly Kala hadn't been on best terms with any gods with the exceptions of his stepmother and Yama. When no one else could get near him because of his incessant screaming, Saraswati was the one who never winced. Later on when Kala needed help figuring out how entries were recorded into the book of time, it was Yama who acted as his ever-faithful mentor.

Anyway Varuna looked like he wanted to give both of them a hug. Instead he sent a tidal wave over half the continent. Well, that's just the kind of god he is. Back in the Vidabhar palace the lord of the ocean gave the princess a bird's eye view inside the wave where she saw the energies building into a concentrated bank of power and fury. The princess got blow-by-blow images of countless humans, animals, insects, plants and earth getting washed away in a titanic deluge of death.

In distress Damayanti surveyed the cataclysmic devastation in the hearts of so many souls. Then something happened. It seemed as though the combination of Kala's actions and the karmic effect generated by the tidal wave pushed her over the edge.

Right there Varuna and Kala got to observe a mysterious moment where she went from being Damayanti the princess with all this life history of personal glory and loss to this empty being with absolutely no history and no future. She had arrived in the present moment. And the two deities marveled at her transformation.

One after another Damayanti's gateways opened. And all that history came pouring out of her. From an energetic point of view it looked as though she was dying. As though she had accomplished everything she had set out to do in this lifetime. And here she had decided to leave the body.

Kala wasn't sure whether to rejoice because she would be closer to him up in heaven or grieve because she was leaving behind her two beautiful girls. It did not take long for him to decide. Damayanti had to stay put. The wheel of dharma would be undermined if she left her body. It wasn't her time yet. And, as an authority about such matters, the lord of time was coming down hard on this one.

Varuna was seeing the same thing. Together the pair of gods talked the princess off the ledge. Varuna apologized for the tidal wave saying he'd take it back if he could. The opening of her gateways had revealed the ephemeral nature of this existence. It exposed the suffering of countless sentient beings. She did not seem all too pleased to come back. But Varuna and Kala were firm in their resolve.

Kala had never worked with the aqua lord before. So they stumbled here and there composing their strategy of defense. Damayanti was adamant about refusing to take back the weight of her personal history. As far as she was concerned, she was done with being the beautiful princess and all the blah-blah-blah that went with the package. In the end Varuna came up with a solution.

"As a Brahman, I can offer you sannyasin," said Varuna. "If you are truly ready to renounce your life."

Damayanti was delighted. So Kala shaved her head. Varuna conducted a puja where he chanted a litany of Sanskrit prayers. Out of nowhere Varuna materialized an orange robe. And he gave her the name Prem Ma. Kala was thinking more along the lines of Bhakti Ma. But Prem Ma, which meant *Mother of Love*, was perfect. That is how the princess died. And how a sannyasin was born.

So my girl shaved her head. Put on an orange robe. And changed her name. What's the big deal? As a teen Damayanti wore terracotta robes with tiny crystals that she had sewn into hidden pockets. While other girls dreamed of finding prince charming, she was dissolving her dreams in the light of yoga.

Fortunately when Damayanti sprinted down to the palace lake and Great Swan asked what she wanted, my girl did not go running back into the palace for the answer. She looked inside herself and discovered a journey to open seven gateways. I say fortunately because I was the king who did not have the answer until I searched in my girl's questioning eyes. And she became my conscience and wayshower to my outer and inner guru.

One day after the swayamvara I put my forehead on the earth by the palace lake and begged Great Swan to let me shave my head and put on the orange robe. She told me that surrender, which is the first stage of renunciation, was an inner reflex that I could practice while fulfilling my responsibilities as a king, husband and father. My guru is wise. And I am not so foolish as to impose my impetuous wishes upon life anymore.

A father learns about surrender on the day of his daughter's swayamvara. But my surrender wasn't real because I never let her go. Every day my heart got heavier. Her choice of renunciation came out as a surprise. I did not think I was strong enough to lose her a second time. This time I feel as though it worked. It took a day of sitting on my throne feeling sorry for myself. I was alternating between feeling trapped inside the box of my mind and repeating the mantra.

Om Shakti Om ... Om Shiva Om

Then I realized my sons were grown up. My wife was living through their dreams. I was free again to follow my daughter.

So why shouldn't she show others the way? Me included.

Now I have no dreams. I live to serve. Now I have no wife, no sons and no daughter. I live with everyone as my family. And I get the benefit of all worlds. Because Prem Ma reminds me of my daughter. And she destroys my illusions with enduring love. Praise be to the one.

Om Shakti Om ... Om Shiva Om

Everyone down there is walking toward a wasteland. The destination won't be pretty. At least that's what the human mind believes. Fortunately Prem Ma and her Vidabhar posse did not have any past associations with the land in the south. So when they arrive they will rebuild the jungle with a sense of open wonder. Mother earth possesses a remarkable capacity to give birth to life anew.

From his heavenly palace in the celestial realm Lord Indra shifted his attention to the twin saints Parvata and Narada who had once again come to pay their respects.

"Okay, it's confession time," he shouted in a voice loud enough to insure everyone in heaven could hear him. "I'm one of the knuckleheads that got behind this freight train of stealing a mother away from her child. And I'm a god. So I am supposed to know better. Right?"

Narada asked the lord of heaven if there was any end to his thread of mischief. Indra clapped his hands and quizzed the saint. Was there an end to the sound of his two hands clapping?

Tapasvini flew into the court followed by her apsara sisters and gandharva brothers. Virasen was among them.

"Round up the usual suspects!" boomed Indra. "We're going down to earth to clean up Varuna's mess." Indra assured the saints there was always an end. Kala and Prem Ma had patched things up. Now a new cycle was starting. And Indra didn't want to miss it.

52. Chasing a Woman on the Trail of Life

His last memory was Shiva giving him the name Kailash and answering the queries of his million-question mind. He was gazing at his guru with so much love. Six of his seven gateways were open and he knew he was much closer to realizing his goal of reuniting with his beloved than ever before. Because he had let go of the goal. He had surrendered to his guru. Now it was Shiva's job to fulfill or destroy it. And Kailash's job was to love who and where he was completely.

The next thing Kailash knew he was standing on a narrow shaded trail running along the basin of a wooded valley. Walking briskly in his direction was a chubby dark skinned woman dressed in a spotless white sari carrying a satchel over her shoulder. Kailash thought to himself. *Better get out of her way. Or she'll run me over.* The woman was moving with singular purpose.

So Kailash was almost embarrassed to interrupt her day. But he figured Shiva put me here for a purpose. And the woman must be part of it. Maybe he was here to be part of her purpose.

Kailash considered it rude to shout at a perfect stranger. Especially a woman. So he waited until she was about ten feet away to clear his throat and introduce himself. But he underestimated the speed of the woman. She motored right past him without so as much as a *Namaste* or *Hari Om*.

Now it was Kailash who felt that she was the rude one. He chased after her wondering *how dare this common woman fail to acknowledge him*. Couldn't she see his glaring need? Didn't she know he was Kailash a disciple of Lord Shiva recently descended from the sacred mountain that was his namesake?

He yelled for her to stop. But she didn't. More rudeness. What sort of woman was he dealing with here? With few options Kailash continued his frenzied chase for the rest of the afternoon. Staying close required complete focus because of the thick brush on the trail. While the woman never once broke into a gallop, Kailash was amazed how it was possible to cover so much ground while walking. The trail had forks. And he could never see a fork more than a few feet before it came upon him.

The disciple of Shiva had to keep his mind in the present moment or risk getting lost down one of the side trails. He felt a keen awareness of his destiny depending on each step he took. He could not afford to lose sight of the woman for more than a moment. But it was impossible to keep her in visual range.

If someone could just clear all the low lying branches and brush out of the way, his task would have been considerably easier. If the woman could just slow down her pace, his task would have been considerably easier. If the trail had been wider and straighter without forks, his task would have been considerably easier. Even after receiving the exalted spiritual boons of Lord Shiva, Kailash could not change any of his external circumstances.

Life was speeding past him. Every moment was one more tick ... then one more tock on the clock of existence. He felt his mortality as he struggled to keep up. While he was still a young virile man, Kailash realized nothing was certain. He could lose his way so easily. The purposeful actions expressed by other people in their lives could take them away from him in the blink of an eye.

He recalled Damayanti and her purposeful movement in clearing the outgrowth of the jungle from the Nishada palace garden to create a meditation sanctuary. This purposeful action led Virasen, Uttani and others to practice yoga meditation beneath the shade of Damayanti's banana tree. If not for the coaxing of Sumitra, he could easily have missed out on the practice. Would he have ever made it to Mount Kailash without repeating the mantra? Every moment was an opportunity he could seize or let slip by. The net result was his mind becoming highly agitated. And he felt powerless to do anything but put one foot in front of the other on the trail ahead.

When the woman reached her destination, Kailash could not close the gap between them because a group of forest dwelling village elders were waiting to escort her under a canopy enclosure. No one acknowledged the presence of Kailash because their attention was glued on touching the hands and feet of the woman as she made her way to a raised altar. Here

invariably claim credit for the healing which is the first misstep away from healing. What we do is act as conduits so universal energies can flow through us into the gateways of others.

The first level of healing awareness is to diagnose in an analogue fashion. Open gateway or closed gateway. Energy flowing or energy stuck. Yes or no. At this level there is little nuance. The healer either feels energy flowing. Or the absence of the flow informs the healer that the gateway is closed.

The first stage of this level is to treat the entire body as a single gateway. Energy is either flowing through the entire body or stuck throughout the entire body. The second stage is to discern individual gateways in this same fashion as either open or closed."

The woman pointed her hand at individuals to select volunteers. One was a boy in his late teens who sprang to his feet and ran up at once. Before Kailash knew what was happening, hands were lifting him off the earth and pushing him toward the altar. He was the other volunteer. So the woman did know about his existence. Kailash was hoping she would allow him to remain upfront as her assistant. Naturally after his considerable spiritual experiences he considered himself to be just shy of an expert in his awareness of healing energies.

People at the gathering gasped with pity at Kailash because his steps were so excruciatingly slow. Then it occurred to him that he had forgotten about Kala's curse. How had he kept up with the woman on the trail with this crippled body? Not once had he stopped to think of it on the trail. Had he been healed of the curse? And if so, had the curse come back when he seated himself and closed his eyes? Nothing was making sense. By the time he stepped up on the altar, the disciple of Shiva was completely exhausted.

The woman directed the boy to diagnose Kailash. Was his body open or closed? She did not tell him how to do it. The boy turned his palms open to Kailash and closed his eyes. He took in several long slow breaths. Then he pronounced Kailash to be closed.

Next the woman directed the boy to determine which of the seven gateways were closed and which were open. Again the boy turned his palm open to Kailash and closed his eyes. Again he took several long slow breaths. Then he said that one, three and five were open while two, four, six and seven were closed.

The woman explained that while he had absolutely no training as a healer, the boy had gotten the diagnosis correct. She turned to Kailash and asked if he wanted healing. The disciple of Shiva did not know how to answer. His million-question mind was working itself into a frenzy. What magic spell had the woman cast over him back in the forest? Maybe she still had him under her control which would explain why he had felt so exhausted. How had he chased her on the trail when she moved with such incredible speed? Was she one of those dark healers known to steal energy from weak-minded desperate people? Was he desperate for healing?

Kailash nodded his ascent. What happened next came as a total surprise. Where he expected the woman to open her palms to him, as the boy had done, she instead wrapped her arms around Kailash in the most enveloping embrace he had ever received from another human being. His first thought was that this woman must be Shiva in disguise. Energy gushed through him at the same caliber of intensity he had received in the lap of the lord of destruction. How was it possible for an ordinary woman to be such an extraordinary healer? She was the Ganga river of healers. Definitely not the village brook variety. In his ear the woman whispered the mantra over and over.

Om Shakti Om ... Om Shiva Om

Her words entered his body like Shiva's words. The sound carried energy. His body slumped against the woman like a tiny boy melting into the bosom of his mother. If she was a dark healer, he was powerless to prevent her from stealing his energy. The woman kept Kailash right there immobile in her energy field while she resumed the lecture. He thought it was strange to feel the vibration of every word while simultaneously hearing the woman talk about the subject of healing.

"At these two stages of awareness in the first level, healers can provide wonderful service to humanity so long as they refrain from using personal energy to do the healing and refrain from taking personal credit for doing the healing. Just as this boy was able to give a correct diagnosis without holding a degree from a healing school, he could with proper direction do great healings if the four cornerstones that I mentioned were important enough to him.

Healers do not heal. Healers help people heal themselves. This is the first lesson for every healer. As a matter of fact, it is the first lesson for any level of spiritual development. And it is the last lesson as well. More healers get tripped up on this lesson than any other. Because the personal mind loves to grow its self-importance, which is another way of saying personal power, by taking credit for the work of God.

So the first order of business for an honest healer is to see God in all the energy flowing through the body of the healer, the body of the patient and the body of the universe. Actually I see Goddess Shakti in all the energy movement. Some healers reference God energies as male: Shiva. Some healers reference God energies as female: Shakti. And there is a third category of healers that reference God energies as pure undifferentiated oneness: God. All are correct.

The key is to open and surrender to the purest essence of God. You will never be able to control Shakti, Shiva or pure oneness. If you are modifying the energy flow to grow your personal power, then you are not healing. Even if you call it healing, you are doing something dishonest and definitely outside the realm of spiritual development.

The best way to guard against this pitfall is to establish your yoga practice so you are regularly re-establishing an honest humble energy relationship between your body-mind-soul ... and the universal body-mind-soul. If you get lazy with your own practice, you will become an energy vulture preying on the patients who come to you for healing.

Please be honest. Please be humble. Please stay close to Shakti. She will always take care of you. Always trust her intelligence over your own mind. This is what it means to surrender to the purest essence of God."

The woman asked the gathering if there were questions. With his million-question mind Kailash wanted to show the woman that he was listening to her words. He wanted to be acknowledged for possessing a mind capable of processing deep thoughts. So much of what the woman said was similar to the guidance of Shiva that Kailash felt his guru must have been here with them. He wanted to ask her if it was so. In his heart he heard his guru laughing and saying that of course Shiva was there. Wherever there is Shakti, so too will you find Shiva.

"The curse?" sputtered Kailash. "How did I keep up with you on the trail? If you healed it, why did it come back? Is this place real? Or am I hallucinating?"

The woman laid the body of Kailash down on the earth in front of the altar. When he tried to get up, she put her hand on his shoulder. Without saying a word she made it clear that he was not ready to move yet. She put a finger to her lips and smiled mischievously indicating that now was not the time to speak. So he laid down between the woman and the gathering of villagers. He closed his eyes. And he listened.

"The second level of healing requires a much more sophisticated energetic discernment. Just as two cooks can prepare and taste the same dish. One will say that it is great because it is hot, filling and better than eating a pile of dung. The other will vomit because he finds the combination of spices or the freshness of the ingredients to be less than satisfactory. The former might achieve the first level of cooking but he will never reach the second level without heightening his discernment. The second cook must be able to taste the difference between grade evaluations such as: poison, awful, bad, mediocre, good, excellent and exquisite foods. Then this cook must train to be able to prepare ingredients to make foods at these different grade evaluations depending on his desire to serve the needs of his customers.

If you wish to heal at the second level you must develop a discernment like that of the finest master chef where you can discern between many grade evaluations of energy. This level of healing requires constant attunements to purer and purest energies. And you must do it while constantly surrendering the credit to Goddess Shakti. Or Shiva. Or the One. So if you are the finest master chef and customers rave about the exquisite dishes you prepare ... that no other chef on the continent can prepare ... and people tell you how special you are ... will you take credit for the dish? Or will you say? *Give the credit to Goddess Shakti. She grew the ingredients and she guided my hand every step of the way.*

To aim for the second level of healing is dangerous. You must be dedicated. And you must be humble. But let's focus our attention on the first level because all newcomers must start at the beginning. And remember you can perform wonderful honest authentic miracles of healing at the first level."

The woman directed the gathering to break up into pairs. The teenage boy came up and asked to be Kailash's partner. For the next three days the woman gave healings and lectures about healing. From all directions people descended on the forest village by the brook. She turned no one away. At the end of the first day I heard someone refer to her as Amma. I realized I had found a teacher who could show me how to radiate the universal body, mind and soul. I knew I was in the right place.

My first impressions of Amma as a healer was that she did everything patiently and persistently. She did not cut corners. And she taught me not to cut corners. The first cornerstone was to recite mantra twice a day. The second was to remember Shakti. The third was to love all sentient beings. And the fourth cornerstone was to serve all sentient beings. As long as I kept all four corners straight and honest, I knew I was blurring the separation between God and human. I was on the path laid down by my guru.

54. Maze of Death

Before the calamity of Varuna's tidal wave, the land surrounding the ashram had been a vast untamed jungle roughly three times the size of Vidabhar. The balance of life here tilted heavily toward the plant and animal devas whose lineage of masters were as old as the land itself. It wasn't that there were no villages or hunting tribes. There were people residing in the jungle who spoke their own languages and dwelled within the culture of a jungle consciousness in which the vast majority avoided all contact with the outside world. These jungle people comprised only a tiny fraction of the sentient beings residing here.

Now the land was barren. The devastation hit the plants and animals with a severity impossible to comprehend even for the witnesses observing the aftermath. Prem Ma entered the jungle with great trepidation. Her pace slowed to a state of emotional paralysis. Where there had been ancient forests of teak, sandalwood, sal, mahogany, ashwaganda, banyan and many other varieties, there were thousands upon thousands of trees tossed askew in monstrous random piles of death. It looked and felt sinister.

What so disoriented Prem Ma were the crazed communications coming from the plant devas. Many of them hovered over the fractured land without registering what had happened. The teak deva was still searching for her trees. The helter-skelter remains of dead teak trees were unrecognizable to the deva. So she kept calling out to her children.

"Teak trees, where are you? I am blind. Why are you not answering? Stop playing this game of hide and seek! Talk to me! I'm desperate and alone!"

Hearing the teak deva, as Prem Ma had the capacity to do, was heart wrenching. What could Prem Ma do? What could she say? And the entire land was populated by plant devas pleading their own soliloquies that went unheard by their countless deceased plants. Where was Prem Ma supposed to start? Who would she try to heal first? And how?

The destruction was, as Bhima had described it, a maze of death. Kala considered removing Prem Ma from this place. He dreaded seeing her suffer. When she turned to him for help, Kala took his mother into his arms. He had already sent out a call to Dwapara.

'Bring in as many flocks of vultures as you can. We've got lots of work to do. And it's not a pretty sight.'

Since the tsunami his staff had been working overtime. Every day the lord of time and his team saw birth and death side by side in a symbiotic balance. So he did not flinch at the devastation.

Uttani huddled with Sumitra and Samadhi who had never seen their mother in such a bewildered state. Naturally the girls were frightened as was the rest of the Vidabhar contingent. Prem Ma was their shepherd. And now their shepherd was lost.

The amount of time and work it would take to clear even a small section of this land was far beyond the scope of the Vidabhar party's resources. Bhima went ahead in search of a path through the maze of death. All of them moved with reverence as though walking on hallowed ancestral ground.

Prem Ma sat on the open earth. She closed her eyes and entered into the dreamtime of the plant realm. But instead of the familiar dreamtime, the swami had entered an eerie restless place of unsettled spirits. Prem Ma called out to the teak deva, as she was the first one Prem Ma had been able to discern in the cacophony of lost devas calling out to their departed children.

"Teak deva, Come to me. I will help you find your way."

The teak deva could not believe what she was hearing. A voice had responded to her plea. As she moved toward the voice, she saw Prem Ma who introduced herself as a friend and loved one of all the plant devas and plant realms. The teak deva asked to guide her toward her trees.

"I'm sorry. But they are all dead."

The teak deva failed to register any sign of hearing what Prem Ma said. And she started to drift away when Samadhi went up to the teak deva and jumped into her arms. The girl started to cry. And the plant deva joined her.

Prem Ma teared up thinking 'That's my girl.' Of course now that she was a renunciate Prem Ma wasn't going to be advertising this thought out in the world. But here in this ghoulish place Samadhi had charged in to help her mother and perform the action that the responsible adult was too locked in her mind to perform.

Prem Ma sidled up to them and joined the hug. The three of them mourned the death of the teak trees and so many more deaths that only Kala as the lord of time along with his team of vultures might ever come up with a number to account for the loss.

The teak deva thanked the girl and the swami. She told them that she felt free to move onto to a new jungle where teak seedlings were needing protection. She would go now and say a quick prayer for the land to heal and soil to become fertile again for plants of other species. Samadhi and Prem Ma pranammed to the teak deva and the earth and to each other. Here Prem Ma said that they could be mother and daughter as long as she didn't tell anyone out there. It would be their *little* secret of enduring love. Prem Ma lifted Samadhi into her embrace where they celebrated their clandestine reunion.

"Mommy, I want to shave my head and wear an orange robe just like you," pleaded Samadhi. "Do they let little girls do that here in the jungle?"

"I don't know," replied Prem Ma. "But I'll find out."

When Prem Ma and Samadhi came out of meditation the scene had shifted considerably. There were black birds everywhere picking through the decayed remains to free up the trapped spirits of the land. Kala had opened his book of time and was making notations with remarkable speed. In all directions Dwapara was squawking out orders like a crow who thrived on adversity. When you were in a pinch, Dwapara was definitely a bird you wanted on your team. And today definitely qualified as being in a pinch.

A dark skinned woman wearing a white sari walked through the maze with a serene energy belying the devastation around her. At once Prem Ma felt the kinship of a sister and rose from the earth to meet her. Prem Ma was surprised when the woman forgoed introductions or namastes and instead went straight for a great all-enveloping embrace which was the signature for everyone who came to know her as Amma.

The two women did not want to let go of each other. So Amma just waved for other members of the Vidabhar team to come forward and join in a group hug. Sumitra and Samadhi snuck through the forest of legs to get between Amma and Prem Ma. Now there was a place where the energy was sweet.

Behind Amma was a can-do army of men skilled with the ways of heavy-duty forest work. Captains were shouting out orders and the men fanned out with a chaotic order like ants moving in seeming randomness but with an invisible means of communicating with each other. They cut down and dragged limbs. How they choose what to cut and where to drag was a mystery to the Vidabhar foremen who though highly skilled in growing a wide array of plants were completely out of their element in this maze of death.

55. Periphery to the Center

On the fourth day Amma set out on the trail for her next destination. As quickly as he could Kailash scampered after her. But this time he was limping with a hunchback body. So she moved a lot slower.

When Kailash asked her to explain why he had been able to walk at her brisk pace the first time, Amma said it was a gift from Shakti. She wanted him to keep the faith. The curse was not meant to be permanent. As Kailash heard the words, he was reminded of the naga Karkotaka who had bit his hand by the mountain stream. He had said the same thing. The curse was not meant to be permanent.

Through the *tapas* or fire of his yoga practice, Amma said, Kailash had purged the gambler from his energy matrix. Never again in this incarnation would he feel any attraction to race horses or throw the dice. Never again would he feel disgusted with himself for what he had done in the past. The former prince had learned what he needed. The cycle of playing games of chance was finished.

When he looked inside, Kailash felt that this healer was speaking the truth. The iron pit which had resided like a forever clenched fist inside the third gateway was no longer there. Now he felt an easy soft center that allowed the flow of energy. Could it be true? Was Kailash creating a more receptive center within himself?

Now a new cycle was opening up which required a concerted effort on his part to shift his axis of power from the periphery to the center. Kailash asked Amma to explain what she meant. She said that all the actions he had taken in his life had been motivated by the need to prove himself worthy of praise, acclaim, power and love. Kailash thought about it. He was learning to be honest with himself. Both Shiva and Amma were keen on honesty. So he had to admit that, as unflattering as it was, what she had just said was accurate. He was constantly looking for external approval to validate his worth.

Amma said anyone requiring external validation was living with their axis of power on the periphery. For such a person, merging with God was impossible.

The new cycle was an invitation for Kailash to step up his devotion to Shiva. As she explained in her lecture, the essence of love is God. To discover the meaning of these words Kailash would need to occupy the center of his own sphere of power. No longer could he dwell on the periphery. In his moments of energetic awareness Amma was directing Kailash to pay attention to this distinction and shift more fluidly from thoughts generated at the periphery to love arising from the center. This shift could work only when the gateways of the heart and mind were both open.

Amma asked if Kailash thought Shiva was seeking anyone's else approval each time he sat for meditation in his lofty Himalayan abode. Did Shiva need Shakti's love in order to feel worthy of drawing in his next breath? If so, what would happen if Shakti ignored Shiva? Or Shiva got distracted in his devotion to Shakti? If not, how did Shiva establish his worth?

"The task of the devotee is to merge with the object of devotion. The task of the disciple is to merge with the guru. So you've got your marching orders. Now let's walk in silence."

Kailash was dying to ask more questions. How do I merge with the object of my devotion? How long will it take to merge with my guru?

Amma chided her student to practice now what she had just instructed. This teasing was her way of whacking him upside the gateway of his mind. She had caught him operating from the periphery. Now he had to catch himself.

This distinction of operating from the periphery versus the center would expand the visceral awareness of energy for Kailash. When he did catch himself, there was a natural shift like a gravitational pull toward the center of love. He stepped forward on the trail and took in a long slow breath. Here is where he made the energetic shift. Here is where Kailash merged with Shiva. And the mantra recited itself.

Om Shakti Om ... Om Shiva Om

56. My Guru is to Love God

Since her first day at the ashram Prem Ma had been sneaking furtive glances at the dark skinned saint. Prem Ma wondered if Amma ever slept because it seemed that she was always on the move issuing instructions like a field marshal operating a military campaign. Every captain and devotee had to answer to Amma if their efforts were falling short. She was just as generous in lavishing praise where it was needed.

For a great saint this woman seemed to keep herself awfully busy. It didn't seem as though Amma gave herself even a moment to sit and meditate. Slowly the labor teams were making progress. New supplies and men were arriving daily. Always Amma was keeping her finger on the pulse of every cycle of activity. And always Prem Ma was on the lookout for an opening to approach the woman whom everybody was looking to approach.

After lunchtime Prem Ma had observed a routine where Amma went on a short stroll by herself. So like a singer searching for the entry rhythm in a new song Prem Ma watched Amma closely throughout her meal. When the saint rose to signal her transition, Prem Ma did not wait for permission. She moved in step with Amma. When the two women had the rhythm of forward motion under their feet Prem Ma asked, "Why did you choose such a remote place to build your ashram?"

"The location chose me," shouted Amma howling with laughter. "I was born here in the jungle."

Prem Ma had difficulty wrapping herself around this reality.

"Born here? Where are the crops? The fruit and nut trees? How do you grow vegetables here?" Prem Ma had grown up in the civilized world of a highly organized kingdom. This was like living on another planet.

"We live on indigenous root vegetables and other plants. Not so different from what people eat in Vidabhar" said Amma. Again she was laughing uproariously. "I eat Shakti. She's my favorite food. What's yours?"

Since they were presently living in the middle of a disaster zone Prem Ma thought it irreverent to indulge in idle chatter when there were so many daunting tasks needing to be accomplished. She tried to steer the conversation to practical matters. Prem Ma presented a brief bio of her accomplishments in Vidabhar and Nishada. She asked for permission to launch a healing initiative among the plant devas. Prem Ma had heard about a team of skilled Amma healers roving through the jungle and she was intrigued. What were Amma's healers like? She proposed borrowing these healers to combine with her skills as a plant liaison to start restoring the dreamtime back to a balance between spirit and matter. But Amma would hear none of it.

"You need to laugh, sister. Since your arrival you haven't been yourself." The saint spoke with a certainty as though she had known Prem Ma as an intimate friend for many years. "Everyone else can see it. But they look to you for support. So they don't say anything. But I don't need your support. So I'll just speak the truth. Okay?"

Prem Ma asked Amma about her guru lineage. With whom had the saint studied? What were the spiritual practices of the ashram?

"My guru is to love God," said Amma bending over because she was laughing so hard. "And my practice is to serve others. Is that an impressive enough lineage for you?"

Arm-in-arm the two women walked around the jungle carnage that the teams of forest men were stacking in organized piles of uprooted trees. Later they would scavenge for timber to construct the new ashram. Whatever they could not use would eventually be burned or buried.

Members of the Vidabhar team had fanned out across the ravaged jungle to conduct a detailed survey of the land. Together they were preparing a comprehensive long term agrarian plan laying out a myriad variety of plants best suited for the soil and climate. This was precisely the area of expertise where Bhima and his team of Vidabhar foremen shined brightest. If a silver lining could be seen in the disaster, it would emerge from this fresh new proficiency of crops and trees arranged and negotiated in consultation with the plant devas none of which would have been possible prior to the clearing of the jungle by the tidal wave.

"I don't know if I made the right decision back in Vidabhar," started Prem Ma who was going to launch into all the variables that had led her to choose renunciation. She tried to recount the story of her karmic debt to Kala. But Amma cut her off.

"Don't worry. Shakti and Shiva are behind all this drama. If it means anything to you, you have their blessings." The ashram newcomer was astonished by the resolve in the woman's voice. As though she conducted regular conversations with Shakti and Shiva. Like dearest friends. Of course the blessings of these deities meant a lot more than *anything* to Prem Ma. Amma kept talking as though she was downloading a message from them right now. "They stand firmly behind your decision to become a renunciate."

Prem Ma hastened to raise concerns about Nala. No reports had reached her ears. Had he perished in the bitter elements of the Himalayas staggering under the weight of conducting a pilgrimage with a crippled body? Each time she looked inside her own heart, Prem Ma felt he was still alive and well. Maybe he had even reached Kailash and had finally achieved his dream of becoming a disciple of Shiva. That would explain why no one had seen or heard of the exile prince.

She wanted her beloved, who had been her husband, to find out about her decision to take sannyasin from her own lips. But the circumstances with confronting her past debt to Kala and Varuna's tidal wave had conspired to force her hand. She didn't feel that she could hold the false scepter of worldly power in her hands anymore. She felt she had outgrown the dream of love from her childhood. She had taken this step as a necessary progression in her march toward unlocking the secret within her own soul.

Once again Amma spoke of what was simmering in the mind of Prem Ma before she could get out all the words.

"Again, sister. Stop worrying. And start trusting again. We've got him covered."

Prem Ma wondered what Amma meant when she used the subject *we*. But she let it pass. Prem Ma decided it was time to stop pushing life and be more humble. She took in a long slow breath. And she asked Amma to please show her the way to trust life again. Prem Ma admitted she had been trying too hard since donning the orange robe.

Amma kept coming up with surprises. This time she pulled out a simple unadorned ragdoll. The kind you would see in the arms of a jungle village girl. Amma kissed and hugged the ragdoll. Then she presented it as a gift to Prem Ma.

"I want you to play with this doll. Talk to her as though she is your mother Goddess Shakti. I invite you to be so much in your heart that the doll feels alive and real. Let your gateways open. Be a girl again. It's okay. I know. You think you have to be serious because you took sannyasin. But you are mistaken.

I have swarms of sannyasins in my ashram. And I don't allow them to be serious all the time. It's not how God lives. God loves. So start loving again. You don't have to grow your hair and put on fancy clothes to love people. And you won't break your vows if you love people.

"Can I stay here as a swami when all this tidal wave clean up is finished?"

"We'll see. First you have a doll to play with. And I've got a jungle full of swamis barking out orders like drill sergeants and loving every second of it. I might have a rash of orange clad men joining the army when all of this clean up is finished."

The two women giggled. Prem Ma snuggled the doll into her bosom.

"That's it, my darling child. What's the point of opening all these gateways if you forget the love?"

One by one the gateways had been flying open during the conversation. Prem Ma wondered if she had found her next teacher. Her next guru. But she already had a guru whom she respected and loved. Gurus were not something you just switched like stepping midstream from one ferryboat into another.

"Can a woman have two gurus in one lifetime?"

"Can a mother have a thousand children in one lifetime?" giggled Amma. Prem Ma thought this woman said the most peculiar things. In a short time she had come to adore the way Amma saw reality. "You're thinking again," chided Amma. "Better stop it. Or I'll rat you out to your guru."

Prem Ma hugged the doll. And Amma hugged Prem Ma.

57. Ashram Contract

On the third leg of the journey Amma once again slowed down so Kailash could keep up. The saint asked the disciple of Shiva if he would like to continue all the way to her ashram in the south. Kailash replied in the affirmative. He still had so much to learn.

Amma launched into a laundry list of pre-conditions to which Kailash was required to adhere as part of a residence contract. Kailash thought it made sense that a community of devotees would need strict guidelines to maintain the sort of purposeful living that he had been observing this woman model every moment day and night. The conditions had no wiggle room for debate or negotiation.

One, you must practice complete silence at the ashram unless you are addressed. Even then you are only allowed to ask questions about how to perform your service.

Two, the only person at the ashram to whom you may ask questions is me. No one else.

Three, you are there to serve Shakti. Not your personal self-importance or the self-importance of others. So you are not allowed to socialize. Surrender everything you think, say and do to Shakti.

Four, repeat the mantra at all times. Especially when serving others.

I realize these last two conditions have qualities more of guidelines because who can repeat a mantra at all times or surrender every thought to Shakti? But aim high while you are in the ashram. To reside in such a place is a rare privilege. Don't miss it!

Nala took in a long slow breath. And he recited the mantra.

Om Shakti Om ... Om Shiva Om

"These restrictions are necessary to heal the curse. You must trust that I am not exercising control over you to gain personal power. If you can't, don't go to the ashram.

If you choose this path, it will not be easy. At times you will hate me. That's okay. Just don't break the rules. And remember to surrender everything to Shakti. Am I being clear?"

"Yes."

Under the shade of a banyan tree Amma stopped. She sat on the earth and leaned back against the main trunk of the magnificent tree. Around them many stout limbs from the main trunk had grown out and then reached down into the earth to tap their own roots. So the one tree appeared to actually be more like an entire grove complete with scores of secondary trunks each on its own strong enough to support further outward growth.

Amma instructed Kailash to lay his head on her shoulder and close his eyes. Under the thick spacious canopy provided by the banyan Kailash felt that Amma and he had retreated into the sanctuary of an ancient living temple.

Here Amma proceeded to give Kailash a final attunement. The purity of energies was so exquisitely refined that Kailash felt his own energy system go into an automatic state of shutting itself down. His intuition told him to stay awake. The disciple of Shiva wanted to remain close to Amma. But his physical body was shutting down in order to receive the tremendous inflow of energy. As had happened before Kailash could not resist for long.

His last memory was feeling his seventh crown gateway open. The sensations were exalted. Previously he had heard this gateway described as a thousand petaled lotus. Now he could actually feel the many petals. He could not count as many as a thousand. But the gateway was comprised of layer upon layer upon layer of these subtle finely honed sheaths for which the description of a thousand petaled lotus seemed entirely apt. He marveled at the beauty of the opening. All the while he wondered. Could this awakening actually be happening to him?

The Nishada gambler prince seemed like an old classmate from another lifetime ago. He wondered if he had received this gift earlier in life, would he still have frittered everything away? Or would he have recognized the precious crossroad that life presented each instant of this existence? Would he have valued these thousand petals of awakening more than the desperate need to win something that was never real in the first place?

Right now Kailash was living at the center as Amma had instructed him to do. Right now the prospect of living at the periphery seemed like a quaint childish endeavor that had outlived its purpose. From the center Kailash felt like he was a drop in a rainbow river of love. He felt that he had become the embodiment of his guru Shiva. He wished he could just stay under the banyan tree with Amma forever. He took in a long slow breath. And he recited the mantra before losing consciousness.

Om Shakti Om ... Om Shiva Om

Immediately Amma turned around and applied herself to a new task. So off Kailash went. As he walked in his tortured stop-start stop-start rhythm, he heard it mentioned that Amma had been supervising many teams of laborers clearing the jungle for weeks without taking rest. The story did not jive with his reality. Amma had been walking to remote villages and performing healings with him over the past weeks. He had lost track of the days. Something was wrong here. How could she be in two places at the same time? Now he really wanted to start asking questions.

Another conversation Kailash overheard mentioned a team of Vidabhar laborers led by a Swami Prem Ma and the former-King Bhima supervising an enormously elaborate agricultural plan to rehabilitate the jungle wasteland into a series of fruit and nut groves, crops and amazing meditation gardens. Kailash dropped to his knees. He could not control the emotions moving through his trembling body. Bhima was here. Where was Damayanti? Had she remained in Vidabhar waiting for him with the girls? But who was better equipped to implement this sort of ambitious plan than his beloved? Now he really wanted to start asking questions.

Kailash felt himself at one of those crossroad moments again. What should he do? Get to the bottom of these unanswered questions arising from his million-question mind? Or do what Amma had instructed? What would his beloved advise him to do? What would his guru Shiva do if he were me? Kailash asked himself what he wanted most right now.

The answer was clear. He wanted to remain in the ashram. And he had made an agreement. Kailash made no attempt to stop the trembling in his body. Instead he closed his eyes. He took in a long slow breath. And he recited the mantra.

Om Shakti Om ... Om Shiva Om

Eventually he rose to his feet and limped toward the healing ward. These first ones were the most difficult steps he could recall having made in his long and jagged journey toward the opening of his seven gateways. Once he built up some forward momentum it got easier. He had come to Amma's ashram to trust her. Not to fight her. He had come to surrender to Shakti. Not to win back Damayanti. He had come to serve people in need. Not to serve himself.

He cautiously asked the first person to point out the captain. He was initiating a conversation but it was directed toward serving others. He limped in the direction to where he was pointed. Kailash asked if he could serve on the healing team.

The captain demanded to know his qualifications. Where had he trained as a healer? Who was his guru? How long had he studied? And what were his specialties?

"Shiva is my guru. My training comes from the repetition of the mantra. And my specialty is opening up the gateways of divine love for people in need."

The captain smirked at Kailash. Not another one of these useless spiritual wanna-be's. Ashrams attracted all kinds of idealistic dreamers who talked a great game but were usually found snoring under a tree while the people in need were left waiting. What stood out about this guy was the obvious fact that he was a cripple. How was he going to heal others if he could not heal himself?

Kailash would get one day to prove his stripes. The captain said that Kailash better know how to clean and dress a wound. If Kailash could tend to the sick competently, he could stick around. If he was applying to this healing team to avoid the heavy lifting involved with the labor teams, the captain promised to assign Kailash to the most onerous job in the ashram which was the latrine detail.

Before the disciple of Shiva had time to familiarize himself with the tools available in the healing ward, his first patient arrived in the body of a scrawny bag-of-bones ten year-old girl with a burning fever. She was carried into the healing ward by a bewildered man who looked in need of healing himself. Just as he had been seen Amma do many times, Kailash took the girl into his arms. He scanned her body and picked up that five of her gateways were locked up tight. The other two were barely letting light through. Without healing she would not survive the night. He took in a long slow breath and recited the mantra.

Om Shakti Om ... Om Shiva Om

He held her close while he felt the cosmic energy move through his body into her body. It took a long time before the blocks in her energy fields got unstuck. At first the girl was scared. She knew she was dying. And she thought Kailash looked like a freak show attraction which of course he did. When she closed her eyes, though, she didn't see a cripple. She saw a wonderful rainbow display of lights that was getting stronger and stronger.

Kailash got three of her five closed gateways to open into the optimal range. Then the other two opened to near-normal. Now the body was open enough to start healing itself. He took in a long slow breath and again recited the mantra.

Om Shakti Om ... Om Shiva Om

The energy continued to grow stronger. And the girl stopped resisting. She let Kailash take all her weight. The rainbow shaft was pouring up his spine. And he stopped resisting. Kailash silently told the girl that he loved her. Even though she was older than his girls, he imagined he was holding Sumitra. He hoped he wasn't cheating the girl. It didn't feel like he was because he wasn't taking any of the energy. He just let the love flow through the girl. And he didn't want anything from her. When the rainbow shaft started pouring up her spine, he imagined that he was holding Samadhi.

With experience Kailash would learn that children were quicker to heal than adults because they were quicker to trust. Children didn't have all the built-in mental lines of defense that adults believed safeguarded them from the adversities of life. Those first steps Kailash had taken toward the healing ward, when his million-question mind craved to get all his questions answered, were part of his healing. He was learning to trust that life was here to support him in his service to God.

The instant he let go of the girl, she bounded away with a gallop that brought tears to the haggard man's eyes. After confirming that he was the girl's father Kailash would not let him leave without also receiving healing. The medics and other healers in the ward took note. Kailash was indeed earning his stripes.

Through the ashram grapevine word spread quickly about a crippled healer who did not use medicine to heal. Rumors got out that he used mantras given by Shiva. Another rumor that got a lot of mileage had it that Amma must have personally trained the cripple because he used her same method of hugging the people who came to him for healing. And his therapy worked.

When his patients asked how he had healed them, Kailash would say he had not healed anyone. He was just a servant of Shakti. And she was doing the healing. Not him. Days passed into weeks. And the work of healing the sick continued especially as his reputation grew.

Most days required traveling into the jungle to serve patients too sick to travel themselves. The captain had come to rely on Kailash to handle the difficult cases. Most nights Kailash worked as long as people needed him. With each patient who came into his embrace, Kailash became firmly convinced that he was healing something in himself by serving others.

The love for Shakti was getting stronger than the love for anything or anyone else. Because the rest of reality might be nothing more than an illusion projected by his own mind. While Shakti was too pure and too vast for his mind to project. Shakti became the object of his devotion. And he even lost his need to win her love. For it seemed silly to waste any energy in needing love.

The love was here. What need was there for more of it? The love was boundless. This was the love between Shiva and Shakti. He started out as Shiva seeking Shakti. And he ended up merging one into the other so that the distinction between them seemed pointless. He was Shiva-Shakti. He was male. And he was female. He was the seeker. And he was the sought. He was the lover. And he was the beloved. He was the many. And he was the one.

in the newly created ashram garden. Amma was initiating the Swami Prem Ma along with an unknown man and two girls. In fact there was little else that anyone around him was discussing.

Many times Kailash almost blurted out the questions running nonstop through his head. Who was this Swami Prem Ma? And why the mystery surrounding the man? Who could the two girls be other than his Sumitra and Samadhi? When Kaliash closed his eyes and searched in his heart, he could see. It was them. And this Prem Ma had to be his beloved. But why had she shaved her head and taken sannyasin? How could she do such a thing?

After all she was married. She was a wife and a mother. Kailash could create an enormous scandal if he raised an objection. He had rights here. In the full public view of all the world the princess had draped her lotus garland around his neck. How could she take the lotus garland back? Her orange robe and shaved head seemed like an abomination. Her renunciation was an attack on the sanctuary of love.

So what did Kailash do? He asked himself what he wanted more. To stay in the ashram and trust Amma ... Trust Shiva ... Surrender to Shakti? Or Man-Up ... Stop being a spiritual doormat ... Talk to Damayanti-Prem Ma-whatever-her-name-was ... Embrace Sumitra and Samadhi into his arms and tell them again and again how much he loved them?

All his life he had dreamed of taking the lord of yoga as his guru. Now that it had happened he wondered what cruel twist of fate had conspired to put him in this place. Whatever choice he made would be wrong. If he followed Amma's ashram contract, which he had vowed to do, he would be abandoning his girls and his beloved. If he broke his vow, he would never heal Kala's curse. Amma had said the contract was being imposed to cure the curse. If he broke the vow, he would have to leave the only piece of paradise he had ever found on earth. If he broke the vow, he risked losing his guru.

One patient after the next moved forward in the line. Kailash performed his duties of healing as he had been taught to do. He was as effective as ever opening the gateways of people in need. To do it he had to start with himself. And it was with a somber hue that the rainbow shaft ignited. But ignite it did. Kailash stayed true to his vow. He closed his eyes. He took in a long slow breath. And he recited the mantra.

Om Shakti Om ... Om Shiva Om

Like her daughter Uttani felt most alive with dirt in her hands. She closed her eyes and entered the dreamtime. Things were so much improved and getting better every moment of every day. The mango and almond devas were dancing in anticipation of row upon row of saplings ready to set roots. Bhima and Prem Ma had decided it should be Uttani to ask the devas to bless the first planting in the ashram groves.

This woman who had uprooted her life from the familiar terrain of Nishada and Vidabhar was the epitome for what the ashram stood. She lived Amma's four spiritual cornerstones: energy, love, God and service. Hoisting a fertile clump of earth into her hands Uttani petitioned Surya the sun god to bless the earth and all her sentient beings with his sacred light. When Surya brought his hands together in prayer, all the ashram attendees did the same including Amma and chanted his holy name.

Uttani nodded to Bhima. The former king poured holy water gathered from the river Ganga onto the dirt in the woman's hands. And he poured the holy water onto the surrounding earth. Uttani petitioned Goddess Ganga to bless the earth and all her sentient beings with her sacred water. When Ganga brought her hands together in prayer, all the ashram attendees did the same and chanted her holy name.

Since the arrival of Prem Ma and her Vidabhar team in the Maze of Death the plant devas had been awaiting this moment. These spirit beings existed to protect the plants to which they were entrusted. So it was with great love that they did not wait for her invitation. They simply rushed to embrace Uttani.

All the attendees closed their eyes. They took in a long slow breath. And they recited the mantra.

Om Shakti Om ... Om Shiva Om

Prem Ma bowed her head. The girl ran her tiny fingers with frightened delight across the stubble of her mother's scalp.

"You're letting it grow," whispered Sumitra.

Prem Ma did not wish to burst into tears. So she just nodded.

"Can we keep it our secret? You and me?"

Sumitra sensed how difficult it was for her mother. She wrapped her short arms around her mother in a protective gesture. "It's okay, mommy! Whatever you do, I still love you."

Prem Ma yielded into Sumitra. It was pointless to hold back anymore. The love between a mother and a daughter trumped the love she felt for God. When she burst into tears, Prem Ma dissolved and Damayanti returned from the dead. And Sumitra joined her not knowing what the consequences would be of her mother's actions.

Together the mother and daughter burst open their gateways. Rainbow shafts of light ignited as one. And it was good. Damayanti instantly knew that she was making the right decision. She took Sumitra's hand and closed her eyes. She took in a long slow breath. Together the mother and daughter recited the mantra.

Om Shakti Om ... Om Shiva Om

"Boss, I think we've got things under control," croaked the black crow.

Kala closed the book of time and turned to his apprentice. "I don't know what I'd do without you. This last job was a real mess."

"Varuna has a flair for the dramatic."

"Everything came together perfectly. Just as my stepmother predicted. Long ago she asked me to be patient. And she asked me to trust the enduring nature of love. So I did."

Kala closed his eyes. He took in a long slow breath. And he recited the mantra.

Om Shakti Om ... Om Shiva Om

Ashram swamis chanted sacred prayers and poured pure butter onto sacred fires. From the jungle saints and yogis had been wandering in. Without a word these men and women with sacred ash smeared across their foreheads had seated themselves around the periphery of the ashram. In the atmosphere the vibration of love was on the rise.

Pushpaka had arrived carrying the celestial ensemble. Like the swayamvara many years ago emissaries of every realm had come to take their place. Elephants, bears, monkeys, lizards, and tigers were just a few of the animals eager to witness the event. The naga Karkotaka would not have missed it for anything in the world. Garuda flew in along with Kailash's brother eagle. The many kings and queens who donated men and resources to the jungle rescue operation arrived to inspect the results being celebrated so joyously. Indigenous peoples with customs and languages completely of their own making arrived settling into small clusters of encampments.

Lotus flowers rained down from the heavens. Amma walked every inch of the ashram grounds and greeted everyone with her signature hugs. Arriving with much less fanfare than at the original swayamvara Vibhishana the rakshasa demon king simply walked into the ashram. Like so many others he was thrilled to get a hug from the jungle saint.

Overhead a flock of swans circled and landed in the gentle waters of the river. Great Swan and Hansaram were among those waddling onto the shore. Amma motioned for everyone to gather in the new ashram garden. Places had been designated for the honorees, deities and other luminaries.

At the altar Damayanti was wearing a plain white sari. The neatly folded orange robe was in her hands. Sumitra recalled the story of her mother wearing Maya's orchid of illusions in her hair. She wished she had an orchid for her mother. And then she remembered that there were orchids growing behind the altar. Forgoing any sense of propriety she ran in her white sari to the orchid patch where she asked the orchid deva if she could pick a single flower. The orchid deva was thrilled Sumitra had asked permission and gladly contributed her finest orchid to the cause.

Not knowing when the ceremony would begin Sumitra sprinted through the garden careful not to damage the newly planted flowers. She gazed ahead at her mother with a mind for how beautiful the flower would look in her hair. In full stride Sumitra tripped and cracked her head on the altar. Everyone assembled in the garden heard the thudding sound of bone on stone. And the dead silence after. For a moment no one moved. Then Amma took control. She ordered the healer to be summoned and that no one else could touch the girl.

The ceremony was suspended. All attention went to Sumitra. Damayanti disobeyed Amma by taking the hand of her daughter. She wanted to embrace Sumitra. Only a short time ago Sumitra had come to her rescue. And now she refused to be powerless to do the same. She would not wait for some healer. Right now who was better to heal Sumitra than her own mother? She closed her eyes. She took in a long slow breath. And she recited the mantra.

Om Shakti Om ... Om Shiva Om

She tried to ignite the rainbow shaft. But nothing happened. She turned to Amma who could of course heal Sumitra. She was famed as the greatest of all healers. But Amma shook her head and said, "Only the crippled healer can save Sumitra."

"Healer," shouted the captain of the healing ward, "Amma needs you. A girl is dying. Hurry!"

Many times Kailash had been called to go to one in need. So he didn't think too much of it. But as he limped toward the captain, Kailash realized he had never heard such distress in the man's voice. Nor had the captain ever specifically invoked Amma's name. He had said that a girl was dying. Kailash had to hurry. But his crippled body would only carry him so fast.

Kailash wished he could hurtle his body through the air as he had done in leaping to his descent from Himalayan cliffs to get back to his beloved. What would he do if he arrived too late? The healer composed himself and kept limping.

As he approached the garden, Kailash had a crazy thought that this place reminded him of the garden back in Nishada. And as he approached the impressive crowd huddled close around what he assumed to be the dying girl, he had another crazy thought that this gathering reminded him of the swayamvara crowd back in Vidabhar.

As fate would have it, the lord of time was the first one to identify the healer as the exile prince Nala. He waved his entire body fiercely at the cripple and screamed, "Faster! Faster! You must run faster!"

Kala had come to embrace dear Sumitra and precious Samadhi as his nieces. He could not bear the possibility of this dear child suffering in the moment when he was being released from the suffering of his childhood. It could not be allowed to happen that Sumitra might perish. Not when he had waited so long for this day.

So many times had Kala suffered the cruel torment of struggling to move faster in that very same hunchback crippled body. But never so much as this day. The bitter irony of the circumstance was that he had been freed from it. And he had been responsible for subjecting Nala to reside inside it. And now he had the perfect body but was powerless to heal Sumitra.

Now Kala went into a mad dash at the cripple and scooped the hunchbacked healer up onto his shoulders. He would not stand by and just watch. Carrying Kailash the remaining distance the lord of time begged for forgiveness, "Brother, while you and I have not met in this lifetime, I must beg your forgiveness. Please heal Sumitra!"

Kailash stood stunned. Before him were Sumitra, Samadhi and Damayanti as well as Amma, Great Swan, Bhima, his mother Uttani, Lords Indra, Yama, Agni and Varuna. And they were all glaring at him.

His first thought was 'Why me?' Surely these great deities could heal Sumitra with far greater skill than he. Why was Amma just standing there? And she was his teacher. Even Sumitra's mother was an extraordinary healer in her own right.

Why were they waiting for him? A cripple who could not even heal himself.

Among all these great luminous beings Amma was the one who spoke with divine authority. "Kailash, what are you waiting for? Do your job! She will only respond to your embrace."

When he hesitated, Damayanti grabbed his hand and pleaded, "Please, we've all tried to bring her back. But nothing has worked. I'm her mother. Please! You're my last hope!"

It took him a second to figure it out. Damayanti and Prem Ma were the same woman. The entire time he had been serving people here at the ashram, she had been here too. And she did not recognize Kailash because of the curse. All these thoughts flashed through his mind as he scanned the energy field of his unconscious daughter.

Get centered. She needs me. Keep my gateways open. So I can help her. These thoughts raced against the time it took to see that her third, fourth and seventh gateways were shut. Otherwise she was fine.

With the tenderest embrace of a loving father Kailash lowered himself to ground level and transferred the support of the earth for his body. In slow motion he took her weight and cradled her body.

rainbow shaft of light shot up the gateways of Damayanti. In a moment the rainbow shaft enveloped the lord of time. Mother and son came together as one.

"A long time ago I abandoned my son Kala after bringing him into this world. By the grace of Shakti and Shiva, he has forgiven me. And I have learned to trust the wheel of Dharma turns for the benefit of all souls. May my love for Kala grow stronger each day! Kala, I love you!"

Amma passed the garland to both Damayanti and Kailash who hoisted it high. Now the rainbow shaft shot up through Kailash and this light too enveloped the lord of time. Speaking in a hushed voice between the two of them Kailash said, "A moment ago you asked me to forgive you. Now I do the same. Please forgive me, Kala, for taking your mother away."

"I forgave you the moment I saw you limping toward Sumitra. What I did to myself out of ignorance was cruel. But it was my choice. Now you must forgive yourself."

Damayanti and Kailash lowered the lotus garland around the neck of Lord Kala. From the earth the rainbow shaft shot up and enveloped all sentient beings. Healing energies poured out over the land. The archetype of mother and son was strengthened in the universal body. The immortals, devas, humans and animals cheered for Damayanti and Kala.

The hunchback crippled body cracked open. Like the worn skin of a snake, Kailash stepped out of Kala's curse into the rainbow light of a new body more radiant than his previous one. The girls broke rank from the line to grab their Daddy. And no one ... no saint or god was going to peel those girls away.

Our heroic beloveds draped the second garland around Sumitra's neck. She looked so regal and exalted completely healed from her divinely serendipitous tumble. Damayanti and Kailash draped the third garland around little Samadhi's neck. Her drawings in the dirt were part of the forces of nature that dreamed these beloveds back together. So this second swayamvara would forever be known as Samadhi's Swayamvara.

Amma and the lord of time held hands and rose high into the sky. Slowly their bodies began to spin forming a vortex between heaven and earth. This saint who had brought everyone to the ashram in the jungle transformed in mid-air. In a burst of the purest white light she emerged as Goddess Saraswati. She was the stepmother who held light when others held only darkness. Without calling attention to herself she was the wayshower through the million veils of illusion back to truth.

In the aura of love Saraswati and Kala embraced. Together they ascended into the highest spheres of heaven where Kala was reunited with his father Brahma.

All the gods and goddesses shouted with love in their hearts. "May the secret of enduring love be revealed anew each time this story is told and celebrated! Praise to the one! Praise to love!

Om Shakti Om ... Om Shiva Om!

Acknowledgments

Thirty years ago after graduating from Northwestern University with Philosophy B.A., I was seated next to my dad Demetri driving down Memorial Drive in Cambridge. He turned to me and asked what I was going to do with my life. As a teenager my dad came to Boston from Greece via the merchant marines to become a classic self-made entrepreneur without a high school diploma. So he had high hopes for me with my newly acquired college degree.

"I'm going to write a novel of spiritual truth," I replied. Just to be clear, this goal was my sole object of pursuit. I didn't care about girls, money or people thinking well of me. In the years ahead my one-pointed focus would lead to a completely out-of-balance life. "Great!" Demetri shouted with unreserved Hellenic gusto. He slapped and then rubbed his hands. "My son is going to write the modern Platonic Dialogues!"

Both of us started looking for a parking spot. We were going to see an Ingmar Bergman film. In matter-of-fact fashion my dad asked if I knew how to write. When I admitted I didn't have a clue, he jammed on the brake. My dad's jaw dropped. "What did you study in college?" he howled. Four years of college bills had put a strain on his life. "Didn't you learn how to write there?

"No dad," I said calmly. "At Northwestern I learned how to think. Life is going to teach me how to write."

So my acknowledgments must start with deepest thanks for my mom Connie and my dad Demetri. Thirty years is a long time to wait to taste the harvest of a son's life labor. Countless times both of them gave or lent me money for rent, food & pay for my library addiction. When I moved into an ashram for six years, while neither of them thought was a good idea, they didn't give up on me. When I opened my yoga studio, while neither of them thought was a good idea, they didn't give up on me. When I told them about self-publishing this novel, both of them told me in no uncertain terms that they wanted to hold a copy of the book in their hands before they died. Thanks Mom & Dad. Hope you like it.

Thanks to Skye Wentworth for acting as my publishing & PR guru. Michael Moon for the 'Beloved Swans' front cover photo. Jacquie Spector for back cover photo. Carter Wentworth for book cover design. Satya Sardonicus for gateway template. Thanks to editors: Lori Monaco, Michelle Fremont & Jen Schaefer. Thanks to EJ Ouellette for recording the audio book and composing/performing the Om Shaki Om music logo. Thanks to HotCore Yoga studio members for supporting my literary pursuit.

Thanks to my spiritual teachers: Maharesh Mahesh Yogi, Norbu Nomkai Rimpoche, Yogi Amrit Desai & my Kripalu family, Gurumayi, Mata Amritanandamayi, Bikram Choudhury & Ma Chetan Jyoti.

Thanks to Swami Rama Ashram along the banks of the holy Ganga River in Rishikesh, India where I wrote all the original text.

Thanks to the women with whom I've been blessed to share heart, body & soul. You have been my greatest teachers.

Note to Sanskrit scholars & enlightened yogis: please forgive any mistakes I have made in retelling an ancient Vedic tale through a modern idiom. My intent has been to share my enthusiastic love for this ancient culture so that present day readers might embody the wisdom of yoga in tandem with the awakening of the divine feminine.

www.hotcoreyogapress.com

Volume 2 – Coming in 2015